NIGHT RIDE FROM KIRTLAND

NIGHT RIDE FROM KIRTLAND

Book One in the Series
OLD CHARLIE AND THE PROPHET

DANIEL BAY GIBBONS

Sixteen Stones Press

HOLLADAY, UTAH

Book layout, typography and cover design ©2015 by Julie G. Gibbons. Photo credits, "Pferd auf dem Gehrenberg bei Wendlingen, Deggenhausertal," by Dietrich Krieger; published by permission of the author under the terms of the GNU Free Documentation License; "Kirtland Ohio Temple," by Michael Whiffen, published by permission of the author under a Creative Commons Attribution license, and "Old Wheel" under license from iStock. Sixteen Stones Press logo designed by Marina Teležar.

Sixteen Stones Press
Publisher website: www.sixteenstonespress.com

Night Ride from Kirtland
(Book 1 in the series, *Old Charlie and the Prophet*)
by Daniel Bay Gibbons

Series website: www.oldcharlie.com

Hardback ISBN 978-1-942640-05-9
Paperback ISBN 978-0-9906387-9-7
eBook ISBN 978-0-9906387-8-0

DEDICATION

To Annie

CHARACTERS

THE NOVEL IS TOLD FROM THE POINT OF VIEW OF THESE MAIN CHARACTERS:

Old Charlie, a 12-year-old black stallion

Julia (Julia Smith), adopted daughter of Joseph & Emma Smith, age 6

Little Joseph (Joseph Smith, III), oldest son of Joseph & Emma Smith, age 4

Wycliffe (John Wycliffe Rigdon), son of Sidney & Phebe Rigdon, age 7

George (George Robinson), son-in-law of Sidney & Phebe Rigdon, age 23

Lovina (Lovina Smith), daughter of Hyrum & Jerusha Smith, age 10

Lucy (Lucy Smith), youngest sister of Joseph Smith, age 17

Arthur (Arthur Millikin), blacksmith's apprentice, age 20

OTHER ANIMAL CHARACTERS

Major, a large mastiff do belonging to Joseph Smith

Sam, a white stallion belonging to Hyrum Smith

Bluebird, a filly belonging to Hyrum Smith

Jim, a black stallion belonging to Joseph Smith

Raven, a saddle-bred stallion belonging to William Smith

Champ, a gray gelding belonging to Sidney Rigdon

Dominic, Arthur Millikin's horse

OTHER HUMAN CHARACTERS

The Joseph Smith, Sr. Family

Joseph Smith, Sr., father of the Prophet, age 56

Lucy Mack Smith, his wife, age 52

Lucy Smith, youngest daughter of Joseph Smith, Sr. and Lucy Mack Smith, age 17

The Joseph Smith, Jr. Family

Joseph Smith, Jr., the Mormon Prophet

Emma Smith, his wife, and their children:

    Julia Murdock Smith, age 6

    Joseph Smith, III, age 4

    Frederick Smith, age 1

    Alexander Smith, born during the story

The Hyrum Smith Family

Hyrum Smith, Joseph's brother

Jerusha Barden Smith, his wife, and their children:

    Lovina Smith, age 10

    John Smith, age 5

    Hyrum Smith, Jr., age 3

    Jerusha Smith, age 1

    Sarah Smith, born during the story

The Sophronia Smith Stoddard Family

Sophronia Smith Stoddard, Joseph's sister, and her daughter:

    Mariah, age 5

The Samuel Smith Family

Samuel Smith, Joseph's brother
Mary Bailey Smith, his wife, and their children:
>   **Susannah Smith**, age 2
>   **Mary Smith**, age six months

The William Smith Family

William Smith, Joseph's brother
Caroline Grant Smith, his wife, and their children:
>   **Mary Jane Smith**, age 4
>   **Caroline Smith**, age 1

The Katharine Smith Salisbury Family

Katharine Smith Salisbury, Joseph's sister
Wilkins Salisbury, her husband, and their children:
>   **Lucy Smith**, age 3
>   **Solomon Smith**, age 2
>   **Alvin Smith**, born during the story

The Don Carlos Smith Family

Don Carlos Smith, Joseph's brother
Agnes Coolbrith Smith, his wife, and their children:
>   **Agnes Smith**, age 1
>   **Sophronia Smith**, born during the story

The Sidney Rigdon Family

Sidney Rigdon, counselor to Joseph Smith
Phebe Brooks Rigdon, his wife, and their children:
>   **Athalia Rigdon**, age 16, married to George Robinson
>   **Nancy Rigdon**, age 14

Eliza Rigdon, age 13
Sarah Rigdon, age 12
Sid Rigdon, age 9
Wycliffe Rigdon, age 7
Lacy Ann Rigdon, age 5
Carvel Rigdon, age 2
Dorcas Rigdon, age 1

OTHER CHARACTERS

Mary Fielding, an English convert in Kirtland
Warren Parrish, Joseph Smith's former secretary
Vinson Knight, a member of the Kirtland bishopric
Polly Beswick, cook to Joseph & Emma Smith
Aunty Grinnels, cook to Hyrum & Jerusha Smith
Old George, handyman to Hyrum & Jerusha Smith
William, Samuel, and Don Carlos Smith, brothers of Joseph
     Smith
Nathaniel Millikin, Arthur's uncle
Brigham Young, Luke Johnson, John Boynton, Mormon Apostles
Alexander Badham, Kirtland blacksmith

Note: Old Charlie, Jim, Sam, and Major were actual animals, described in historical records. All other animal characters are fictitious. All human characters in the story were actual historical persons.

TABLE OF CONTENTS

PROLOGUE

ISRAEL SMITH

INDEPENDENCE, MISSOURI
Wednesday, September 10, 1913

The morning sunlight slants through the branches of the maple trees and shimmers on the windscreen of the black Model-T Ford. The rumble of the engine causes squirrels to scatter on the suburban lawns and the rear tires to stir up a wake of red and yellow autumn leaves on the street. The driver is a young man, not yet in middle age, with steel-blue eyes and a high, intelligent forehead. He is dressed in a high-collar, wool suit with a white shirt and green silk tie. There is a soft and well-worn leather briefcase on the seat beside him. He glances anxiously at his watch—five minutes before ten o'clock—and then presses the accelerator closer to the floorboards. He realizes he is going to be late, and he knows how much his father abhors tardiness, in boys, and especially in grown men. It is a sensibility ingrained in Israel Smith since his boyhood.

His boyhood. Israel realizes he is no boy, but he still feels like one in the presence of his father. He is thirty-six years old, married, and with a son of his own. Until this year, 1913, Israel was living in Iowa, where he was distinguished member of the Iowa Bar Association. There he had a respectable, though not-so-lucrative law practice. He lived happily in the small country town of Lamoni with his wife Nina and little baby Joseph, just a year old this week. Until now, Israel's days were filled with the routines of land conveyances, contracts, wills, trusts, court appearances, depositions, and summonses. His nights and weekends were devoted to a quiet family life and religious devotion.

But now, in the summer of 1913, Israel A. Smith, Esquire, has closed down his Iowa practice, sold his home, and relocated his little family to Independence, the bustling Missouri State capitol. The previous week Israel sat for and passed the Missouri Bar exam and was sworn in as an attorney and counselor-at-law before the Missouri Supreme Court.

It is not the practice of law, however, that has brought him to Missouri. Israel Smith, Attorney-at-Law, has come to answer a summons from his eighty-one-year-old father— Joseph Smith, III, President of the Reorganized Church of Jesus Christ of Latter-day Saints, and son of the Mormon Prophet, Joseph Smith, Jr., and Emma Hale Smith. Israel has come to Independence to help his father dictate a history of his long and remarkable life. The dictating began yesterday, the aged father speaking slowly and the young attorney writing. Israel knows that they are embarking upon a long and laborious, but interesting experience. One of the great experiences of Israel's life.

Israel parks the Model T in front of a modest wood-frame house at 1214 West Short Street. Briefcase in hand, he walks quickly up the familiar grass-lined, cement walkway to a deep front porch, which wraps around both sides of the house. His feet echo on the wooden porch, and he turns the knob on the familiar oak-paneled front door with its large pane of frosted glass. Entering the cool front hall, Israel calls out, "Father! I'm here."

A feeble voice comes from the front room: "I'm in here, my boy! You're late!"

"I know, Father," Israel says, walking into the room. "I'm sorry."

In the front room a venerable old man with a long, snow-white beard sits in a leather easy chair. The walls are covered with bookcases. Portraits of Joseph and Emma Smith hang on the wall. A pendulum clock ticks quietly. By the old man's side is a small side table covered with papers and books, one of which he sets aside as the young man walks into the room. A silver-headed cane rests close at hand against the leather chair.

"Hello, Father," Israel says as he kisses the old man on the cheek. The young lawyer then takes his seat at a small writing desk, which has been set up beneath one of the windows, where the morning light is brightest. Israel opens his briefcase and pulls out a small sheaf of cream-colored paper, a dip quill pen, and an inkwell. A few of the pages are already covered in Israel's carefully written Pitman shorthand. Though he has had some training in Pitman shorthand many years before, he is somewhat rusty and has been spending late nights in Independence brushing up on his word signs and phrase outlines.[1] Israel places the written pages from yesterday in a pile to his left, with another pile of clean, unmarked pages on his right. Israel carefully fills his pen with black ink from the little bottle. Finally, he looks up at his father, takes a deep breath, and says, "All right, Father. I'm ready now."

"Very well, my boy," says the old man. "Now remind me where we were yesterday."

Israel picks up the last written sheet and reads aloud:

"I was born in the early morning of November 6, 1832, in the little town of Kirtland, Ohio. My earliest recollections of men, things, and events, therefore begin at Kirtland. The house we occupied stood on the west side of the street, which runs from the Temple down to the Chagrin River and was not very far from the ford across this little stream. The comforts of life were meager and makeshift. The life which my parents had been compelled to live, constantly harassed by persecutions and moving about from place to place on what was then the frontier of civilization, had inured them to hardships and overwhelming difficulties."

Israel stops reading. "That's where we stopped. You asked me to remind you to talk about your father's horses next."

"Oh, yes," says Joseph Smith, III. "The horses!" The old man tips back his head and closes his eyes and smiles. Then he begins speaking, at first haltingly, and then with great fluency and strength:

---

[1] Israel A. Smith, "My Father's Last Years," in *The Saint's Herald*, November 6, 1934.

"All my life I have been very fond of good horses. Many memories of my childhood and youth are connected with the horses we owned and which were largely under my personal care, as I grew older. Some references to some of these animals may be of interest.

"It must have been in the year 1841 that Father brought home a large sorrel horse, which he had purchased and named Tom Carlin, 'in honor,' I supposed, of Thomas Carlin, incumbent of the gubernatorial chair at Springfield."[2]

The old man pauses, chuckling softly, his eyes still closed.

"This horse was given to me, but he was too large and clumsy for me to ride easily. I usually preferred Old Charlie, the horse that came with us from Kirtland to Missouri and from Missouri to Illinois, pulling our wagon carefully across the rolling prairie and the frozen Mississippi.

"Charlie had been with the family through many vicissitudes and was naturally greatly endeared to us. He was a handsome, large, black animal, with a singular white star on his forehead. High-spirited and proud in carriage, he was gentle and noble in disposition, and would carry me as quietly and safely as any old hack would do. I used to ride him about the streets, go where I pleased in the city, and never suffered the least injury from him, even when I was quite small. In fact, he seemed to like to have me with him, and he made a very good pal for me, indeed.

---

[2] *The Saints Herald*, December 11, 1934; the language quoted in the prologue is a near verbatim transcript of Joseph Smith III's words dictated in 1913.

The old man falls silent. Finally Israel speaks up. "Father, you said that Old Charlie pulled the wagon from Kirtland to Missouri and then from Missouri to Illinois. What can you say about those journeys?"

Joseph Smith, III, thinks for a moment, and then says,

"My memories of the journey from Kirtland to Missouri in the spring of 1838 are confused. I can remember that across the center of the covered wagon in which we rode there was a division made by fastening up blankets, and that Father occupied the back part of the wagon to hide from his pursuers. I remember we reached a river, and that the roads running through the low lands were of the kind known as corduroy—rough logs laid crossways to keep the wheels out of the mud. Some who had been riding in the wagons walked over these roads, and I also did so, for a ways, stepping carefully over the rigid poles holding to the hand of my mother. My adopted sister, Julia, was one of the companions of this journey, and my brother, Frederick, who was born in June 1836, was another.

"Of the exodus from Missouri to the Mississippi River at Quincy I have a definite and clear recollection. Our team was composed of two large black horses, Charlie and another horse called Jim. Charlie was particular about his teammates and would not work with an inferior companion. Jim must have perished soon after our arrival in Nauvoo, but Charlie survived and was used by Father as a riding horse. We reached the river. The weather had become extremely cold and the river was frozen over, so that we crossed upon the ice. Charlie, the more intelligent animal of the team, was hitched to the tongue of the wagon and the driver, walking behind him, held the end of the tongue in his hand, guiding the horse across. This was considered the safest way to

make the crossing for it was feared the ice might not be strong enough to bear the weight of the double team and the loaded wagon.

"Carrying in her arms my brothers, Frederick and Alexander (who had been born in Far West the preceding June), with my sister, Julia, and myself holding onto her dress at either side, my mother walked across the frozen river and reached the Illinois shore in safety. This, then, was the manner of our passing out of the jurisdiction of a hostile State into the friendlier shelter of the State of Illinois in 1839."

Father Smith falls silent again, so Israel prompts him. "What can you say about Charlie during the Nauvoo period?"

"Old Charlie was absolutely afraid of nothing. He was Father's favorite riding horse in the Nauvoo Legion. I have seen him stand close beside the cannon when it was fired, and all the notice he appeared to take of it was that as the smoke rolled about him and its scent was in the air, he would lift his head high and blow a veritable trumpet-blast of a breath through his nostrils— answering the description of the horse in Proverbs—or was it Job?"

The old man picks up an old leather Bible and leafs through the pages. Israel watches for several minutes as his father searches for the verse. "Ah," he finally says, "Here is the passage." And then he reads aloud:

"Hast thou given the horse strength?
Hast thou clothed his neck with thunder?
Canst thou make him afraid as a grasshopper?
The glory of his nostrils is terrible.

He paweth in the valley, and rejoiceth in his strength.
He goeth on to meet the armed men.
He mocketh at fear and is not affrighted,
Neither turneth he back from the sword.
The quiver rattleth against him,
The glittering spear and the shield.
He swalloweth the ground with fierceness and rage,
Neither believeth he that it is the sound of the trumpet.
He saith among the trumpets, 'Ha! Ha!'
And he smelleth the battle afar off,
The thunder of the captains, and the shouting."[3]

The old man closes his Bible.

"That could be a description of Old Charlie. I have seen the drummer of the Nauvoo Legion, carrying the big bass drum against his breast, walk up close to the horse, thundering and beating as loudly as he could, but the only effect it had upon the animal was to exhilarate him.

"We were excellent friends and playfellows. He used to allow no one to ride him except Father, Mother, Lorin Walker (his attendant in the later years), or myself. In spite of this spirited notion he was essentially a family horse, and an ideally faithful servant. A loyal and gallant courier!"

The old man's voice drifts off and falls silent. The scratching of Israel's pen continues until he catches up with the dictation. He looks up at his aged father. The old man smiles sadly, gazing vacantly out of the window. The trees

---

[3] Job 39:19-25

on the lawn are aflame with yellow and orange leaves. A single teardrop runs down the old man's cheek.

PART I

"HAST THOU GIVEN THE HORSE STRENGTH?"

"Hast thou given the horse strength?
Hast thou clothed his neck with thunder?
Canst thou make him afraid as a grasshopper?
The glory of his nostrils is terrible.
He paweth in the valley, and rejoiceth in his strength.
He goeth on to meet the armed men.
He mocketh at fear and is not affrighted,
Neither turneth he back from the sword.
The quiver rattleth against him,
The glittering spear and the shield.
He swalloweth the ground with fierceness and rage,
Neither believeth he that it is the sound of the trumpet.
He saith among the trumpets, 'Ha! Ha!'
And he smelleth the battle afar off,
The thunder of the captains, and the shouting."[4]

---

[4] Job 39:19-25 (Within the immediate family of Joseph Smith, Jr., this scripture was deemed a fit description of Old Charlie)

OLD CHARLIE – SEPTEMBER 27

KIRTLAND, OHIO
Wednesday, September 27, 1837

Joseph Smith: "I started from Kirtland on the 27th of September, in company with Brother Sidney Rigdon, to fulfill the mission appointed us on the 18th of September by a conference of Elders, in establishing places of gathering for the Saints; Brothers William Smith and Vinson Knight accompanying us."[5]

Well, I s'pose all the lucky horses in Kirtland is ridin' out to Zion with Brother Joe and me this mornin'.

In my twelve summers I reckon I've had pretty durned good luck—leastways, better than most other horses. My legs is still strong and steady—I can outrun most other horses on any flat road in Kirtland or roundabouts. But when it comes to hills, there ain't no critter, horse or otherwise, what can keep up with me. I've seen a heap of summers, more than most horses, but my black coat is still sleek. I aim to live a long life with Brother Joe, and I expect

---

[5] B. H. Roberts, ed., *History of The Church of Jesus Christ of Latter-day Saints*, Second Edition, Revised (Salt Lake City: Deseret Book, 1976) (hereinafter "HC") volume 2, 518

my old age will be right peaceful in his pasture and stable, right back there in Kirtland. Wherever I go with Brother Joe, even when there ain't no stable, I feel right peaceful. It's the kind of peace a horse feels when he sees the waving of the long grass and feels the wind in his mane. When Brother Joe fixes me up for ridin' and then mounts the creakin' saddle on my back, I feel right peaceful and steady. His strong hands pat my neck and his liftin' of the reins and the pressure of his boots in the stirrups perk me right up for a good ride, and then I always know that I'm luckier than all the other horses here roundabout.

This morning it was crisp and clear, with the smell of wood smoke from the houses in the air and the red leaves kinda driftin' down from the branches of the trees. I was jest standin' in the cool grass when I heared the creak and bang of the back door of the house, so I wandered over and see'd Brother Joe walkin' toward the stable carryin' his saddlebags and bedroll. His boy, Little Joseph, was jest toddlin' right behind him, wearin' a broad brimmed hat, jest like his Pa's. Brother Joe's big white dog, Major, was follerin' right behind him, a hangin' his tongue out. Major's a right powerful dog, and right useful in watchin' out for things about the place, 'specially when Brother Joe's not around to keep his eye on things.

Well, Brother Joe called right out to me, "Come on, Old Charlie! We've got a long ride today." I was already stampin' my feet and expectin' a nice ride, and I knowed what was coming next. Brother Joe said, "Here's somethin' for you, Old Charlie," and he reached in his pocket and brung up a red apple for me from Lady Emma's orchard. I took it right in my teeth, clean like, from his hand and polished it off proper while he scratched my ears. Then he brought me over to the fence to get me all saddled up. Little Joseph climbed up on a rail to watch. Brother Joe laid the blanket on my back and hefted the saddle over my back and tied on his saddlebags and other gear, while Little Joseph reached out from the fence rail and kind of stroked my neck and talked to me, jest like his Pa does. Then Brother Joe rigged up my bridle and set the bit in my mouth, nice and snug and easy, and cinched everythin' up nice. Little Joseph, was trying to help with all of the straps and clasps, but couldn't reach 'em all. Then Brother Joe lifted the boy off the fence and up into the saddle and led me out into the lane in front of the house. I could barely feel the weight of the little feller in the saddle, holdin' tight to the horn, his feet not even touchin' my flanks. But I knowed it gave the little feller a thrill, 'cause I could jest sense it from the way he set in the saddle and kicked his legs, like we was off to the races.

A horse with a rider, also all packed up for a long journey, was waitin' at the hitchin' rail in front of Brother Joe's place. It was Raven, a big black saddle-bred stallion belongin' to that young feller, Brother William. He's Brother Joe's own flesh and blood brother, and he's got hisself a nice place right next to Brother Joe's along the Chillicothe Road.

Raven's what you would call an excitable horse, and he snorted at me, which was usual, and then turned his head away. Brother Joe and William were talkin' low together, laughin' now and then, until Lady Emma came out of the house with the other youngsters. There was Brother Joe's daughter Julia, all bright in her yellow dress and her hair tied up in little strings, and the little boy Freddie in her arms. Lady Emma and Julia was both huggin' and kissin' Brother Joe, and he jest picked up the little feller, Freddie, from Lady Emma's arms, and held him tight for a few seconds. Then he lifted Little Joseph down from my saddle, hugged him, and set him on the ground, and we was off.

Across the road and up a ways from Brother Joe's house is the big fine place of Brother Sidney. He's an older feller with a deep voice. Seems like he's most always right with Brother Joe. He was ready to go hisself, and he rode out of the yard on Champ, his fine gray gelding with a curious sorta' dark mane.

Well us three horses and our riders buck trotted a short way further down the road, and from out of one of the side streets come the feller called Vinson on a little brown mare I didn't recognize. The mare whickered right out loud. Well, Brother Joe and the three men jest set there in the saddle talkin' a bit. I heard them talk about ridin' to a place they call Zion, and so I knowed for sure we was all in for a mighty long ride, since I've been to Zion and back with Brother Joe before. Brother Vinson's little mare kind of blew out of her nose at me—pfffttt—real friendly, but I pushed her away as I'm always watchin' Brother Joe from the corner of my eye, ready to get on when he jest says the word. I knew all of these horses, 'cept the little mare, as they was over at our place plenty of times while their masters come up to talk with Brother Joe. It seems most days Brother Joe is seein' one feller or another at our place in Kirtland.

And then we were off at a nice clip, gallopin' easy south along Chillicothe Road, past the house of Brother Hyrum— he's another of Brother Joe's own flesh-and-blood brothers. I looked out to see if Hyrum's white stallion, Sam, was about the place. But he warn't nowhere to be seen. Fact is, I ain't seen Sam in Kirtland since the high summer.

Well, we was jest leavin' Kirtland and headin' out into the open country when suddenly Brother Joe reined me back some. "Do you hear that, William?" Brother Joe asked. "Listen."

"What is it?" said Brother William.

"Charlie's shoe," said Brother Joe. "Right fore, I'd wager. Hate to have him throw a shoe out on the road."

Well, the four men talked amongst theirselves, and then we all turned back toward Kirtland. We rode past the white temple and past Brother Joe's place down toward the village, four horses and their riders, jest as the mornin' sun was gettin' things nice and warm. I was steppin' gingerly, 'cause sure enough I could hear the clink-clink of my shoe as I stepped. Brother Joe and the others was talkin' back and forth friendly-like. I see'd that Raven was tossin' his head this way and that, and Brother William was already havin' a time of it keepin' him under control. From the hill we could see the village, the whole outfit, laid out below us. Houses left and right, the brown roads lined with trees, the blue water of the river, twistin' this way and that amongst the buildin's of the village. We passed Brother Joe's store, the hotel, and all the stores. Usual weather, all calm, and nary a cloud. Lots of folks comin' and goin', as usual. Up ahead by the river I heared the hammerin' sound and smelt the fire smell from the liv'ry stable.

Out front Brother Joe dismounted and handed my reins to a young feller who come out of the open doors of the liv'ry. He was covered in dust from his boots to his head—hair, face, clothes, jest one heap o' dust. He had a dirty little hat pulled low down over his eyes; in fact, the hat brim was down so low you couldn't see the feller's eyes at all.

"Mornin', Arthur," Brother Joe said to Dusty Hat. "Have Badham check Charlie's shoes, will you? Right fore sounds loose."

"Yes, sir," said Dusty Hat, and he led me right into the liv'ry stable by the bridle with Brother Joe follerin' behind. Brother William and Raven waited outside.

Inside the liv'ry it was all fire and smoke and a clankin' sound of metal. The blacksmith, Mr. Badham, was standin' by the fire with a big leather apron tied around his big belly. I knowed him, as Brother Joe has him fix my shoes from time to time, which ain't no fun at all. Mr. Badham had a big hammer and some of them metal tongs in his hands, and there was black smudges on his bald head.

"Mornin'," said Mr. Badham. "Check his shoes?"

Well, I was right nervous as Dusty Hat led me over by the fire. Mr. Badham lifted up one of my hooves and then the other, and then fetched his pliers and pulled the nails right out of my right fore. Then he turned to the fire, and hoisted a big handle down, which caused the fire to start to roarin'. That made me nervous some, but Dusty Hat held me right still. Then Mr. Badham set my shoe in the fire for a spell, then started to hammerin' it a few times. Then he plunged it in a barrel of water, and the steam jest rose up with a mighty hissin' sound. Well, finally, he come back and lifted up my right fore, and set the nails back in, and clinched 'em off. And I was done.

Brother Joe stood for a bit with Mr. Badham and Dusty Hat, jest a talkin'. He was tellin' 'em something about a red wagon. Mr. Badham was jest noddin' his head and then fetched up a piece of paper and started to make lines and marks all over it with a little stick, which he got out of his pocket. Well, that went on for a while, Mr. Badham drawin' his lines, and Brother Joe pointin' to the paper with his finger now and then, and the two of 'em jest talkin' away about a red wagon, with Dusty Hat jest standin' by, listenin'.

Finally, we was finished, and Brother Joe led me back outside, where Raven and Champ and the mare was waitin', and the four of us took off up the way we come, past Brother Joe's place, past the temple, and soon enough we was out on the open road. Four lucky horses ridin' out with Brother Joe on a long journey for Zion, and I'm the luckiest of 'em all.

ARTHUR – SEPTEMBER 27

KIRTLAND, OHIO
Wednesday, September 27, 1837

Joseph Smith: "I started from Kirtland on the 27th of September in company with Brother Sidney Rigdon, to fulfill the mission appointed us on the 18th of September to a conference of Elders, in establishing places of gathering for the Saints; Brothers William Smith and Vinson Knight accompanying us."[6]

From Kirtland's The Messenger and Advocate, *1837: "Our Village—Nothing can be more gratifying to the saints in this place and their friends and brethren abroad than to contemplate the scene now before them. Every Lords day our house of worship is filled to the overflowing with attentive-hearers, mostly communicants. In the evening following the singers meet under the direction of Brother L. Carter and J. Crosby Jr. who give instruction in the principles of vocal music. On Monday evening the quorum of high priests meets. They transact the business of their particular quorum, speak, sing, pray, and so worship the God of heaven. On Tuesday evening the Seventies . . . [Speak] of the goodness and power of God. On Wednesday evening the rooms are occupied by the quorum of Elders . . . On Thursday P.M. a*

---

[6] B. H. Roberts, ed., *History of The Church of Jesus Christ of Latter-day Saints,* Second Edition, Revised (Salt Lake City: Deseret Book, 1976) (hereinafter "HC") volume 2, 518

prayer meeting is held in the lower part of the house . . . [It] is conducted by Joseph Smith senior, the patriarch of the church. During the week a school is taught in the attic story of the house, denominated the 'Kirtland High School.' . . . On the streets are continually thronged with teams loaded with wood, materials for building the ensuing season, provisions for the market, people to trade, or parties of pleasure to view our stately and magnificent temple. Although our population is by no means as dense as in many villages, yet the number of new buildings erected the last season, those now in contemplation and under contract to build next season, together with our every day occurrences, are evincive of more united exertion, more industry and more enterprise than we have ever witnessed in so sparse a population, so far from any navigable water in this season of the year[7]."

Joseph Smith, III: "I remember I was promised a little wagon, to be built by a wagon-maker living not far from our house, up on the hillside. The name of Alexander Badham is connected in some way with the memory."[8]

Arthur Millikin saw Joseph Smith's splendid coal-black stallion through the open doors of the blacksmith shop. The horse's name was Charlie, Arthur remembered, and he stood outside with several other horses pawing the dust and tossing his head. Arthur had often helped his boss to shoe animals for his customers and knew most of the best horses in town, but this horse called Charlie was special. Strong,

---

[7] *Messenger and Advocate,* January 1837
[8] *The Saints' Herald,* November 6, 1934, 1414

powerful, smart, and a little headstrong, Arthur always treated this particular horse with respect.

Arthur was standing at the lathe, working the foot treadle and turning a spoke for a wagon wheel. Arthur loved the smell of freshly cut wood and watched as the wood shavings peeled cleanly away from the spoke and over his hands onto the dirt floor. On the other side of the shop, Arthur's boss, Alexander Badham, stood at the anvil hammering a glowing piece of metal, the metallic clang ringing loudly, and the orange sparks flying.

Joseph Smith had dismounted Charlie and was standing in the street. Arthur stopped the lathe and ran outside. It was his job to bring horses in for shoeing.

"Mornin'," said Joseph Smith. "It's Arthur, right?"

"Yes, sir," said Arthur shaking his hand, which was strong. Joseph's clothing was plain—a faded black leather vest over an even more faded and frayed red shirt, soft leather boots, and pants of brown homespun. His blue eyes had a hint of humor in them, but still they seemed to look right into Arthur's soul. Arthur swallowed and turned away. He hoped that Joseph Smith couldn't see into his soul. There were more questions there than answers. And some of the questions had to do with this friendly man with the powerful handshake and the piercing blue eyes. Some people called him a prophet. Arthur wasn't completely sure about that.

"Have Badham check Charlie's shoes, will you?" said Joseph Smith, smiling. "Right fore sounds loose."

"Yes, sir!" Arthur took Charlie's reins and led him into the blacksmith and wagon shop. Charlie tossed his head and looked around, the whites of his eyes blazing. The sound of Mr. Badham's hammer and anvil stopped, and he came over to talk with Joseph Smith. Arthur went back to his lathe, but watched as Mr. Badham reset the shoe on Charlie's right fore, all the while chatting with the man many called a prophet.

Arthur caught snatches of conversation over the rumble of the lathe.

"Make it the finest little miniature carriage in the county," Joseph Smith was saying. "Just the size for my little boy . . . pint-sized . . . two seats . . . room in the traces for one small pony . . . red paint . . ."

Arthur tried to focus on his work. It was Wednesday morning, not even the midpoint of a long week. Arthur was twenty years old and just finishing his three-year apprenticeship in the shop of Mr. Badham. Three more months and Arthur would be free to begin his life, start working for pay, build a home, maybe even marry a wife! His life's work would begin in three months.

But what kind of work? Arthur's mind drifted as he turned the lathe and listened absently to the conversation of the Boss and the Prophet. Arthur suddenly had this thought. He could open his own little shop on the other side of the village. He now knew more about making wagon wheels than anyone else in Kirtland village. He knew the various kinds of wood needed to make the hubs, spokes, and rims of a good wagon wheel, all of which should be of good quality and thoroughly dry. He knew how to create exactly mortised hubs, how to fashion the spokes, how to bend the rim into a perfect circle, and then, most importantly, how to trim the hubs to fit the spokes. He knew that unless he applied care and accuracy to his work, the wheel would not be completely round and would bounce and wobble when mounted on the wagon. He could make wagon wheels and sell them to Mr. Badham, who could then concentrate on making wagons. *Yes,* thought Arthur. *I can make wagon wheels. Maybe even marry me a wife!*

Arthur finished the wagon spoke and stopped the lathe. He could suddenly hear Joseph Smith's voice clearly.

"I'll be back from Missouri before Christmas," he said with a loud voice, shaking Mr. Badham's hand. "Next year I want to buy a pony for Little Joseph. He'll be five years old in November, after all. Time that boy had a horse of his own. Little Joseph will have the time of his life as he drives around the village in his own red carriage pulled by his own pony."

"Yes, sir," said Mr. Badham. "Arthur and I will have it all ready for Christmas."

Joseph Smith's blue eyes turned to Arthur, and he nodded at him. "Make it the finest little carriage in the county, Arthur!"

"Yes, sir," said Arthur, smiling.

"But don't tell anybody about it," said Joseph Smith, smiling and lowering his voice. "It's a secret. For my boy."

"Yes sir," said Arthur. "I won't tell anyone."

Arthur and Mr. Badham followed Joseph Smith into the street and watched as he mounted the big black stallion. The other three men mounted up as well.

"Well," said Joseph Smith holding the reins. "Wish us well. We're off for Missouri! We're going to find more places for the Latter-day Saints to gather." Joseph Smith waved at them, and the four horsemen rode down the street and out of the village.

Arthur watched them ride away and walked back inside. The wagon shop was a marvelous place, filled with carriages and wagons in various stages of construction, and the back of the shop was lined with high brackets containing woods being seasoned for use in wagon making. Just now there were six projects under construction in the shop—a large carriage for the Congregational minister in Kirtland, a four-seat buggy for Sidney Rigdon, and several farm wagons. The little red wagon for the Prophet's son would be the seventh project.

Mr. Badham was already seated on a high stool at his drafting table, sketching the wagon. Arthur turned back to the wheel he was making. He loved the feel of the tools in his hands, and every time he slipped on the leather apron and went about his work, he felt good and let the worries and cares of the day slip away.

Just now, there were plenty of worries and cares in his life. First, there were big troubles in Kirtland village. There had been financial trouble with the Kirtland Bank, and a good number of people had lost a considerable amount of money, including Arthur's uncle, Nathaniel Millikin. Uncle Nathaniel had been a signer of the Articles for the Kirtland Safety Society under the leadership of Joseph Smith, and it had now gone completely under water, as Uncle Nathaniel said. "If Joe and Hyrum Smith and all the rest of them are really prophets and seers," his uncle said, "how come they didn't see the crash a-comin'?" In late night conversations in the Millikin house, Arthur had heard men, even some of the leading men of the Church, who were talking openly that Joseph Smith was a false prophet and a heretic. "Let's return to the Old Standard!" some had said. "Let's throw out the scoundrels and return to a true religion."

Arthur wasn't sure if he agreed with his uncle. He was a baptized Latter-day Saint. He went under the waters of the river in a baptism, sure enough. But he still wasn't exactly sure if Joseph Smith was what a lot of people claimed him to be—a prophet, a real prophet, like Moses or Abraham. Following the lead of Joseph Smith had become real complicated for Arthur, and it had already created trouble at home. He now felt it best not to speak his mind in front of his uncle, and it also got him thinking about what he would do when his apprenticeship would end in three months time. Then he could leave his uncle's house and stand on his own two feet. Maybe even marry him a wife!

A wife. For a year now he had been quietly watching Lucy Smith, the youngest sister of Joseph Smith. She was now sixteen years old and suddenly grown from a little girl into a beauty with dark flowing hair and shining blue eyes. Every time Arthur saw those blue eyes in Church meetings in the Kirtland Temple, or on the street, he felt the blood rush to his face, and his mouth seemed to freeze, preventing him from saying anything. He wanted to speak to Lucy and tell her how he felt, but that was just plain craziness, Arthur thought. Crazy that a blacksmith's and wagon maker's measly apprentice could attract the gaze of those fiery blue eyes. Arthur wanted to speak to her, but he was a young man of action, not words, and the right time and circumstance never seemed to arise. Maybe it never would. Every day Arthur cursed himself for his stupidity and vowed that he would speak to Lucy, but then when he saw her, his tongue seemed fixed to the roof of his mouth like a spoke mortised into a wheel hub.

LOVINA – SEPTEMBER 27

KIRTLAND, OHIO
Wednesday, September 27, 1837

From August until October of 1837, Hyrum Smith went on a mission to Missouri, leaving his wife, Jerusha Barden Smith and their four children, ten-year-old Lovina, five-year-old John, three-year-old Hyrum, Jr. and eighteen-month-old Jerusha. The mother, Jerusha, was also pregnant and expected to deliver a baby in the autumn. At home in Kirtland, Hyrum left his pregnant wife and small children in the care of two special helpers, who for many years lived with the Hyrum Smith family and acted as domestic servants. These were George Mills (called "Old George" by the family), a destitute veteran of the British and Canadian armies who helped with farming duties and caring for the horses and livestock, and Hanna Grinnels (called "Aunty Grinnels" by the family), an older woman who had been taken into the Smith home out of charity in 1833, but remained with the family as a servant for many years. Despite leaving his family in apparent good hands, Hyrum Smith, upon his departure for Far West in August of 1837, felt an unaccountable "spirit of foreboding."[9]

---

[9] Pearson H. Corbett, Hyrum Smith—Patriarch (Salt Lake City: Deseret Book, 1963) 161 and 213 (note 4).

On September 27, 1837, the day Joseph Smith rode from Kirtland to join his brother Hyrum in Far West, ten-year-old Lovina Smith was the oldest child in the family, and the emotional mainstay for her mother, who was eight months pregnant.

Lovina Smith watched through the curtains of the front room window as her Uncle Joseph rode past on his big black stallion, Charlie. Sidney Rigdon and two other horsemen rode with him.

"Where's Uncle Joseph going, Mama?" she asked, standing between the parted curtains. Her mother was sitting in her rocking chair by the fireplace.

"Far West," said Lovina's mother, Jerusha Smith.

"Will he see Papa there?"

"Yes, of course. And perhaps he'll return with Papa before Christmas."

"That is my wish for Christmas and the New Year," said Lovina. "To have Papa back home for good."

"Well, it won't be for good, I'm sure," said Mama. "But I promise you, your father will be home for Christmas."

"Will he, Mama? Will he truly? That is my fondest wish, that at Christmas Papa may be home, in this very room, surrounded by all of our family? Do you promise it will be so?"

"I promise, Lovina," said her mother. "I promise."

Lovina watched as the horsemen rode south down the Chillcothe Road on their way to Far West. Then she turned to look at Mama, big with child. The rocking chair creaked quietly, the fire crackling in the hearth. Lovina went and sat on the floor by her mother, who stroked her daughter's hair gently with one hand, the other resting on her round belly.

An older woman came to the door, her gray hair pulled back in a knot behind her head. "I've put little Jerusha down for her nap," she said softly to Lovina's mother. "I'll start the jam-making now."

The older woman's proper name was Hanna Grinnels, but the family all called her "Aunty Grinnels." Aunty was a convert to the Church who had been taken in, destitute, by Papa several years before. She had lived all this time under their roof, at first exchanging her room and board for work, but in recent years she stayed for the love of Lovina's family. Lovina and her little siblings—five-year-old John, three-year-old Hyrum, Jr., and twenty-month-old Jerusha—were devoted to Aunty Grinnels, and she to them.

"Oh, Aunty," said Mama. "Wait for me. I want to help with the jam."

"No, ma'am, Sister Jerusha!" said Aunty Grinnels, holding up her hand in mock warning. "You're not moving from that chair this morning. I'll manage just fine with your young lady and with help from young John and Hyrum Jr."

"Thank you, Aunty!" said Mama, settling back into the rocking chair.

"I'll go outside and fetch—" Lovina said as she started to stand up, but was interrupted by her mother.

"Quick, child," said Mama suddenly. "Give me your hand."

Lovina turned in surprise. Her mother was smiling and reaching for Lovina's hand. She gave it to her mother in confusion. Mama took Lovina's palm and placed it over her belly, holding the girl's palm flat against the fabric of Mama's dress.

At first Lovina felt nothing, but then a sudden movement fluttered beneath her hand, like the sensation of a baby bird beating its little wings. "I can feel something moving!" said Lovina, her eyes large with wonder.

"It's your sister," said Mama.

"The baby?" said Lovina.

Mama nodded, smiling at her oldest daughter. "She's kicking a lot this morning. She must know that her big sister is close by."

"It's my sister?" said Lovina. "How do you know? Maybe it's a boy."

"Maybe," said Mama. "But I think it's a girl. But we shall see, won't we?" She leaned over and kissed Lovina on the cheek.

"John! John! Where are you?" Lovina stood in the barn and called for her little brother. She walked down the length of the ground floor looking for signs of the little truant. The horse stalls were empty, except for one holding her favorite, the sweet filly she called Bluebird. She paused to stroke her nose. "John! I know you are in here. We need to help Aunty put up the jam."

The horse stall for her father's favorite horse, the white stallion called Sam, was empty and dry. Her father had been gone so long on his mission to Missouri, and she missed him. Papa was an important man in the Church, and the oldest living brother of the Prophet, her Uncle Joseph Smith.

He relied so much upon his brother Hyrum. It made Lovina proud, but she missed him terribly when he went away.

"John!" she called again.

"It may be that he's hidin'," said a voice behind her. She turned to see Old George, standing in the doorway of the stable with a shovel in his hands. A bristle of white whiskers covered his neck and his wrinkled cheeks, and his blue eyes were bright.

"Where is he?" asked Lovina.

"I'm not supposed to tell," said Old George, winking at her. "Orders from the General." Old George held his shovel by his side like a musket and saluted smartly with his right hand. Old George's dirty coveralls and round belly hardly made him look like a military man, but Lovina knew he often pretended to be a soldier for the sake of her little brother, John. Old George was a destitute veteran of the British and Canadian armies who had lived with the family for years. Lovina's Papa had taken him in, as well as Aunty Grinnels, out of pity for his poverty. Old George took care of things in the barn and the yard, feeding and watering the livestock, brushing down the stallion Sam and the other horses and taking care of their saddles and bridles and other tack, cutting and stacking firewood, planting and tending the corn, potatoes, carrots, parsnips, onions and other vegetables in the garden, and so forth. He was an interesting old man. Lovina knew that Old George was not a member of the Church, but he was a good, gentle, and kind man. Hyrum Smith had a propensity for taking in people who had nowhere else to go or no money to sustain themselves. He had taken Old George in and offered him a home in 1833, when Lovina was only six years old, and so she had known him much of her life. He had been with them ever since. But Old George was no substitute for a father.

"I have a message for the General," said Lovina to Old George. "It's from headquarters, but I must deliver it personally. Can you tell me where the General is?"

Old George leaned his head forward to whisper. "He's up on the mountain, in the lookout nest." Old George's eyes darted in the direction of the hayloft and back to Lovina. Then he winked at her.

Lovina winked back at Old George and then began to climb up into the hayloft. It was late afternoon and a shaft of sunlight illuminated the pile of hay. The air was filled with the sweet aroma of hay, and she heard the meowing of a kitten somewhere beyond the great pile. At the top she glimpsed John's head. He had constructed walls around a central nest of straw. She peered over the wall at her little brother. He was wearing the little sailor's cap Papa had given to him and had a stick thrust through a rope tied around his waist, like a sword in its scabbard.

"What are you doing up here, John?" she asked. "Aunty Grinnels needs our help making jam."

"I'm just building a safe place," he said. "A safe place for me and my army—and for the whole family."

Lovina climbed over the wall of straw and sat down by her brother. Putting her arm around him, she said, "I know, John. I know. We all need a safe place."

LITTLE JOSEPH – SEPTEMBER 28

KIRTLAND, OHIO
Thursday, September 28, 1837

Joseph Smith journeyed from Kirtland, Ohio, to Far West, Missouri, from September 27, 1837, until his return on December 10, 1837. During those forty-four days, his wife Emma Smith was left alone at home in Kirtland with their three children; six-year old Julia Murdock Smith; four-year-old Joseph Smith, III; and one-year-old Frederick Granger Williams Smith.[10]

Also remaining in Ohio during the Prophet's absence was Major, the family's faithful watchdog. Joseph Smith, III later remembered this incident about Major: "I remember this dog particularly from the fact that upon one occasion (after he had been fighting and had had his ears chewed until they were sore), the baby was set down by him as he lay upon the floor. The baby pulled his ears, which hurt him so that he growled fiercely. Father punished him severely for this, boxing his ears soundly. This treatment resulted in his never afterwards lying quietly when a child was placed near him. He would spring to his feet immediately and go away, evidently never forgetting the punishment he had received for growling at the baby."[11]

---

[10] HC 2:518-28
[11] Saints Herald, November 6, 1934, 1414

The morning had dawned cold and cloudless, with a crispness in the air that hinted at the end of summer. Little Joseph closed the back door carefully and walked outside into the yard. His breath came in drafts of steam in the cold air, and he rubbed his hands as he walked across the yard to the stable. Inside, the black horse called Jim nickered, and the boy set to work with the pitchfork, just the way Father had taught him, placing fresh feed between the poles, being careful not to poke the horse with the sharp points. Jim ate the feed eagerly, sending blasts of air from his nostrils. Little Joseph breathed in the smell of the horse, the feed, and the manure on the floor. The sun came up and sent shafts of light into the open door of the stable, glinting off of the metal bits and harnesses hanging from nails on the posts and walls.

Little Joseph loved this place better than any other on earth. He loved horses, and soon he would have his own horse. Yesterday his father, Joseph Smith, Jr., had ridden off on a long journey to Missouri, riding his favorite horse, a big black stallion with a white patch of fur on his forehead, shaped almost like a star. Today Old Charlie's box was empty, but Little Joseph could still smell his presence in the stable. He tried to picture what it must be like to ride across the countryside for a thousand miles, or nearly that much, with his father. Little Joseph had the same name as his father, and he loved horses just like his father. Yesterday, as he watched Father ride off on Old Charlie, Little Joseph had yearned to run after them, but Father had said, "You're the man of the house now! Take care of your mother and sister and little brother. And take care of Jim!"

In the shelter of the stable were Father's farm wagon and an old four-wheeled carriage, which the family always used for excursions around about town or out into the countryside. Charlie and Jim made a handsome pair, two black stallions pulling the carriage, both big and strong. But Charlie was the smarter of the two.

Little Joseph hoped to one day have his own riding horse. The night before Father left for Missouri he had overheard a whispered conversation between Mother and Father.

"But he's only four years old, Joseph," Mother had said quietly from their bed. Little Joseph had been passing in the hallway in his bare feet, going to the outhouse early in the morning. The planks of the floor had been cold on his feet, but he paused outside his parents' door to listen. "Four years old! That's not nearly old enough."

"He's almost five, Emma," whispered Father. "I was riding in a saddle before I was five. He's up to it. I promise."

"I don't know," said Mother. "He could get hurt and never ride again."

"He won't get hurt," said Father. "Little Joseph is born to ride. He takes to it naturally."

"No, Joseph," said Mother. "He's too small for his age."

"He'll grow," said Father. "And first I aim to get him a little horse carriage he can ride in until his legs are long enough for the saddle."

"A carriage?"

"Yes, a miniature carriage. I mean to have Alexander Badham build him one. Something fine, with two seats, so he can take his sister or little brother out for rides in the village. I picture something red."

"A red carriage?" said Mother. "You will spoil these children."

"A red carriage," said Father. "And then a pony to pull it."

Little Joseph looked at Father's wagon in the stable, and tried to picture a little red carriage sitting beside it. *A red carriage and a pony, all my own*, thought Little Joseph, smiling.

Little Joseph sat at the kitchen table. The bench was smooth, unvarnished wood. Beside him was his older sister, six-year-old Julia. Mother sat across from him, holding one-year-old Freddie, who was clacking a pair of wooden blocks together happily. Major, a huge white mastiff, walked into the room and lay down on the floor next to the kitchen hearth, where a small fire was crackling merrily on this cool autumn morning. Major was bigger than Julia, Little Joseph, and Freddie put together, weighing over two hundred fifty pounds and standing taller than Father on his hind legs.

A plump, cheerful woman, also over two hundred fifty pounds, was standing at the iron cooking stove stirring a pot of hot porridge. This was Polly Beswick, who boarded with Joseph and Emma Smith and helped around the house.

"Porridge is ready," said Polly, smiling at the children, then whispered, "I've even put a bit 'o sugar in it!" She wrapped a towel around the handle of the pot and carried it to the table.

"When will Father come back from Far West?" asked Julia, holding up her wooden bowl while Polly ladled hot porridge into it.

"Weeks," said Mother, hoisting Frederick from her right side to her left. "Months. Who knows? It's eight hundred miles to Far West, dear."

"He's gone to the far west on Old Charlie," announced Little Joseph loudly, to no one in particular.

"It's not called 'the' far west, Joseph." Said Mother. "It's called 'Far West.' That's the name of the city. And maybe sometime we can travel there with your Father."

Little Joseph's eyes got big. "You mean we can to the far west—I mean 'Far West'—next time with Father?"

"I didn't say next time," said Mother. "I said 'sometime.'"

Polly laughed, and mother smiled.

"Say a blessing on the food, Julia," said Mother. They all bowed their heads and closed their eyes.

"Heavenly Father," said Julia. "Bless Father on his journey with Old Charlie. Bless Mother and me, and Little Joseph and Freddie, and Polly, and Old Charlie and Jim, and Major, and all the saints. We thank thee for this food. Please bless it. In the name of Jesus Christ, Amen."

"Amen," said everyone.

"Why can't we go to the far west soon?" asked Little Joseph.

"'Far West,' dear," said Mother. "Because our home is in Kirtland, not Far West. Kirtland is where you were born, Joseph. God willing, you may live your whole life here, and die here as a happy, happy old man."

"But I don't want to *live* in Far West, Mother," said Little Joseph. "I just want to visit there, like Father, then come back home to Kirtland. If you don't want to go with me, I could just follow Father to Far West on my own."

"How would you even get to Far West?" laughed Julia. "It's eight hundred miles away and you're only a little boy."

"I would go in my new red carriage."

"What carriage?" asked Julia.

Little Joseph looked up at his Mother to see if she was angry. His cheeks and neck began to turn red. "I heard Father tell you that he was going to have Mr. Badham build me a carriage."

Mother looked sharply at her son. "When did you hear that?"

"Yesterday morning," said Little Joseph. "Early. When I was getting up to go out to the outhouse."

Mother shook her head and smiled.

"When I get my red carriage, I'll also get a pony. Then I can hitch him up and follow Father on the road to the far west."

Mother stood up and walked over behind Little Joseph. She kissed his cheek quickly and smoothed the boy's hair. "Well, there's no carriage made yet, and besides, it's a secret. So don't you be telling your father that you know anything about it when he gets home. It's his surprise. Do you promise not to tell?"

"Okay," said Little Joseph. "I promise."

"And meantime, Joseph," said Mother, "I need you here in Kirtland. You're the man of the house until your father comes back. Now, finish eating your breakfast."

Polly asked, "What can I be doing to help you, today, Sister Emma?"

"Oh, Polly," said Mother. "I don't even know where to begin. Joseph has been away more time this year than at home, it seems. And while he is gone the pressures never let up. The situation of his business is very difficult, and there is no prospect right now of getting a single dollar. We're lucky to have our bread."

"I can catch food for you, Mother!" announced Little Joseph.

"What food would you catch?" she laughed.

"Wild animals!" he said.

"Well I'll cook up anything you catch, Joseph!" said Polly, patting the boy on his head. "Things will be better," she said to Mother. "I know they will be better when your husband returns."

"I hope so," said Mother, and she placed Frederick on the floor where he could play with the blocks that he had dropped from the table. Major immediately got up and walked away.

"Why does he always do that?" asked Polly. "Every time you set that baby down on the floor, the dog gets up and walks off."

"Right after Freddie was born," said Mother, "Major got into a fight with a pack of dogs down on the Chardon Road. He got the best of the fight, but his ears were sore. Soon thereafter, one day, I put little Freddie on the floor to play, and he crawled over to Major and pulled his ears. The old dog growled, and my husband boxed his ears soundly. From that day to this, he can't abide to be on the floor with a little child, from memory of that boxing, I guess."

"I'll remember never to go growling around Brother Joseph," laughed Polly.

"Mama," said Julia. "Can I go across the street to visit Lacy Rigdon?"

"I suppose," said Mother. "Just don't get your dress dirty."

"Can I go outside, Mother?" asked Little Joseph.

"Yes. Just be careful."

Julia pulled her shawl over her dress, and Little Joseph put on his cap and coat, and the two children, brother and sister, ran out the front door.

Julia – September 28

KIRTLAND, OHIO
Thursday, September 28, 1837

Julia Murdock Smith: "Until I was a child of five, I was happy."[12]

Joseph and Emma Smith's oldest surviving daughter, Julia Murdock Smith, was adopted. She and a twin brother, Joseph Murdock, were born on April 30, 1831, to John and Julia Murdock, a Latter-day Saint couple living in the Kirtland area. Julia's mother died immediately after the birth. With striking coincidence, that same day, April 30, 1831, Emma Smith gave birth to a set of twins, Thaddeus and Louisa Smith, who both died within a few hours of birth. The Murdock twins were given to the Smiths by their father, John Murdock. Julia's twin brother, Joseph, died a year later after being exposed to the cold on the night Joseph Smith was tarred and feathered by a mob.[13]

Julia grew up not knowing that she was adopted and believing that Joseph and Emma Smith were her parents. According to her account, when Julia was about five or six years old, one of her playmates told her that she was not really a Smith, but had been adopted at birth. This

---

[12] Letter from Julia Murdock Smith Middleton to John R. Murdock, November 2, 1858, in John R. Murdock, An Abridged Record of the Life of John Murdock (Typescript, copy in possession of author), 99-100

[13] *See, generally,* S. Reed Murdock, *Joseph and Emma's Julia, The "Other" Twin,* (Salt Lake City: Eborn Books, 2004) 1-25

disclosure devastated little Julia. She was never quite the same after learning of her adoption, and the issue weighed heavily upon her thoughts throughout her life. Julia later wrote that she often felt a "sting" when she would hear people say to Emma: "Oh, is this your adopted daughter?"[14]

Julia Smith watched her little brother run down the hill toward the river. From here she could hear the faint rush of the river waters, as well as the sound of carriage wheels, hammers, saws, distant voices, and the vague echo of music drifting up from the village below.

Julia and her parents lived on a hilltop overlooking a network of roadways, shops, stores, and homes below. Behind her were other homes besides Father's white frame house, including the one belonging to her Uncle Hyrum, and the substantial mansion belonging to the father of her best friend in all the world, Lacy Rigdon. Across from Lacy's house was the Kirtland Temple, the center of all of their lives.

Julia walked in a ladylike fashion across the road toward the Rigdons' house. Mother had taught Julia that she should always be ladylike, even at age six. *Your father is an important man*, Mother had told her. *People look up to him, and they look up to you, for you are his daughter and his eldest child. You are the eldest child of a great man.*

---

[14] *Joseph and Emma's Julia*, 25; see also Sunny McClellan Morton, "The Forgotten Daughter: Julia Murdock Smith, in *Mormon Historical Studies*, vol. 3 no. 2, 35-60, Fall 2002

Julia turned and looked back at their home. It was a little white-framed house, two stories high with a long covered front porch in the front, and it stood on a little hill above the road. In back was her mother's little orchard, the vegetable garden, and the pasture and stable where Father kept his horses, Old Charlie and Jim. Julia knew that her father and mother were not wealthy, like the Rigdons and the Johnsons, but Julia didn't care. She thought her home was the most beautiful place on earth. It was the one place on earth where she felt completely safe and loved.

Just yesterday, when Julia had stood on the kitchen bench to kiss Father lightly on his unshaven cheek, he had swept her up in his arms and danced a waltz through the little rooms of their main floor. Then he had deposited her on the front porch, where she stood with Mother and her two brothers to watch him tie his saddlebags onto Old Charlie, mount up, and ride away.

Today it was a nearly perfect September morning, with flowers still blooming along the borders of Mother's garden and the trees still filled with green leaves, which rustled in the wind. Julia felt the wind in her dark hair and suddenly had a powerful sense of happiness. She knew that here, in Kirtland, in this little white house, surrounded by her father, mother, and her little brothers, she belonged!

She skipped off across the street and past the great temple to the house of her best friend, Lacy Ann Rigdon, who at age five was just a year younger than Julia.

The Rigdons' house was much nicer than the little white house owned by her father and mother. For one thing, there were more Rigdons than Smiths. Lacy's father, Sidney

Rigdon, was the counselor to Julia's father in the Church's First Presidency, and President and Sister Rigdon had nine children. Julia had memorized all of their names, in birth order: Athalia, Nancy, Eliza, Sarah, Sid, Wycliffe, Lacy, Carvel, and Dorcas. Lacy's oldest sister, Athalia, was already fully-grown at age sixteen and had recently married Father's secretary, George Robinson. Julia wondered at what age she would marry. Sixteen sounded like the right time.

The Rigdons' house had a big middle part and then two long wings, filled with rooms, spreading out on both sides. It also had a long, deep front porch, like the porch of a palace, it seemed to Julia. It was directly across the street from the Kirtland Temple, with its high tower looking down directly on Lacy Rigdon's house. Julia thought Lacy's house was the grandest building in Kirtland, aside from the temple.

She stood on the front porch and knocked, and Lacy answered. "Let's play in my room," she said, taking Julia's hand and running up the staircase. They passed Lacy's big brothers, Sid and Wycliffe, on the staircase. The boys were talking loudly and had fishing poles in their hands. They were followed by three-year old Carvel, who was trying to keep up.

"Where are you going, Carvel?" a voice sounded from below. Julia looked through the staircase bannister and saw Lacy's mother, Sister Phebe Rigdon. She was sitting in a rocking chair in the front room with a quilt over her knees. Julia thought she looked tired.

"I'm going fishing!" cried little Carvel.

"No, he's not," said Sid, the oldest brother. "Wycliffe and I can't watch him; we'll be fishing. Besides, the river's too deep."

"I want to go!" said Carvel.

"Your brother is right, Carvel," said Sister Rigdon. "You best wait until your father can go with you before you go fishing."

Carvel started to cry. Sid and Wycliffe looked at each other and shrugged, then headed out the front door.

"Come sit by me, son," said Sister Rigdon in a kindly voice. "I'll read you a story."

Julia and Lacy continued up to the top of the staircase. "He's always crying," said Lacy. "I'm glad I don't have to share a room with him." They went into the big upstairs room Lacy shared with her older sister Sarah. Lacy closed the door.

Lacy Rigdon had more clothes and toys than anyone Julia knew. In the center of the room she shared with her twelve-year-old sister Sarah was a wooden rocking horse. Lacy climbed up onto the horse's back and started rocking. Julia picked up one of Lacy's pretty dolls and smoothed its blue, hand-sewn dress.

"You have a lot of brothers and sisters," said Julia, sitting on a little, wooden chair. "I only have two little brothers, but maybe my mother will have more children soon."

"My mother might have more children, too," said Lacy, watching Julia's face.

"How many children can one mother have?" asked Julia. "Your mother has already had nine babies, but my mother only had me and my two little brothers, not counting some babies who died."

Lacy said nothing, but kept rocking on her horse, throwing her head and long hair back as she rode. "Hey, Julia," she finally said. "I've learned some secrets since we last played."

"What secrets?" asked Julia, stroking the hair of the doll in the blue dress.

"I don't know exactly," said Lacy. "I didn't understand it all. But I heard some secrets."

"What about?" asked Julia.

"Things. Mostly about your father, but also about you," said Lacy, continuing to rock back and forth. "I heard my father talking with Brother Granger in our parlor two days ago, the night before your father rode away on his old black horse with my father on his fine horse."

"His old black horse is called Charlie, and Father says he's the finest horse in all of Ohio."

"He may be a good horse," said Lacy, "but he's not as fine as *my* father's horse. His horse is called Champ, and he's a true thoroughbred champion. He cost my father two hundred dollars."

"Well, never mind that," said Julia. "What secrets did you hear about my father?"

"Well, like I said, the night before our fathers rode off to Missouri, Brother Granger was here. He said that your father has had another big lawsuit filed against him."

Julia flushed with anger and embarrassment. "I know that," she lied. "But it's nothing, only persecution, my mother said. Father has lots of enemies, because he preaches the true gospel."

"But my father says that your father doesn't have any money."

"Well, we have enough," said Julia, her face turning red. "And besides, money isn't everything, you know."

"It is if you don't have any. And Brother Granger said your father might even go to jail if he can't pay the money!"

"We have enough money," shouted Julia. Suddenly she didn't want to be here in this big house, playing with all these toys. "I've got to go, Lacy."

"Before you go, I want to tell you one other secret," said Lacy, still rocking on her wooden horse.

"What's that," said Julia.

"Joseph and Emma Smith aren't really your parents!" said Lacy.

"What?" said Julia.

"Joseph and Emma Smith aren't even your parents."

Julia was silent as this began to sink in. "What do you mean?"

"They're not your real parents. They're your little brothers' parents, but they're not your parents."

"Of course they're my parents," shouted Julia. "I'm the oldest child in the Smith family!"

"No, you're not! Your little brother Joseph is the oldest. You're not even a Smith."

"Yes I am! Joseph Smith is my father and Emma Smith is my mother! I'm their oldest child, and we live in the white house across the street! They're my real parents, and you're cruel to say they're not! I want to go now, because you're stupid!"

"I'm not stupid," shouted Lacy. "I heard my father and mother talking about it when they didn't know I was listening. They're not your true parents, and Joseph and Freddie aren't your real brothers!"

"Yes, they are!"

"No, they aren't. You've got two other parents that didn't even want you. They gave you to Joseph and Emma Smith when you were just a little baby."

Julia felt the tears spring into her eyes and fall down her cheeks.

"I hate you!" cried Julia. "I hate you!" She threw the doll across the room at Lacy and ran down the stairs and outside into the bright sunlight.

LITTLE JOSEPH – SEPTEMBER 28

KIRTLAND, OHIO
Thursday, September 28, 1837

Joseph Smith, III: "My earliest recollections of men, things, and events begin at Kirtland. The house we occupied stood on the west side of the street which runs from the Temple down to the Chagrin River and was not very far from the ford across this little stream. Memory has a picture of my going down to the creek with a number of other boys who engaged in fishing for the small edible fish in the stream. Seeing their success I, too, wanted to fish. My mother, to gratify me, procured a little pole and attached a thread thereto, with a bent pin for a hook, and away I marched to the creek."[15]

Mother!" he shouted, bursting into the house.

"Whatever is wrong?" asked Mother.

"Nothing. I just wanted to ask if I can have a fishing pole. I'm going to catch you some food for dinner!"

"A fishing pole? But you don't know how to fish."

"Yes I do! I watched Oliver Huntington catch a fish down at the river!"

---

[15] *Saints Herald*, November 6, 1934, 1414

Mother smiled, and Little Joseph thought he saw a tear in her eye. "Well," said Mother. "Let's see what we can do to make a fishing pole."

Little Joseph followed his mother outside to the porch, where she often sat on a wicker chair, sewing and visiting with her family members or friends. There was an overhanging willow tree, and from this Mother snapped off a low hanging branch, and stripped the autumn leaves from it. Then, sitting in her wicker chair, she unraveled a length from a ball of thread in her sewing basket, then took out a pin from her pin cushion. This she bent into a hook, and attached it to one end of the thread. The other end she tied securely around the end of the pole.

"Here you go, my fisherman!" she announced, handing the little boy the homemade pole.

Little Joseph took the pole and ran off excitedly for the river.

Little Joseph stood amid the crowd of boys on the bank of the Chagrin River, watching the water flow over the stones, which acquired strange, wavy shapes beneath the movement of the clear water.

Little Joseph extended his fishing pole over the water, and the hook dangled above the surface.

"Hey, you need some bait on that hook," laughed Wickliffe Rigdon. He was a big, heavyset boy with dark hair, which he combed from left to right, like his father.

"What's bait?" asked Little Joseph.

"A worm or something," laughed Wickliffe.

"Well, I don't have any bait," said Little Joseph, and he dropped his hook into the water.

All the boys laughed, and Little Joseph felt angry. He stood there on the bank with the pole in his hands, then he felt a little jerk on the pole. He could feel the vibration in his hands. Then he felt nothing, but a moment later he felt it again, and then the fishing line dipped violently in the water. Little Joseph almost lost hold of the pole, but he gripped it tight and lifted it. He had a fish on the hook!

"I can't believe it," shouted Wickliffe. "The little snot actually caught one without bait!"

All the boys now gathered around, shouting. Little Joseph pulled up and toward the shore and withdrew a six-inch fish from the water, slapping the water with its tail and wriggling with all its might. He brought it to shore and then tried to pick it up in his hands. It wriggled free.

"Here," said Oliver Huntington at Little Joseph's side. "Just put your fingers under its gills, like this." He showed Little Joseph how to hold the fish without dropping it.

"I'm going to show Mother," shouted Little Joseph, running up the hill, holding the fish, still fighting and waving its tail.

"I've got one! I've got one!" shouted Little Joseph, running back into the house.

Polly Beswick placed her hands on her wide hips and laughed out loud.

"Well, I never!" said Mother.

"I told you I'd help catch food for you!" said Little Joseph.

"And I promised that I would cook any food you caught," said Polly, reaching for the frying pan.

WYCLIFFE – SEPTEMBER 29

KIRTLAND, OHIO
Friday, September 29, 1837

Wycliffe Rigdon: "Kirtland was where my first recollections began. I remember well the building of the temple. It was finished in 1837 and was dedicated. . . . The upper story of the temple was used for schools. I went to school the last year we remained at Kirtland. Elias Smith, who was probate judge of Salt Lake in 1863, was my teacher. . . . Mormons were not permitted to remain at Kirtland a great length of time after completion of the temple. In less than two years from its completion Joseph Smith and Sidney Rigdon were forced to leave Kirtland on account of their starting of the Kirtland Bank. . . . They gave their notes for the silver needed to start the bank. It ran but a short time as they could not get the silver to redeem the bills, the bills came back to the bank faster than silver could be gotten to redeem them with, and the bank went down. . . . One Warren Parrish, who used to be a good Mormon and who got notes in his possession and had apostatized from Mormonism, got angry with Joseph for some reason unknown to me and told Joseph that he had notes which Joseph and Sidney had given upon which they had borrowed money to start the bank with. And they were about due. And if the notes were not paid at maturity, he would sue them and get judgment against Joseph and Sidney, and if judgment was not paid, he would put them in jail where they would stay until judgment was paid. There was a law in the State of Ohio to the effect that if one got a judgment on a debt against another and it was not paid, he could be

thrown into jail and remain there until he paid it. As they could not pay judgment, all they could do was to get out of the state."[16]

The windows of the big two-story house looked across Chillicothe road to the temple. The temple was the first thing Wycliffe Rigdon saw every morning as he awoke in the second-story bedroom he shared with his older brother, Sid. He parted the curtain and gazed at the soaring walls of the temple across the street from the Rigdon house. It was Wycliffe's morning ritual to look out and watch the first sunlight strike the walls of the temple, which stood like the pointer of some great sundial in the city of Kirtland.

By late afternoon the temple overshadowed the Rigdon house, just as it overshadowed the thoughts of the family. Among Wycliffe's earliest memories was the construction of the temple, which was one of the largest buildings in the state of Ohio. He remembered watching out of this window as hundreds of men worked from early morning until ten or twelve at night on the temple. His father, Sidney Rigdon, and the Prophet Joseph Smith himself had worked as hard as anyone. Joseph Smith had hitched up his own horse, a magnificent and powerful black stallion, to drag blocks of stone from the quarry onto the construction site.

The day the temple was dedicated was a great time of rejoicing for the members of the Church in Kirtland. That morning, Wycliffe had sat by his window as usual and had seen at dawn already many hundreds of people waiting by the doors of the temple. When the doors were opened at

---

[16] J. Wycliffe Rigdon, "History," typescript in author's possession, 27

eight o'clock, the sanctuary on the first floor had been filled quickly. The room was designed to hold five hundred people, but the saints doubled up on the available seating and one thousand filled the room. So many members wanted to attend the dedication, that they could not all get into the building on the first day, so the ceremony was continued on a second day. Wycliffe was five years old at the time, and he had crowded into one of the wooden pews with his older sisters—Athalia, Nancy, Eliza, and Sarah— and his older brother, Sid. His younger siblings Lacy and Samuel had been too young to attend, and his sister Phebe was not born yet. As the first counselor in the First Presidency of the Church, Wycliffe's father sat beside Joseph Smith in one of the highest pulpits designated for the Melchizedek Priesthood on the west side of the temple. The sight of his father sitting in this high position gave Wycliffe a feeling of awe. He was in awe of his father, just as he was in awe of the temple.

Wycliffe's father had preached the sermon on the first day of the dedication, taking his text from Matthew 8: "The foxes have holes, and the birds of the air have nests; but the Son of man hath not where to lay his head." Even at age five, this verse was familiar to Wycliffe, as his father made sure that all of the children read scriptures out loud in the home every day. Morning, noon, and night, on weekdays and holidays, Sid and Wycliffe were fed with the milk of the Word. Wycliffe had been named after John Wycliffe, the fourteenth century English religious reformer who had translated the Bible into English. His brother Sid had been named for Algernon Sidney, the seventeenth century English reformer and martyr. Wycliffe and Sid spent many hours sitting with their father in his study, reading scripture and discussing politics and religion. His father would often pause to gaze at the temple as they came and went from the house, saying, "This is the first temple in modern times which has been built and dedicated to the service of the Living God."

What a glorious time the saints experienced in that temple dedication. When Wycliffe joined in the shouts of Hosannah with a thousand saints, he felt a thrill pass through him. After the dedication, the people came to church every Sunday because they wanted to come. You could not keep them away, and a great many strangers also came to hear the Mormons and especially Wycliffe's father preach. His father usually preached every Sunday morning, and Wycliffe was proud that great crowds, both members and strangers, came to hear him.

But that was nearly two years ago. Now, in the fall of 1837, all was not well with the saints who met each week in the temple. Wycliffe's father had told his sons that Warren Parrish, formerly a key leader of the Church, and a large number of followers believed that the gospel as preached by Joseph Smith and Sidney Rigdon in 1837 had somehow departed from the "pure truths" they held sacred. Wycliffe often passed Warren Parrish's house in Kirtland village. It stood next door to the house of Nathaniel Millikin, another dissenter. The Parrish faction was attempting to gain control of the Kirtland Temple, Father Rigdon had told his sons, because they believed that its possession would give them a greater claim to legitimacy.

As Wycliffe watched, the sun cleared the horizon, illuminating the walls of the temple and casting a reflected orange glow into the boys' bedroom. Sid stirred in the bed and rubbed his eyes. "What time is it?" he asked.

"Just after seven o'clock," said Wycliffe. Downstairs he could hear the voices of his mother and older sisters. Through the walls he could hear the younger children—Lacy, Samuel, and Phebe—making a tremendous racket, jumping on the beds it sounded like. There was a great crash, then dead silence followed by whispering.

"Lacy!" called mother up the stairs. "What is going on up there? Are you all right, dear?"

The Rigdon children sat on long benches on either side of the table with their heads bowed for the prayer. Wycliffe's oldest sister, Athalia and her husband George Robinson were seated together at one end. Generally Father called on someone to pray, but since he was traveling to Missouri with the Prophet, Wycliffe's mother called upon six-year old Lacy to pray.

"Oh, Mother," Lacy said, "Not again. It's Sid's turn. Or Wycliffe's."

"Okay, dear," said mother. "Sid, why don't you pray today!"

Sid and Wycliffe exchanged glances, but Sid said a quick prayer. Their mother was too apt to give in to her precocious young daughter. Generally Mother was very competent and neat in all her household arrangements. But when Lacy demanded something, she avoided confrontation. She moved quietly through the house in her bright colored dresses, a slender woman with dark hair drawn back neatly into a bun. Her complexion was clear, her aprons spotlessly clean, and Wycliffe never thought of her without something in her hand—a ladle, a broom, or a skein of yarn.

"How is school going, boys?" asked George Robinson between bites. Wycliffe idolized his brother-in-law. He was thirty-three years old and had just been appointed as the General Church Recorder and acted as a scribe for Joseph Smith and Wycliffe's father in the First Presidency. When he had married Wycliffe's oldest sister, Athalia, Wycliffe felt like he was gaining a new oldest brother. Athalia was only sixteen years old, and it was still difficult to picture her as a married woman, not the oldest in a house of children. Wycliffe also thought that the girls vastly outnumbered the boys in the family, and it was nice to have another man at the table.

"We're working on Murray's English Reader," said Wycliffe to his brother-in-law. "I'm already on section eight."

George Robinson smiled at the boy. "I know your father will be happy the way you are taking to your reading. How is it going for you, Sid?"

"It's all right," said Sid. Wycliffe knew that this was not entirely true. His older brother was nine, two years older than Wycliffe, but was already behind him in his reading and arithmetic. Sid hated sitting in a classroom all day, studying English grammar and the multiplication tables to be learned by heart. What Sid loved was working with his hands. He was the one most willing to bring in the wood before they left for school, to help with the milking, or to give the cattle their feed. Sid was also handy around the horses. He was the only one of the children who could even approach Champ, father's new fiery and unpredictable gray gelding.

Wycliffe knew that Sid was his mother's favorite son. He whittled pegs for her to hang her apron on inside the milk house, and he could build a fire in the kitchen hearth better than Father. Sid took a great pride in the house, the barn, the stable, and the kitchen garden.

"Finish up," said Mother. "You'll all be late for school. Oh, and Lacy, I thought you were going to wear your older pinafore, not your Sunday best."

"No," said Lacy. "I'm going to wear this one."

"But dear," said mother. "You'll soil it when you play at recess."

"But I want it!" said Lacy. "Please!"

"No, dear. I'm sorry."

"No!" said Lacy, thrusting her lower lip out. Wycliffe noticed that his sister Athalia rolled her eyes. All of the children watched.

"I'm sorry, my dear," said Sister Rigdon. "It just won't do to wear that dress."

Lacy began crying. There were real tears rolling down her cheeks, but Wycliffe knew from experience that she could turn them on and shut them off at will.

Mother looked sympathetically at her daughter. "Oh, I know how much you want to wear the yellow dress, but you must not. Do you understand?"

Lacy did not respond, but threw herself off of her seat and down upon her back on the floor and began kicking her heels on the floor.

"Oh Lacy," said mother. "Please don't do that."

Lacy answered by wailing even louder and then finally bumping the back of her head on the floor.

"Lacy! Oh Lacy, please don't! You'll hurt your head, sweetheart!" cried Mother in alarm.

Lacy continued to scream and bumped her head even harder on the floor.

Finally Mother said, "Oh, all right dear. You can wear your yellow dress."

Wycliffe excused himself and went upstairs to the room he and Sid shared. In the corner was a little desk his father had given him, where Wycliffe kept his books. He sat down and opened the little leather Bible. Inside was an inscription: "To my beloved son John Wycliffe Rigdon," and it was signed, "Sidney Rigdon." Wycliffe turned the pages, and stopped on this verse, "Honor thy father and thy mother, that thy days may be long . . . ."

LUCY – SEPTEMBER 30

KIRTLAND, OHIO
Saturday, September 30, 1837

Lucy Mack Smith: "The persecution became so hot, that Joseph regarded it as unsafe to remain any longer in Kirtland and began making arrangements to move to Missouri."[17]

Henry Caswell: "I walked over to . . . the residence of the prophet's mother. On entering the dwelling, I was introduced to this eminent personage as a traveler . . . She welcomed me . . . And told me that here I might see what great things the Lord had done for his people. ' I am old,' she said, 'and I shall soon stand before the judgment-seat of Christ; but what I say to you now, I would say on my death-bed. My son Joseph has had revelations from God since he was a boy, and he is indeed a true prophet of Jehovah. The angel of the Lord appeared to him fifteen years since, and shewed him the cave where the original golden plates of the Book of Mormon were deposited. He shewed him also the Urim and Thummim, by which he might understand the meaning of the inscriptions on the plates, and he shewed him the golden breastplate of the high priesthood. My son received these precious gifts, he interpreted the holy record, and now the believers in that revelations are thousands in number. I have myself seen and handled the golden plates; they are

---

[17] *History of Joseph Smith by His Mother*, 350

about eight inches long, and six wide; some of them are sealed together and are not to be opened, and some of them are loose. They are all connected by a ring which passes through a hole at the end of each plate, and are covered with letters beautifully engraved . . . ."[18]

Papa had left the house before dawn to ride out to the wild maple groves along the south banks of the Chagrin River to oversee the cutting of winter firewood, Mama told Lucy as she awoke in her soft bed in the early morning. The older woman was standing by the window in the early sunlight with a book in her hands. "Samuel and William and Don Carlos came over for Papa in the lumber wagon. They'll hunt for deer in the morning, then bring down trees and cut logs and load the wagons in the afternoon. We should have some venison and cords of new wood by nightfall. There are herds of deer—big bucks even—along the river, I'm told."

"I've never been on a deer hunt," Lucy said, rubbing the sleep out of her eyes and stretching. Gracie the cat jumped lightly onto the quilt on Lucy's bed and stretched out her long, gray body, then began to purr gently.

"Of course not, child," said Mama. "That's a man province. We've got our own work to do today. Remember, we're meeting Sophronia and Katharine and the sisters-in-law over at Emma's house to lay in wild elderberry jam."

"I remember," said Lucy, smiling. Mama turned to her from the window, holding the book, which Lucy saw was

---

[18] Henry Caswall, "The City of the Mormons" (London: Printed for J.G. F & J. Rivington, 1842), 26-27

the Book of Mormon. "Have you been reading this morning already, Mama?"

"Yes, child," Mama said. "I've been thinking of your brother Joseph on his journey. You get yourself ready, while I sit at the table and read a spell."

Gracie jumped to the floor as Lucy got out of bed. She yawned and then sat by the mirror hanging on the wall of her room and brushed out her long dark hair until it shone. Then she washed her face in the basin and picked out her nicest everyday dress. She had been looking forward to today all week. She dearly loved the little purple elderberries and the jam they produced, but she was especially excited that her little nieces and nephews would be there. She didn't especially care for the jam making, but knew that she could use the excuse of the children to escape from the house, where her older sisters and Mama would be working.

At age sixteen, Lucy felt that she occupied a unique position in her family. She was far younger than her older brothers and sisters. Sophronia, Hyrum, Joseph, Samuel, William, Katharine, and Don Carlos were all married, with houses and families and children of their own. Lucy was still living as a child in her parent's home, but was more of an age with her numerous nieces and nephews.

Her nieces and nephews. They were Lucy's pride and joy—her jewels. She loved being around them more than anything in the world. Lucy felt like a shepherdess among them and would recite their names to herself, like a shepherdess would count her sheep. There were fifteen of them—ten girls and five boys—with one more baby on the way.

As Lucy dressed for the day she counted her flock: first there was her oldest brother Hyrum's brood—Lovina, the eldest of her parents' grandchildren at age ten, then John, Hyrum, and little Jerusha—and Hyrum's wife, Jerusha, was expecting a baby any day now. Lucy's sister Sophronia had five-year-old Mariah. Sophronia was a widow, her husband having died the previous year. Her famous brother Joseph and his wife, Emma, had Julia, Little Joseph, and Frederick. Samuel and his wife, Mary, had two little daughters, Susannah and Mary. Her brother William and his wife, Caroline, had two little girls as well—Mary Jane and little Caroline. Next came the family of her sister Katharine and her husband, Wilkins Salisbury. They had one daughter, Lucy, almost three, and a chubby little boy, Solomon, who had just turned two. And her youngest brother Don Carlos had a beautiful baby, Agnes, who was named after her sister-in-law, Don's wife, also named Agnes.

This was Lucy's little flock—ten girls and five boys— and she smiled as she thought of spending a whole day with them. *Fifteen pearls on my necklace,* she thought, *and a sixteenth pearl in just a few days.* As she looked in the mirror, she gave a final brush to her dark hair and smoothed out the plain, blue dress—it brought out the deep blue of her eyes—and finally arranged an imaginary pearl necklace around her neck.

Emma Smith's kitchen was filled with the voices of children, as Lucy Smith's fifteen nieces and nephews filled every square inch of the room, it seemed. Mama was already at work at the sideboard washing elderberries in a bucket of water, and Lucy's sisters and sisters-in-law—Sophronia, Emma, Mary, Caroline, Katharine, and Agnes—were putting on their aprons. The only sister or sister-in-law missing was Hyrum's wife, Jerusha, who was home, getting ready to deliver the new baby. The air was filled with the sweet conversation of sisters and the joyful chattering of small children.

"You're quiet today, Julia," said Lucy to Joseph and Emma's oldest. Julia was sitting in a little chair in the corner, staring out the window. Usually Julia was the most vivacious and talkative of all her nieces and nephews. But today something was on her mind. "Are you all right?"

Julia didn't say anything, but stood up and walked into the sitting room.

"That apron is too small for you, Agnes!" cried Caroline. "Try this other one."

"That's not very kind, Caroline," said Sophronia. "It's not genteel to comment on another woman's figure." There was an explosion of laughter from the mothers in the room, but Mama continued her work without a sound.

"That's all right, Caroline," said Agnes. Lucy thought she had a musical voice, with a hint of an exotic accent, her being from the far wilderness of Maine, and Agnes was always seemingly filled with laughter and good humor. "I don't mind telling you that the apron's a little tight because there be two of us inside it right now."

That news sunk in for a few moments before Caroline Smith screamed in delight and hugged her sister-in-law. "Is it true?" she asked. This finally got Mama's attention, and she turned around from her elderberries, her mouth open in surprise.

Agnes Smith's face had turned bright red beneath her beaming smile. She nodded her head as all of the sisters gathered around and embraced her. "It's true," said Agnes Smith. Don Carlos and I are expecting a new wee one—a brother or sister for little Agnes.

"How soon?" asked Caroline. "Do you know?"

"Next spring," said Agnes, beaming. "May, as close as I can tell."

There was another chorus of womanly approval. *Another sheep for my flock*, Lucy thought as she hugged Agnes. *A seventeenth pearl on my necklace!*

The women were now all sitting at the table sorting out the ripest elderberries in large wooden bowls while the children swarmed around them in the kitchen and spilled out into Emma Smith's large sitting room. Suddenly Lucy's older sister, Katharine started laughing.

"What is it, Katharine?" said Agnes.

"Oh, I might as well tell you," said Katharine. "You're not the only one with two bodies inside one apron."

There was another burst of laughter from all the women.

"You, too?" exclaimed Caroline.

"Yes," said Katharine. "And in late spring. Probably May or June!"

Another round of hugs and excited congratulations followed, until Emma Smith laid her head on the table, her shoulders shaking.

"What's the matter, Emma?" asked Sophronia. "Are you crying?"

Emma Smith raised her head up with a glorious smile on her face. "Not crying," she said. "Laughing along with you all! I have another little body beneath my apron as well!"

Outside the white clapboard house of her brother Joseph and sister-in-law Emma, Lucy Smith led the children in a long parade to the barn. Lucy had brought a long rope and had each child hold on to keep them in line. Lucy and her oldest niece, Lovina, carried the littlest ones, Jerusha and Mary.

"Okay, children!" Lucy shouted. "Left, right, left right!"

"Solomon is doing it wrong!" shouted four-year-old Mary Jane.

"That's okay," said Lucy. Just march as best as you can.

The air was filled with the laughter of fifteen little children. By the time they got to the stable, the little boys in their woolen pants with suspenders were laughing and pulling the rope this way and that, and the little girls in their long cotton dresses and pinafores were screaming and squealing.

In the stable Lucy led them past the horse stalls—the first one occupied by Joseph's black workhorse, Jim, and the second one empty—that one belonged to her brother's favorite riding horse, Old Charlie, who right now was somewhere on the long road to Far West, Missouri. Lucy led them to the back where the huge piles of freshly cut summer grass were stacked.

"I'll lead the way to the fort!" shouted Little Joseph, who scrambled up the biggest pile. On top was a wide flat space well beneath the rafters of the barn. The air was fragrant with the smell of freshly cut grass, and little shafts of sunlight poured through cracks in the barn roof. Lucy had all of the children sit in a big circle.

My pearl necklace, she thought as she started a game of duck-duck-goose with the children. *Fifteen pearls, and four more coming!*

Suddenly Lucy's niece Julia got to her feet, rolled down the haystack, and ran out of the barn.

JULIA – SEPTEMBER 30

KIRTLAND, OHIO
Saturday, September 30, 1837

Mother's orchard was full of whispers.

The warm, autumn wind rustled in the branches, sending down little hovering leaves, red and yellow and gold, one by one, to the ground below. Julia smelled the sweet smell of ripe apples. She could hear Jim moving around in the barn, the cluck of the chickens, and far beyond the soft sounds of the village. From inside the house she could hear the sound of laughter as the women talked and worked. Beneath the trees she could see the pasture fence, one side of the kitchen garden, and one side of the house with its white siding. Suddenly she saw her Aunt Lucy's shoes and the hem of her blue dress. Lucy was hesitating, then came walking beneath Julia's favorite apple tree and looked up into the branches.

"What are you doing up there?" Aunt Lucy asked.

"Nothing," said Julia.

"Well, can I come up there with you?"

"Up here? You can't climb this tree in your dress."

"Want to see me try?" said Lucy. "I've been climbing trees since before you were born."

Julia looked in surprise as her aunt hiked up her skirt, grabbed the lower limbs of the apple tree, and began to climb to the big branches where Julia was sitting.

"There," said Aunt Lucy, sitting carefully next to Julia on a large branch and smoothing out her skirt. "I've taken the little ones back in the house. Now why don't you tell me what the matter is."

"Can I ask you a question," said Julia.

"Of course," said Lucy. "You can ask me anything."

"Will you tell me the truth?"

"Yes, of course I will."

"But you must not tell Mother or Father. Do you promise?"

Lucy looked over and saw the tears in Julia's eyes. This was a serious question. "Of course, sweet Julia," said Lucy, reaching over and taking Julia's hand in hers. "What is it?"

Julia was quiet for a moment, then asked, "Who am I most like? My mother or my father?"

"Well, you have your mother's intelligence. And you have your father's wit."

"No," said Julia. "Who do I most look like?"

Lucy thought a long moment, then answered, "It's hard to say."

"Why is it hard to say? You said that Freddie has Father's blue eyes and light hair."

Lucy hesitated. "Well, your hair is dark like your mother's."

Through tears Julia said, "Lacy Rigdon told me that I wasn't born to Mother, that I have a different mother and father."

Lucy scooted as close to Julia on the apple tree branch as possible, then kissed her on the cheek. "Julia," she said, leaning in to whisper in her ear. "I promised to tell you the truth. I'll tell you part of it, but you must ask your father and mother to tell you the rest. Yes, you were adopted by your father and mother as a baby."

Julia leaned into her aunt's neck and sobbed like a baby. Lucy also sobbed, as she watched the bottom fall out of Julia's world and the person she thought she was vanish before her eyes.

ARTHUR – SEPTEMBER 30

KIRTLAND, OHIO
Saturday, September 30, 1837

Eliza R. Snow: "Warren Parrish, who had been a humble, successful member of the Gospel, was the ringleader of the apostate part."[19]

Arthur sat on the floor of the cabin with his back against the log wall, listening to the men speaking.

"Prophets see the future," Uncle Nathaniel said, sitting on his three-legged stool by the fireplace. The light of the flames lit up his face with an orange and yellow glow. He had a handsome beard and wore a homespun shirt. He was whittling a block of wood with his long bowie knife, and the shavings were falling to the planks of the floor in long spirals. "If they don't see the future, they ain't no prophets in my book."

"He was a prophet once," said John Boynton quietly. "I know he was. He brought forth the Book of Mormon. That's all the proof I need." John Boynton was always more soft-spoken than the others in the room, and Arthur had known

---

[19] Eliza R. Snow, comp., *Biography and Family Record of Lorenzo Snow* (Salt Lake City, 1884), 20-21

him as the best schoolteacher he had ever had. He had held classes in a room at Whitney's Store in Kirtland and later in the attic story of the new Kirtland Temple. That was before Arthur had started his apprenticeship with Alexander Badham in the blacksmith and wagon making shop. Arthur hadn't been through the doorway of a school since, but he always thought John Boynton to be one of the smartest men he ever knew.

"So how come high and mighty Joe Smith didn't see that crash coming," said Warren Parrish. He was sitting at the table with a newspaper in his hands. He had been reading the national news aloud to the other men—news that told of banks going out of business all across America, including especially in the new settlements in Pennsylvania, Indiana, and Ohio.

It was a cool evening, but tempers were hot in the cabin of Nathaniel Millikin. It had only been a few days since Joseph Smith had ridden off to Missouri on his black horse, but Arthur could see trouble coming to Kirtland village, like a big black rain cloud moving over the earth.

A great separation had begun in Kirtland. Many men had begun to stand up and speak in open opposition to Joseph Smith. These men included Joseph Smith's own personal scribe and secretary, Warren Parrish, and the Church apostles John F. Boynton and Luke S. Johnson, and Arthur's own Uncle Nathaniel. Arthur well knew the fire and indignation arising in his uncle's soul, since he shared a roof and a table with his uncle and aunt in Kirtland. There had been many late night talks around the dinner table, or later sitting around the Millikins' fireplace, where Arthur heard Uncle Nathaniel shouting bitter abuse upon the head of Joseph Smith. Tonight Warren Parrish, Luke Johnson, and John Boynton sat around the hearth talking about Joseph Smith's multitude of errors, including especially the failure of the Kirtland Safety Society.

"He's a fallen prophet," said Uncle Nathaniel, "if he ever were one in the first place."

"I don't care whether he was ever a prophet or not," said Warren Parrish. "All I know is that he's not a prophet any longer. He's not my prophet, in any case. He has left the true religion and the true visions of God. The only visions he has now are visions of personal grandeur."

There was a murmur of assent from the other men.

"We need a return to the old standard!" said Warren Parrish. "Paul said 'the righteous will live by faith.' Well, we're not living by faith, except faith in one man, Joseph Smith."

"Problem is all those blind men and women who are still following Joseph," said John Boynton. "Old Father Smith and Brigham Young and the rest of them can't see the awful truth through all of their adulation for the man. And they are persuading the rest of the people to continue to follow a fallen prophet. They don't remember that we are saved by grace through faith, and not from any power in Joseph Smith or the Church."

"We need a reformation," said Luke Johnson, the most quiet of the three men. "I think we all agree on that. Maybe we could speak with Joseph about it—reason with him— when he returns from Missouri." Johnson had a wide, placid face and strong hands. Arthur knew him to be a good farmer and a fine horseman. He had often been in the shop of his boss, Mr. Badham.

"He won't listen," said Uncle Nathaniel. "He never listens, only talks."

"No, he won't listen," said Warren Parrish. "I should know. I've been his scribe and had to endure the torrent of words that come from his mouth. Pretended revelations and all the rest to justify his failures."

"Every Sunday Old Man Smith and the others occupy the pulpit in the Kirtland Temple to continue to preach falsehoods," said Uncle Nathaniel. "They speak only falsehoods and loyalty to a misguided man. Problem is, they have the temple, and we don't."

There was silence in the room for a moment, and then Warren Parrish brought his fist down on the table. "Why do they have the temple?" he asked. "What gives them the right to usurp the House of God from true believers? They are the apostates."

"Apostates from the old standard," agreed Luke Johnson.

"So what are you suggesting?" asked John Boynton.

"Very simple," said Warren Parrish. "We take back the temple."

Later on in the night, Arthur lay in his bed listening to the wind working around the eaves of Uncle Nathaniel's cabin. It was shaping up to become a real storm outside. Arthur thought about the four men who had talked late into the night in the cabin. What they said didn't make a lot of sense to Arthur. He had never read the Bible through all the way in his life, and had only read a story here or there in the Book of Mormon. He didn't know anything about living by faith or being saved by grace. Arthur didn't know whether Joseph Smith or Brigham Young or Warren Parish or his Uncle Nathaniel were right or wrong.

He closed his eyes and tried to put all of those arguments out of his mind. They gave him a headache. He thought instead about the little miniature carriage he was starting to build for Joseph Smith in Mr. Badham's shop. And he thought about the lively blue eyes of Lucy Smith.

As he fell asleep the wind was tearing around the eaves of the cabin and rattling the window frames. There was definitely a storm coming.

Lovina – October 2

KIRTLAND, OHIO
Monday, October 2, 1837

Aunty Grinnels came into Lovina's room carrying a candle. Lovina awoke with a start and sat up.

"What's the matter?" she whispered, so as not to awaken her little sister, who was asleep in a wooden bed along the wall.

"Would you like to help welcome your little sister into the world?"

"Is it time?"

"Yes, child. Your mother thought you might help me and Sister Sessions at the delivery. Come quietly now."

Sister Patty Sessions was in her mother's bedroom, along with Lovina's grandmother, Lucy Mack Smith, and her Aunt Lucy.

Patty Bartlett Sessions, the midwife, had been in and out of the home of Hyrum and Jerusha Smith all weekend, as Lovina's mother felt the pains of childbirth coming on. She visited the previous day and urged that Jerusha Smith receive a blessing, which was given Sunday by Lovina's grandfather, Joseph Smith, Sr., and her Uncle, Don Carlos Smith. Sister Sessions now stood over the bed where Jerusha

Smith lay, with her hair pulled back in a severe bun and the sleeves of her dress rolled up.

"Now, Sister Smith," said Patty Sessions. "Let's deliver this baby!"

"Come sit with me," said Aunt Lucy, taking Lovina by the hand and pulling her to a chair outside the door. "Here we can be out of the way of the midwife and your Grandmama, but be ready to bring anything they need."

After waiting for what seemed like forever, Lovina heard the startling sound of a baby's cry through the door and then exclamations of joy from Lovina's grandmother.

"It's a girl!" cried Lucy Mack Smith.

"I knew that already," said Lovina to her Aunt Lucy.

"How did you know that?"

"Mother told me!"

"Come in for a quick peek," said Aunty Grinnels, beads of sweat on her forehead and a relieved look on her face.

In her grandmother's arms was a little bundle with her face uncovered. Her eyes were closed, and she was already making sucking sounds with her mouth.

"She's hungry," said Aunt Lucy.

Lovina could feel tears in her eyes, and she could not stop smiling.

"Can I hold her?" she asked.

"Not before she gets some food from her mother," said Grandmama."

"Sister Jerusha?" said Aunty Grinnels. "Are you ready to feed your new daughter?"

There was no answer from her mother's bedside. Lovina looked over and saw the midwife, Patty Sessions, bent over the bed.

"Mama?" said Lovina.

Patty Sessions stood up and looked at the women. "Jerusha's taken ill," she said. "Send for the elders to give her a blessing, please."

OLD CHARLIE--OCTOBER 3

KIRTLAND, OHIO
Tuesday, October 3, 1837

Joseph Smith: "I started from Kirtland on the 27th of September."[20]
. . . I arrived at Far West some time in the latter part of October or first
of November."[21]

The first few days on the road to Zion we jest took it nice and easy, thirty, forty mile a day through country I knowed through and through. Most nights we stayed in small towns out in the farm country, green fields, and good stables. Most of the folks we stopped with was what Brother Joe calls the "saints." That's jest a way of sayin' they is mighty good friends of Brother Joe and shows us horses a good time, with fresh feed and green grass under our hooves for a night. But after a few days, less and less of the country seemed familiar, and I knowed that we was ridin' over ground I never seen before. Last night we slept out under the trees a little ways off the road. Brother Joe hobbled me by the other horses near a little stream, and as it got dark we

---

[20] HC 2:518
[21] HC 2:519, 521

jest grazed quietly, while Brother William and Brother Vinson built a fire.

By this time I had got to know them other horses right well—Brother Sidney's Champ and Brother William's excitable saddle-bred horse called Raven, but especially Brother Vinson's mare, which I learned was called Little Roan. She was as patient and sweet a mare as I ever see'd, and was right smart, too. One day we split up on the road so that Brother Sidney could ride into a little town to try to buy some food for the men. Well, we rode all day without meetin' up, like Brother Joe and the others had planned. Along toward sundown, Brother Joe said that they best set a camp even though they hadn't seen Brother Sidney, but as they was dismountin', Little Roan started to snort and pull out over the prairie. Brother Joe and I followed Brother Vinson, and not a mile away we found a little campfire out on the grass, with Brother Sidney and Champ settlin' down for the night. Little Roan jest knowed where they was out over the rollin' hills and dry grass.

This mornin' we was out on the road before it got light, and when the sun started peekin' up over the brown fields, I suddenly realized that I more or less knowed where we was! I wasn't exactly sure that Brother Joe and me had been over that particular chunk of road before, but jest the same I knowed them fields and clumps of trees and that there country—jest the smell of it! It was the same country Brother Joe and I had ridden through years ago when I first went to Missouri with the outfit Brother Joe called Zion's Camp. It was years ago, but jest the smell of that durned farm country brung it all back to me.

When the sun come up proper, we started to gallop, and Brother Joe and the others seemed in proper spirits. I knowed that the other horses—Raven in particular—was feelin' fine, as we had a nice little race over the roads. It made me feel like a colt again, gallopin' free over that familiar country.

Runnin' free beneath the saddle, with a rider like Brother Joe, is kind of like a wind that blows away all the years away. When I'm runnin' in the wind under the clear blue sky and the mornin' sun I sometimes feel like Old Charlie vanishes and I'm once again jest a little colt, with no fears or worries in all the world. The world trembles with the thunderin' of my hooves in the dust and leaves me free and happy. The long gallops over the hills sorta' conquer fear and danger. No one can hurt Brother Joe nor me when we is runnin' free, faster than any other creature, man or horse, on earth. I hear the wind a rushin' past my ears. The leather of the saddle jest creaks a bit and the metal on the bridle clicks in time with the poundin' of my legs.

My mind went back to when I was runnin' free in the grass with my dam. In the big field where I spent my first summers it was all rollin' hills and clear streams and no saddles and bridles. That was a time when I was jest all legs and no horse sense at all. I remember runnin' alongside my mother, tryin' to push my nose underneath her to get at the milk. The wind blew and sent waves over the grass, and I had all I wanted then—milk and grass. 'Course there was other mares and foals in that big field, and one day I ran over to another mare and wanted some milk and tried to push underneath her, but she jest snorted and drove me off.

After a time, I learned the smell of all the different sorts of grass—what was sweet, what was bitter, and I learned where there was good grazin'. Then I learned to explore the big field. I would go head out of a mornin', runnin' over the hill to the river and along the wooden fence line all the way down yonder to the marsh and then back up to my dam and the other horses. Each day I'd run out further and further, though the slightest thing would spook me somethin' terrible—a green snake slitherin' in the grass, or the awful sound of my hooves when they would get stuck in the marsh mud.

There was plenty of other horses in that big field, not just mares and the foals like me what was born there, but plenty of older horses, too. And pretty soon I learned how to behave myself in front of my elders. For instance I learned to let the older horses sniff at me first for a spell, while I showed respect by droppin' my ears and stretchin' out my neck. But pretty soon, I grew taller, and after my first winter in the big field, and the birth of all them new little foals, the older horses showed jest a little respect to me and let me sniff them to get acquainted.

And I grew up fast, like all horses. The day we is born, we can walk along, followin' our dams and even nibble at the grass a bit. After two summers, we is as tall as our dams, 'specially the stallions, like me, and runnin' here and there, every which way, and makin' friends with all them other colts. Horses need friends, sure as sure. A friendly horse is a right nice thing to have close by, to keep flies off your face, to keep you clean of dirt and tangles, to run all around with, and to keep a look out while you've got your head down grazin'. And soon I was runnin' all around that big field with a bunch of other young colts. We was always jest bumpin' each other and racin', nibblin' each other, kickin' around, swishin' our tails.

'Course there was men 'round about too, but they didn't come around much, 'cept to feed us when the snow covered everythin' or to comb us down a bit. Sometimes the men would jest lean up agin' the fence and watch us some. Seemed like mighty good entertainment to them, though why I don't know. Sometimes the men come inside the fence to take the older horses to saddle up and ride, and I see'd for the first time how a saddle gets strapped onto a horse's back. Seemed mighty peculiar at first—strappin' that leather thing on a back, but I got used to seein' it. But in them days saddles and bridles warn't for me and the other colts at all. For me it was jest all playin', racin', or rollin' in the grass, walkin' beside the deep clear water of the stream, or sometimes jest standin' on the little lookout hill makin' a kind of map in my mind of the big field and the stream and the long fence lines. Up on the big green hill, I had a favorite spot, and standin' there I could remember jest about everywhere I ever been and everythin' I ever seen in my whole life. I could remember where the men dropped the hay in the winter for us to eat, forkin' it to the ground out of heavy wagons with these long sticks. I could remember where the best spots was for rollin' around or dungin' or jest loafin'. I remembered where the muddy places was in the marsh along the creek. Up in my spot, when the weather was fine, I was jest on top of the whole durned world. I could see everythin' and everybody.

In those days I was as free as the wind in the grass. And that's the way I felt this mornin' gallopin' down the road with Brother Joe on the way to Zion. I felt as free as the water in the stream or the wind in the trees, feelin' the pressure of Brother Joe's legs in the saddle and the sureness of his hand on the bridle, the pat of his hand on my neck, and every now and then his voice jest sayin', "Good boy, Charlie!"

Lovina – October 13

"Come here, child," said Lovina's mother, beckoning her to come into the sick room.

It was the eleventh day, and Lovina seemed to have forgotten everything about her outside world—the world of friends, church meetings, walks past the temple, Sister Snow's Select School for Young Ladies. All of that. Her world now revolved around this home and its new terrible routines. The nighttime vigils at her mother's bedside. The grave visits of the midwife and doctors. The blessings given by the priesthood. And the care of the new baby, now named Sarah, who amid her mother's frightening illness was already growing. Aunty Grinnels had taken complete charge of the baby, staying with her day and night.

Lovina sat quietly as her mother held her hand. Her grandmother, Lucy Mack Smith, was there in a rocking chair. "Can you leave us for a few minutes, Mother Smith," said Lovina's mother.

"Of course," said Grandmama and left the room, quietly closing the door behind her. Jerusha Barden Smith was lying in a clean bed with white sheets and pillowcases, and a colorful coverlet neatly laid over her. Her pale white hands were lying on top of the bedding, and her hair was combed neatly. But her face was deathly pale. The form of her body, so large a few days ago, was once more lean and flat. "Just hold my hand for a spell," said Mama, reaching for Lovina's hand. Her voice was very weak, and she seemed to have trouble keeping her eyes open.

"Mama, I love you!" said Lovina, squeezing her mother's hand.

"I love you too, child. You are my oldest. I know you are only ten years old, but you must understand what will soon happen and help prepare your younger brothers and sisters."

"What can I do, Mother?" said Lovina, tears streaming down her face.

"Tell your father, when he comes, that the Lord has taken your mother home, and left you for him to take care of."

The house was filled with family on the evening of Friday, the thirteenth of October. Lovina's little brothers, John and Hyrum, sat on the lap of their grandfather, Joseph Smith, Sr. Grandmama was holding little Jerusha on her lap, and Aunty Grinnels was holding the new baby, Sarah. The other members of Lovina's family were there—the aunts and uncles and cousins—and also many of the brethren and sisters from the church. The little children were happy, sitting on laps, held in arms, in spite of the tears falling in torrents from the eyes of every adult in the room.

Lovina looked across the room. The door to Mama's bedroom was open. The bed was empty.

ARTHUR – OCTOBER 29

KIRTLAND, OHIO
Sunday, October 29, 1837

Joseph Smith: "During my absence in Missouri Warren Parrish, John F. Boynton, Luke S. Johnson, Joseph Coe, and some others united together for the overthrow of the Church. Soon after my return this dissenting band openly and publicly renounced the Church of Christ of Latter-day Saints and claimed themselves to be the old standard, calling themselves the Church of Christ, excluding the word 'Saints,' and set me at naught, and the whole Church, denouncing us as heretics.[22] . . ."

Arthur sat in the Kirtland Temple, watching.

He loved to study the pulpits on both ends of the large assembly room in the temple. He loved the richly carved woodwork of those pulpits. He had once heard Brigham Young say that Joseph Smith had not only received revelation to build the temple, but he received a pattern, a plan, or a model also from the Lord, just like Moses received a pattern for the tabernacle and Solomon for his temple. As a woodworker, Arthur understood patterns. Though he was not particularly good with schoolwork and reading, he did

---

[22] HC 2:528

understand wood and felt that he could learn something about God by studying the patterns ordained by Him in the pulpits of the temple.

It was Sunday morning and Arthur sat in the last bench in the main floor assembly room of the Kirtland Temple beside his Uncle Nathaniel. Just now Brigham Young was preaching, standing in the top central pulpit on the east side of the temple. Uncle Nathaniel was listening intently to the speaker, but Arthur's mind was wandering.

As the sermon droned on, Arthur let his eyes run over the pulpits. There were twelve of them on this side of the room, set in four rows of three, and Arthur knew that there were twelve other pulpits behind him, on the west side of the temple. Arthur then looked at the walls and ceiling as Brigham Young spoke. Carved into almost every surface were other symbols: keystones, flowers, vines, and images of rivers and of a tree. He also saw that the sacrament table was shaped like a yoke of oxen.

Arthur's eyes shifted from the images on the pulpits back to the right corner of the room, where he could see the sheen of Lucy Smith's dark hair. There were hundreds of people in the room, but his eyes went back again and again to that head of hair seated between the gray heads of her father, Old Father Smith, and her mother, Lucy Mack Smith. *My Lucy is named after her mother*, thought Arthur, then immediately shook his head. *You idiot*, he thought. *She's not "my" Lucy. Not now. Not ever.* Seated around Lucy and her parents were other members of the Smith family. There were Hyrum Smith's older children, Lovina and John. Lovina was only a few years younger than her Aunt Lucy. Arthur knew that their mother had died while their father was away in Missouri. Lovina was seated in the row directly behind dark-haired Lucy, who kept turning to whisper to her niece, until Lucy Mack Smith lifted her fingers to her lips, and looked sharply at young Lucy. Arthur saw her turn one final time and smile at Lovina, her blue eyes dancing in merriment.

Brigham Young's voice was now rising, and Arthur suddenly took note of what he was saying. "I hereby proclaim, publicly before the world, what I have always said in private. It is this, that I know by the power of the Holy Ghost that Joseph Smith is a Prophet of the Most High God! He is a Prophet and has not transgressed or fallen, as others have declared!"

There were suddenly cries from many men in the congregation. "Heresy!" said John Boynton, sitting on the stand next to Brigham Young. "He's a fallen prophet!" shouted Luke S. Johnson, also sitting on the stand.

Arthur's uncle was on his feet. "We need to return to the Old Standard!" he shouted.

Brigham Young tried to continue, but there were shouts in the room. No one was listening to Brigham Young. There was shouting now from dozens in the room, and the meeting ended in disarray.

As Arthur looked at the extended Smith family amid the confusion in the room, young Lucy Smith glanced in his direction. Arthur quickly turned away his eyes and felt the blood rush to his face and neck. When he turned back, the Smith family had stood up on their feet and was walking together out of the temple.

OLD CHARLIE – NOVEMBER 1

ON THE ROAD IN MISSOURI
Wednesday, November 1, 1837

Joseph Smith: "I arrived at Far West some time in the latter part of October or first of November."[23]

All through them cool days of the fall we was on the move, four horses with riders, ridin' cross country to Zion. There was always plenty of man talk between Brother Joe and the others, but I jest kind of ignored it, fallin' into the routine of ridin' days and campin' out nights, or sometimes stayin' in the stables of houses or inns along the way. The days was real crisp and cool without no rain, and the trees was all ablaze with red and orange leaves until they all fell on the path, and then we crunched the leaves right down into the color of dirt. After a few weeks, there warn't no leaves on the trees at all, just bare branches held high like they was goin' to scratch the blue sky.

Then, 'bout two weeks ago, we seemed to leave all the trees behind and rode out onto the open prairie, which was also full of all the bright colors of dyin' things. The grass was

---

[23] HC 2:519, 521

a yellow gold. There warn't no green to be seen for miles around. We rode sun up to sun down most days for forty, fifty mile, Brother Joe and the others makin' their camps at night underneath all them stars.

The other horses—Brother Sidney's grey gelding Champ, Brother William's big black Raven, and Brother Vinson's mare called Little Roan—mostly kept to theirselves durin' the first part of the journey, but little by little showed their true spirits. Raven and Little Roan were pleasant ridin' companions, but Brother Sidney's Champ was right troublesome. Of all the cussed, ornery horses I ever met, Champ must have been the worst. I really got to hate him on the journey to Zion, and he seemed to like to make sure I did. I figure somebody must have done somethin' to him when he was a colt, but that horse hated just about everybody and everythin' under the sun. He was a strong gelding with a gray coat and dark mane. He was one big horse, and one way or another he was never tired of makin' sure you knew he was big. Little Roan and Raven learned the first day to steer clear of Champ, as they got nipped every time they stepped in nippin' distance. He was really full of hissself, Champ was. He hated all other horses, it seems, and if one come near that he didn't know properly, he'd commence to squealin' and then try to take a bite out of them. I learned to never answer him back. I didn't have to, after all. I'd just toss my head and eat my hay.

Little Roan was another matter. She was always pleasant in her temper and was what Brother Joe once called "a nice, quiet mare." She never nipped or squealed. In fact, I'm sure she never did no harm to a creature in her life. She reminded me of my dam—jest as patient and smart as could be. But, sometimes on the road to Missouri I wondered if she was too quiet. I sometimes wondered if she was goin' to make it all the way. She didn't seem to have the spunk that a horse needed to ride along with Brother Joe. I've been with Brother Joe for all these years, and know how he is and the awful big demands on the horses of the Brethren that want to ride with him. You might go forty, fifty, even sixty mile a day, and then jest when you figure it's time to stop and find some tender grass to eat and take a rest, Brother Joe suddenly needs another five mile or more out of you. Little Roan warn't no quitter, but she had none of the keep-goin' that a ridin' horse needed.

I learned that a horse has got to *love* his rider. He's got to feel what *he* feels. He's got to be *part* of his rider. Poor Little Roan, smart and sweet as she was, warn't never up to that part of bein' a proper saddle horse.

All that fall, as we moved day by day across the open prairies, I could feel Brother Joe was out of spirits, though whenever he was talkin' with the other men he pretended he warn't. I noticed it most the day we crossed the Big River. That was a fearsome day for me and all the other horses, 'specially those what never seen a river that big. Brother Joe called it the Miss-Sipee or somethin' like that. Well, anyway the day we crossed over, we come up to what they called the ferry, and Brother Joe and the others dismounted and led us up onto a big, flat boat. It was quite a time for Brother Sidney to get Champ situated, let me tell you. And then, all the while they was takin' us across the wide, muddy river, Brother Joe stood agin' the rail, just a chattin' away with the

Brethren, and with two or three other fellers who was takin' their wagons across the river. And Brother Joe laughed and was right chipper in his conversation. It was gettin' along toward sundown, and all the surface of the river, as far as you could see, was kind of glintin' in the light. But on the other side, as soon as he mounted back up, I could feel that there was somethin' on his mind. Somethin' that was weighin' down his thoughts.

Funny thing about Brother Joe—he can be the most talkative man alive, but deep down he's got a quietness about him. It put me in mind of the first feller I properly knowed in my life—that was the young feller back in the big field where I was foaled, the one they all called Pete.

Pete lived in the big house next to the field I was born and raised in. I had spent my first two summers as free as a rabbit in that big field, with my dam and a whole herd of other horses and colts, runnin' here and there, eatin', playin', and livin' a free life. Then one day the men moved me and all of the other young foals into a smaller field, beyond a fence I had never been beyond. I was jest playin' with six, eight other foals in the grass when two men sorta' waved their hats in the air, and one by one moved us toward an open gate. Pretty soon, we found ourselves beyond the fence we had knowed our whole lives and where we was born and had growed up, and we was standin' kinda confused in another little field. I didn't know it then, but that was the last time I would ever be in that big field again. We could see our dams and all the other horses through the fence, but one feller came and closed the gate behind us, and we was suddenly closed off in a smaller field. It was a big change, and we didn't know what was was comin' next.

Well, pretty soon a bunch of other fellers walked over to the fence and was all leanin' agin' the rails, talkin' to one another and chewin' on them funny green leaves the men all seemed to love to chew on, and they was jest watchin' us young horses out in the little field. We warn't skeered, jest a mite nervous and wonderin' what was comin' next. Now I know that them men was jest sizin' us up and tryin' to see which foals was strong, or headstrong, or timid, as they was fixin' to teach us to carry a saddle and be ridden. But back then I didn't know what they wanted, and I was right watchful of what they was doin'.

And so there we was, the other colts and me, jest playin', tossin' our heads, bumpin' each other, and high-tailin' it around the field. After a while I noticed that this one young feller—the other men called him Pete—had climbed over the fence, and he was right there in the little field with us. I was nervous about him and so were the other horses, and we jest kind of moved away to the other side of the field. Well this Pete feller jest walked over and set hisself down on a rock plumb in the middle of that durned field. I come to learn later that Pete was the boss's son. He jest sat there on that rock, not movin' or talkin' at all. Well all the other young horses kept up wanderin' around and soon forgot all about Pete, but I didn't. I was watchin' him, and I expect he was watchin' me, too. After a while I noticed that Pete reached in his pocket and pulled out a little knife and a stick, real slow and quiet like, and he started carvin' on that stick. That was right peculiar, I thought. Well, Pete jest sat there, all afternoon, carvin' on his stick, until it started to get on toward evening. Then about sunset Pete got up and walked over to the fence and climbed to the other side. I watched him as he walked up to the big house where the boss man lived. The next day Pete came back and sat on his rock, sometimes singin' quietly, sometimes eatin' an apple, sometimes feedin' breadcrumbs to the little birds, but mostly whittlin' with his knife on a stick. And then at sunset he left.

After two or three days I got kind of curious about Pete, so I quit my playin' with the other foals on the far side of the field, and I wandered over near Pete. He didn't seem to notice me none, so finally I went right up to him to smell him over. Pete didn't move a muscle, but jest sat there while I snuffed him over a bit. Then, real slow like, Pete lifted up his arm and began strokin' my neck, and then he ruffled my mane and scratched my flanks, and all the while Pete was talkin' real quiet and slow, almost whisperin'.

"Beau," he was sayin'. "Hey, Beau. Good boy, Beau," over and over again. And then he pulled an apple out of his pocket and cut it into little pieces with his knife and laid them one at a time on the flat of his palm and held them under my nose. They was the sweetest things I had ever tasted in my life, as we hadn't got no apples in the big field. 'Course, I hadn't had no sugar yet. That came later.

ARTHUR – NOVEMBER 24

KIRTLAND, OHIO
Friday, November 24, 1837

Joseph Smith, III: "I remember I was promised a little wagon, to be built by a wagon-maker living not far from our house, up on the hillside. The name of Alexander Badham is connected in some way with the memory. I remember that I became impatient for the possession of the wagon and one day slipped away from the house and went to the shop. Peering into it through a crack in the upright siding I saw the wagon, nicely painted red and awaiting the finishing touches before it was to be delivered. I must have received the wagon, but, strange to say, I have no recollection of ever having used it."[24]

Arthur Millikin had red paint on his hands, and he was sure his face was red, too. He had been careful not to get the paint on his face, but still he was sure it was bright red—as red as this little wagon he was putting the finishing touches on. It was meant for the little son of Joseph Smith, also named Joseph. *Make it the finest little miniature carriage in the county,* Joseph Smith had said in September when he visited the shop. It sure was that, Arthur thought. It was a

---

[24] *The Saints' Herald,* November 6, 1934, 1414

fine piece of work, first laid out in detail in pencil on Alexander Badham's drafting table, and then cut, laid out, fashioned and turned, and now painted by Arthur and his boss.

The powerful scent of fresh paint was in the air, filling Arthur's nose. It almost made him light-headed—or was it the flashing blue eyes of Lucy Smith. Arthur had just seen those eyes on the street in Kirtland, and that was why he was sure his face was red. He had been sent by the Boss down to Whitney's store for the pot of paint he was now brushing onto the new wagon. As he left the store, Lucy came in with her father, the old man also called Joseph Smith. The old man had nodded at Arthur, who stood holding the door. He swallowed as Lucy Smith followed her father inside, watching those blue eyes. For the smallest moment, just an instant in time, those eyes locked onto Arthur's eyes. In that instant, Arthur felt a panic rise up from his heart and into his throat. He swallowed hard to make sure it didn't burst out and reveal itself to the world. How could she not know he loved her, looking into his eyes. But she merely smiled at him, the briefest of smiles, and passed into Whitney's store.

Arthur's heart was still pounding as he brushed the red paint onto the side panels of the little carriage. Could Lucy Smith know how he felt? How could she not know?

The Boss, Alexander Badham, was on the other side of the shop attaching oak rims to a set of farm wagon wheels. The forge had burned low, as there had been no blacksmithing customers today, and it was a little cold in the wagon shop. A storm had blown in overnight, and it was still wet and cold outside. The big double doors were closed against wind, but it was still chilly inside the shop, and Arthur blew on his hands and fingers from time to time to keep them warm. The only meager light in the shop came from the slanting autumn sun shining through the two windows and a multitude of long cracks in the boards lining the shop.

Make it the finest little miniature carriage in the county, Joseph Smith had said. Arthur had immediately asked the Boss if he could build it, and because of the press of other projects, Mr. Badham had agreed. Arthur was certain it would be the finest little miniature carriage in the county. He wanted the man called Joseph Smith to think so—and the little son called Joseph Smith, and the grandfather also called Joseph Smith to think so, too. But especially he wanted their niece, aunt, and daughter named Lucy Smith to think so. Arthur rather viewed this little wagon as his masterpiece, the culmination of his years of apprenticeship, the proof to Mr. Badham and all the world, that he was now a master at his trade. And he hoped that this masterpiece would help win him a wife.

Arthur applied the red paint in long strokes, making sure there was no grit or bubbles on the surface. The masterpiece was almost finished and would sit in the shop awaiting the return of the man some called a prophet, to make payment and take delivery. Arthur could picture the little boy called Joseph Smith, III, having the time of his life as he rode around the village in his fine, red, miniature horse carriage.

As he worked, Arthur noticed a small bundled-up figure pass under one of the windows and stop. Then he saw a small head dressed in a cap, and a boy's face appearing at intervals through the lower panes of glass. It was Joseph Smith's little boy, obviously jumping up and down to try to see through the window. Arthur chuckled to himself, then watched as the boy's silhouette move to a large crack in the upright siding, and he saw the boy's eye and nose pressed against the largest opening, looking at the red wagon.

Arthur put down the can of red paint and walked to the door of the wagon shop. "I'll be right back, sir," he said, turning to Mr. Badham.

"See that you do, boy," said the Boss.

Outside the wind was very brisk but the sun was beginning to emerge from behind the clouds. Arthur walked to the corner of the building and peered around the corner. There was Joseph Smith's little boy—they called him Little Joseph—standing with his face pressed close to a large crack between two pieces of wooden siding, peering into the blacksmith shop.

"What are you doing?" said Arthur, smiling.

The little boy looked startled. "Nothing," he said stepping back from the wall. "Just looking."

"What are you looking at?"

The boy said nothing and looked at his feet. He was a handsome little fellow, with a wide brimmed hat and a red scarf around his neck. When he looked up at Arthur, he could see that his lower lip was trembling. The little fellow was about to start crying!

"Hey, it's okay," said Arthur. "No one's mad at you. You're the son of Joseph Smith, aren't you?"

Little Joseph nodded his head.

"Is your father home yet? Back from Missouri?"

Little Joseph shook his head.

"Well, when he comes home, tell him I have something for him."

Little Joseph looked up, and Arthur winked at him. The little boy broke into a smile and winked back at Arthur.

"Okay," said Little Joseph. "I will."

WYCLIFFE – DECEMBER 3

KIRTLAND, OHIO
Sunday, December 3, 1837

Eliza R. Snow: "One Sabbath morning, [Warren Parrish], with several of his party, came into the Temple armed with pistols and bowie knives."[25]

Wycliffe Rigdon sat with his family in their pew box, a little enclosure surrounding their family pew, like a fence with a little gate. The room was only half filled. Since the trouble with the failure of the Kirtland Bank and the departure of Joseph Smith and Sidney Rigdon for Missouri, the dissenters in Kirtland had drawn many away, and many were too fearful to attend, preferring instead to wait and see what would happen.

Old Father Smith, father of the Prophet and Hyrum Smith, was conducting the meeting, seated as usual in the pulpits on the Melchizedek Priesthood side on the east end of the lower court. Just before the meeting started, there was a murmur in the room. Wycliffe turned to see that Warren

---

[25] Eliza R. Snow, comp., *Biography and Family Record of Lorenzo Snow* (Salt Lake City, 1884), 20-21

Parrish, Joseph Coe, John Boynton, Nathaniel Millikin, and other dissenters had noisily entered the back of the room, and were taking seats together in the Aaronic pulpits on the east side of the temple.

Wycliffe was surprised to see that Warren Parrish and several of the other dissenting brethren were carrying knives and pistols in their belts. He suddenly had a sickening feeling in his stomach.

"We'll wait for all to be seated," said Father Smith, kindly, from the Melchizedek Priesthood side. He then announced a hymn and prayer. After the prayer, he turned the time over to one of the brethren to preach.

The brother stood up and began his remarks on the west stand. Just after he commenced to speak, Warren Parrish on the east end interrupted him. "We don't believe what you are saying!" he shouted. "You are departing from the pure truths of the gospel, and you shall not preach falsehood in this place."

The brother tried to continue his sermon, but John Boynton, formerly one of the Twelve Apostles, spoke up. "You are preaching falsehood!"

Father Smith stood up. "Order!" he called out. "You brethren must have the patience and respect to hear him preach. After he is finished, you can then have all the time you want, but now you must wait your turn. You must not interrupt the service!"

The brother commenced preaching again, but Warren Parrish and the others commenced again shouting. Wycliffe and the other members of the congregation looked back and forth from the Melchizedek Priesthood pulpits, where poor

Father Smith was trying to call for order, and the Aaronic Priesthood side, where the dissenters were shouting.

Finally, Father Smith said, "All right then. If you will not respect the order of this house, we will call the city policemen to take you out of the house.

At this point, Warren Parrish, John Boynton, and others drew their pistols and brandished their bowie knives and rushed down from the stand into the congregation.

"You just try to stop me from speaking!" cried John Boynton, pointing his pistol in the air. "I'll blow out the brains of the first man who dares to lay a hand on me!"

There were screams among the congregation. People ducked down behind the pew boxes, and a few even tried to escape from the confusion by jumping out of the windows.

Two policemen entered the room, having been summoned by one of the brethren, and took hold of John Boynton and the others. Amid the screams and shrieks of the congregation, a scuffle ensued and a stovepipe was knocked down, striking one of the benches and scattering soot and ashes. Wycliffe watched as a black cloud spread through the room. The bowie knives and pistols were wrestled from the hands of the dissenters and thrown or kicked on the floor to prevent their being used.

After this terrible scene in the temple of God, order was restored, and the day proceeded.

Julia – December 10

KIRTLAND, OHIO
Sunday, December 10, 1837

Julia Murdock Smith was devastated when a playmate told her she was not really a Smith, but had been adopted at birth. Julia was never quite the same after this experience, and the issue nagged at her all of her life. There were times that she was bitter even as a child. She had a powerful need to be part of the family, but there were constant reminders that she was adopted. Joseph and Emma were certainly not to blame for Julia's sadness, as they treated Julia in every way as if she were their daughter.[26]

A fine snow was falling. Julia could feel the flakes on her face. They melted as soon as they touched her skin. It was midday, but you could hardly tell by looking at the sky. The clouds lowered over Kirtland like a sheet of lead. Only the faintest sign of the glowing ball of the sun could be detected behind the gray covering.

Julia was sitting in her favorite apple tree, dressed in her Sunday dress with her woolen cloak wrapped tightly around

---

[26] See, *Joseph and Emma's Julia,* 25

her. All was warm except her legs, as the chill wind played havoc under her dress.

Mother had refused to let the children leave the house or yard today, even though it was the Sabbath. Last Sunday there had been violence in the Kirtland Temple. Men had shouted at one another, and weapons had been drawn— knives and guns. It was frightening, especially to Julia's mother.

Julia's mother. The words stuck in Julia's thoughts and clogged any further feeling, like a clump of muddy debris in the bottom of a flowing ditch. A dozen times every day Julia had the sensation of catching herself thinking old, regular thoughts, but then being suddenly reminded that she was adopted. It was like suddenly tripping over the threshold of the doorway you have crossed a hundred times a day for an entire lifetime.

It was not just the mean invention of Lacy Rigdon. Julia knew that she had been adopted. Her Aunt Lucy had confirmed it. She told her the story sitting in this very apple tree. Julia closed her eyes and remembered her conversation with Lucy.

Lucy said she had been just ten years old and newly arrived in Kirtland with Grandfather and Grandmother. Almost the first news they heard when they arrived was that Emma had delivered a set of twins on April 30, 1831, but that the twins had almost immediately died. They then learned that later that same day, miraculously, another woman, a Latter-day Saint, had delivered another set of twins, but the mother died that day. They were then told that Joseph and Emma had taken the orphaned twins as their own.

"It was the providence of God, Julia," Lucy had said to her. "God took away the first set of twins and received them unto Himself, but then He provided a second set to comfort your Father and Mother. You are one of the second set of twins."

"Did you see the first babies?" Julia had asked.

"No. We arrived a few days after you were born. But Joseph told us that the first twins were beautiful. Two perfect little babes, so very tiny, one boy and one girl. Your Father said that he went into the room where Emma lay and held both little babes in his hands. They were so tiny that each could literally be held in one of Joseph's hands. Your Father and Mother named the babies Thaddeus and Louisa. But within moments, he said that they could tell that the babes were in distress. They were not breathing properly. In the blink of an eye, he said, Louisa was gone. They scarcely had time to mourn, when Thaddeus slipped away. Both of them, dead."

"Thaddeus and Louisa." Julia repeated the names.

"Thaddeus and Louisa," said Aunt Lucy. "It was more than I could stand, Julia, to hear that my niece and nephew were gone. Both of them! Gone too soon! Gone before I could even hold them!" Aunt Lucy had cried great tears as she shared this with Julia, sitting in this apple tree last fall. Then she had finished the story.

"The doctor couldn't tell Joseph why the babes died. 'It was just their time,' he simply said. 'They were too small for this world.' Aunt Jerusha told me that your father wept like a child, and your mother was inconsolable. 'Too pure for this world,' your Father kept saying. 'Too pure for this world.' Oh, Julia, what a dark day that must have been. So very dark. And also so strange, for within hours after the babes slipped away, your parents had news that Sister Murdock also bore twins, a boy and a girl. Then, after the birth, the mother suddenly died, leaving the newborn babes without a mother."

"Was I one of those second twins?"

"Yes. You and a brother named Joseph."

"What was my mother's name?"

"Julia Murdock. She already had three older children who were staying with a neighbor. Their father—your natural born father—had to walk slowly over to that neighbor's house to tell them the news that their mother was gone."

"What became of the three older children?" Julia had asked Lucy.

"I don't know," said Lucy. "But I remember that there were two older boys, Orrice and Johnny, and a little girl named Phebe."

Julia opened her eyes. They were stinging. Was it the cold December wind, or tears? She couldn't tell, but she decided she didn't want to think any more about what Lucy had told her.

Suddenly she heard the sound of hooves on the road. She looked over through the branches of the tree and saw a man wrapped in a black cloak riding a black stallion. She saw the white star on the horse's forehead.

"Charlie!" Julia screamed, climbing down from her cold perch in the apple tree. "Charlie! Father! It's me, Julia!" She ran out into the yard where Father was dismounting. "It's me, your daughter!"

"My daughter," said Father, sweeping Julia up into his arms. "My only and my beloved daughter!"

LITTLE JOSEPH – DECEMBER 15

KIRTLAND, OHIO
Friday, December 15, 1837

Father rode off in the morning on Old Charlie, his hooves echoing through the farmyard as they struck the icy ground. It was strange thing—Little Joseph noticed that Father had not saddled up Charlie, but had just put on his bridle and thrown his leg over the black stallion's bare back.

Little Joseph watched him go from the sitting room window. Mother had asked him to pick up his wooden blocks that were lying on the floor and put them away properly. Little Joseph had been bending over, putting the blocks in their box, when he had seen his father ride out into Chillicothe Road and down the hill toward the village.

"Where is Father going, and why doesn't he have a saddle?" said Little Joseph to his mother.

"It's possible to ride a horse without a saddle," said Mother, smiling at her oldest son. She was sitting in her rocker stitching a piece of green fabric. Julia was also in the room, sitting on the settee, trying to stitch an identically colored piece of fabric of her own. It was nearly Christmas, and Mother and Julia had decided to make new napkins for the dinner table. Little Joseph didn't care much about napkins. It was horses he loved.

"But Father never rides Charlie without a saddle," he said, watching out the window.

"You'll just have to ask your father about it when he gets home," said Mother, smiling.

Two hours later Little Joseph was in the orchard with his baby brother, Freddie. Freddie was walking now, and loved to hold his big brother's finger as he moved carefully over the rough ground. The sun had warmed up the ground, but there was a cold breeze. Freddie tripped on a root and fell, his heavy coat breaking the fall. He stood back up, laughing, and Little Joseph gave him his finger again, and they set off walking.

There was the sound of carriage wheels in the road, and around the corner came Old Charlie harnessed to a little red carriage, with Father seated in the driver's seat, holding the reins. Father was grinning ear to ear.

Little Joseph left Freddie in the orchard and ran to Father. The carriage stopped, and Father got out.

It was the most beautiful little carriage he had ever seen—bright red, with yellow rims on the wheels, and a new padded leather seat. The space inside was small, almost too cramped for Father, who sat holding the reins and smiling at Little Joseph.

"Where did you get it?" asked Little Joseph. Freddie had followed his big brother out into the yard and reached over and took his hand.

"From Badham's wagon shop," said Father smiling.

"It's beautiful," said Little Joseph.

"Can I have a ride in it?"

"No, I'm sorry my boy," said Father. "It's going to be a Christmas gift for someone."

"Is that for me?" shouted Little Joseph.

"It will be," said Father, starting to unhitch Charlie. "After Christmas."

"But can't I drive it now?"

"No. You'll have to wait. In the New Year we'll get you a pony to pull the carriage, and then I'll teach you how to drive safely." Father led Charlie out of the traces and tied him to the fence, then grasped the shafts and pulled the red carriage into the stable. "Until then," Father said, "we'll keep this in the stable."

"May I at least sit in it?" pleaded Little Joseph.

"Yes, you may," said Father. "But only today. Then we need to cover it up until Christmas."

Little Joseph spent the rest of the day and evening sitting in his red carriage, parked in the corner of the stable.

LUCY – DECEMBER 24

KIRTLAND, OHIO
Sunday, December 24, 1837

From the Life of Joseph F. Smith: *"The Prophet Joseph Smith, realizing the necessity of the situation, informed Hyrum that it was the will of the Lord that he marry again and take as a wife a young English convert, Mary Fielding by name."*[27]

From Mary Fielding Smith, Daughter of Britain: *"In due course, and following his brother's counsel, Hyrum sought the hand of the lady whom it was providentially appointed that he should marry. This unusual circumstance, wherein the Lord revealed whom a person should marry, has few parallels. Subsequent events were to prove the rightness of Joseph's pronouncement in behalf of his brother. Mary, definitely, was the proper person for Hyrum. . . . So, in Kirtland, marriage came to Mary when she was thirty-six years old and Hyrum one year her senior. It occurred the day before Christmas, 1837."*[28]

---

[27] Joseph Fielding Smith, *Life of Joseph F. Smith*, (Deseret News Press, Salt Lake City, 1938) 120

[28] Don Cecil Corbett, Marty Fielding Smith: Daughter of Britain (Deseret Book, Salt Lake City, 1966) 44-45

Joseph Smith wrote: "Apostasy, persecution, confusion and mobocracy strove hard to bear rule at Kirtland, and thus closed the year 1837."[29]

Lucy Smith didn't know whether to smile or frown, to laugh or to cry.

It was Christmas Eve, and the sound of singing surrounded Lucy. She stood to the side of the large gathering room in her brother Hyrum's house, where her sister-in-law Jerusha had died less than three months before. Lucy was trying to observe everyone in the room simultaneously. All were there. Papa, Mama, Sophronia, Hyrum, Joseph, Samuel, William, Katharine, Don Carlos, and all of their families. And sixteen nieces and nephews within reach of their favorite, Aunt Lucy. All of her pearls in one small place.

Suddenly Lucy realized she was both smiling and crying at the same time. Her tears were for Jerusha and the sweet little motherless children she left behind, but her joy was to see her entire family together in one place. They were all packed into this one room, singing together a hymn from the little book, *A Collection of Sacred Hymns*, which they each held in their hands:

Why do we mourn for dying friends,
Or shake at death's alarms?
'Tis but the voice that Jesus sends,
To call them to his arms.

---

[29] HC 2:528

We Smiths really know how to sing, thought Lucy. She stood by her parents, Joseph Smith, Sr. and Lucy Mack Smith. They both suddenly looked old in Lucy's sixteen-year-old eyes. Her father's hair had gone white. In his day, he had been notably strong, but his day was done. *He's grown old!* Lucy suddenly realized. And her mother seemed smaller than she had been, as if she was shrinking with the passage of years.

Are we not tending upward too,
As fast as time can move?
Nor should we wish the hours more slow
To keep us from our love?

She had always been the historian, the cataloger, the preserver of family traditions. Her heart rejoiced to see the entire family here together, and her mind instantly embraced each person and their place in the whole. She instantly saw the six families of her brothers and sisters and her sixteen beloved nieces and nephews as one whole, with multiple beloved parts.

Why should we tremble to convey,
Their bodies to the tomb?
There once the flesh of Jesus lay,
And left a long perfume.

On Lucy's right were her brother Don Carlos and his wife Agnes with their one-year-old daughter, Agnes.

On her left were her brother Joseph and his wife Emma, with their children Julia, Joseph, and Frederick.

Then, there was her oldest sister, Sophronia, who was a widow with a little daughter, Mariah. Her husband Calvin had died the previous year. Lucy knew that she was now courting with William McCleary.

Lucy also saw her brother Samuel and his wife Mary, and their two little daughters, Susannah and Mary.

And she saw her brother William and his wife Caroline, with their little girls, Mary Jane and Caroline.

The graves of all his saints he blest,
And softened every bed:
Where should the dying members rest,
But with their dying Head?

Across the room were her sister Katharine and her husband, Wilkins, with their daughter, Lucy, and their little son, Solomon.

And then in the center there was her Uncle Hyrum, newly returned from Missouri to learn of the death of his dear wife, Jerusha. He stood in the center of the room holding his little daughter, Jerusha, with his three older children, Lovina, John, and Hyrum nearby. Lucy held baby Sarah in her arms, orphaned so young.

There were many tears on the cheeks of family members. Lucy knew that they were all mourning the death of Jerusha.

Thence he arose, ascended high,
And showed our feet the way:

Up to the Lord our feet shall fly,
At the great rising day.

Lucy smiled through her tears as she looked into the sweet faces of her eleven nieces and five nephews, ranging in age from newborn up to her niece Lovina, who was the oldest at age ten.

Lucy also smiled as she contemplated that Emma, Katharine, and Agnes were all expecting babies to be born in the coming months. Lucy inwardly counted these new additions to her catalog of loved ones. Twenty nieces and nephews. And she wondered how many of the new babies would be boys, as male grandchildren had been rather scarce in the family to this point.

There were a few others crowded into the room aside from family. There were Uncle Hyrum's longtime family friends and helpers, Old George the soldier, and the woman they called Aunty Grinnel. They stood by the door, watching.

Finally, there was Mary Fielding, a recent convert to the Church newly arrived from England, who stood dressed in her best Sunday frock, with a wreath of flowers in her hair, beside Lucy's Uncle Hyrum. She was to marry Uncle Hyrum today. Lucy looked into the face of her Uncle Hyrum, who was singing in his beautiful baritone voice. Lucy watched as a single tear dropped from his eye and ran down his cheek. This he wiped away with his sleeve and then smiled at Mary Fielding, then around at his children, his parents, and his brothers and sisters.

Then let the last loud trumpet sound,
And bid our kindred rise;
Awake, ye nations under ground;
Ye saints, ascend the skies.

The hymn ended, and Lucy's Papa walked to the middle of the room. His voice trembled as he spoke: "My dear family. Let me just say that Jerusha was a woman whom everybody loved who was acquainted with her. She was in every way worthy. She died in the faith and with love for our son Hyrum and their children. It is a grief of my heart that Hyrum returned home from his mission to find his beloved Jerusha dead, and he is now the sole parent for five beautiful children, including sweet little Sarah, newly born. So, it was with both grief and joy that our son Joseph realized the necessity of the situation, and came to Hyrum informing him that it was the will of the Lord that he marry again, and that he take as a wife our sweet young English convert, Mary Fielding."

There were smiles and tears, and then clapping by the entire Smith clan. They then sang another hymn, this from the section in the little hymnal marked "On Marriage:"

When earth was dressed in beauty,
And joined with heav'n above,
The Lord took Eve to Adam,
And taught them how to love.

On such a grand occasion,
As union had begun

They held a sweet communion,
And joined the twain as one.

And blessed them at an altar,
For chaste and pure desire,
That no unhallowed being
Might offer there "strange fire."

Beware of all temptation,
Be good, be just, be wise,
Be even as the angels,
That dwell in Paradise.

Go multiply—replenish,
And fill the earth with men,
That all your vast creation,
May come to God again:

And dwell amid perfection,
In Zion's wide domains,
Where union is eternal,
And Jesus ever reigns.

The singing stopped and Lucy's aged father stepped forward. "Hyrum and Mary Fielding," he said. "Come forward and join hands."

Hyrum handed little Jerusha off to Aunty Grinnel and faced Mary Fielding, taking her by the hand.

Then Lucy's father said, "We are here to join our son Hyrum and Mary Fielding in holy matrimony. As we have just sung, marriage is an institution of heaven, first solemnized in the garden of Eden by God Himself, by the authority of the everlasting priesthood."

Here her father paused, and wiping tears from his eyes, continued. "Now, do you, Hyrum Smith and Mary Fielding, covenant to be companions during your lives, and discharge the duties of husband and wife in all respects?"

"Yes," said Uncle Hyrum.

"Yes," said Mary Fielding.

"Then," said Lucy's father, "I pronounce you husband and wife in the name of God! May the Lord bless you both!"

To this there was a prolonged cheer and applause, and Hyrum kissed Mary Fielding Smith.

After the wedding supper, the Smith grandparents and parents all sat down to visit, and Lucy bundled up her older nieces and nephews and took them outside for a walk. All the horses and carriages of her parents and brothers and sisters were hitched to the fence. Uncle Joseph's black stallion, Old Charlie gave a friendly neigh. Little Joseph walked over to stroke his nose, and the other boys followed.

There were ten in her little flock, all but the toddlers and babes in arms. Lucy held two-year-old Susannah by the hand, while Lovina held little Solomon. The older girls—Julia, Mariah, Mary Jane, and little Lucy—followed behind.

"Let's march!" said Little Joseph, leaving his father's horse and running ahead toward the temple. The boys, John and Hyrum, followed him, kicking their feet out as they walked and saluting every tree and house along the road.

"Your mother was an angel," said Lucy to her ten-year-old niece, Lovina Smith. "I'll never forget her."

"Nor I," said Lovina, and then fell silent.

"Your life will be very interesting now," continued Lucy. "Mary Fielding Smith is a wonderful woman. She has been a teacher, so she knows how to take charge of children."

Lovina was silent.

"And, of course," said Lucy, trying to fill the silence. "There is Hannah Grinnel to help with the little girls. John and Hyrum look like they will do well." She pointed up the road to where the three boys were trying to hit rocks with sticks they had found by the roadside.

"And, my dear," said Lucy, stopping and embracing her niece, "remember that I am always here." Lovina put down little Solomon and hugged her aunt and sobbed.

PART II

"HE GOETH ON TO MEET THE ARMED MEN"

"Hast thou given the horse strength?
Hast thou clothed his neck with thunder?
Canst thou make him afraid as a grasshopper?
The glory of his nostrils is terrible.
He paweth in the valley, and rejoiceth in his strength.
He goeth on to meet the armed men.
He mocketh at fear and is not affrighted,
Neither turneth he back from the sword.
The quiver rattleth against him,
The glittering spear and the shield.
He swalloweth the ground with fierceness and rage,
Neither believeth he that it is the sound of the trumpet.
He saith among the trumpets, 'Ha! Ha!'
And he smelleth the battle afar off,
The thunder of the captains, and the shouting."[30]

---

[30] Job 39:19-25 (Within the immediate family of Joseph Smith, Jr., this scripture was deemed a fit description of Old Charlie)

OLD CHARLIE – JANUARY 12

KIRTLAND, OHIO
Friday, January 12, 1838

Lucy Mack Smith: "The persecution finally became so violent that Joseph regarded it as unsafe to remain any longer in Kirtland, and began to make arrangements to move to Missouri. One evening, before finishing his preparations for the contemplated journey, he sat in council with the brethren at our house. After giving them directions as to what he desired them to do, while he was absent from them, and as he was leaving the room, he said, 'Well Brethren, I do not recollect anything more, but one thing, brethren, is certain, I shall see you again, let what will happen, for I have a promise of life five years, and they cannot kill me until that time is expired.' That night he was warned by the Spirit to make his escape, with his family, as speedily as possible; he therefore arose from his bed and took his family, with barely beds and clothing sufficient for them, and left Kirtland in the dead hour of the night."[31]

Joseph Smith: "January, 1838—A new year dawned upon the Church in Kirtland in all the bitterness of the spirit of apostate mobocracy; which continued to rage and grow hotter and hotter, until Elder Rigdon and myself were obliged to flee from its deadly influence, as

---

[31] Scot Facer Proctor and Maurine Jensen Proctor, eds., *The Revised and Enlarged History of Joseph Smith by His Mother,* hereinafter "Lucy Mack Smith," 350

did the Apostles and Prophets of old, and as Jesus said, 'when they persecute you in one city, flee to another,' On the evening of the 12th of January, about ten o'clock, we left Kirtland, on horseback, to escape mob violence, which was about to burst upon us. We continued our travels during the night, and at eight o'clock on the morning of the 13th, arrived among the brethren in Norton Township, Medina County, Ohio, a distance of sixty miles from Kirtland. Here we tarried about thirty-six hours, when our families arrived; and on the 16th we pursued our journey with our families, in covered wagons towards the city of Far West, in Missouri."[32]

It was a short night—real short. After dark I was jest standin' in the pasture. Inside the stable Brother Joe's black harness horse, Jim, and his milk cow was all settled down for the night, and I could hear them breathin' quietly. It was a clear, cold night with a little bit of snow on the ground here and there. There warn't a cloud in the sky, and the stars kind of glistened in the black. All sorts of Brethren and their horses had been comin' and goin' all evenin', includin' Brother Hyrum ridin' on Sam, but they had all cleared out. Soon the lights in Brother Joe's big house winked off one by one, and I 'spected that Brother Joe and Emma and all the little ones was all sound asleep. I jest stood a while in the yard lookin' at the house and the sky, and my breath came out of my nostrils like little clouds in the cold.

Then suddenly, in the dark, I see'd a little light through one of the windows, like someone was carryin' a candle from room to room in Brother Joe's house. Then the back

---

[32] HC 3:1-2

door opened, and I walked over to the fence to see. It was Brother Joe and Lady Emma. Major was standin' by Brother Joe, waggin' his tail. Lady Emma kind of reached up and held Brother Joe in her arms a bit and then took a hold of Major's collar and stood in the doorway watchin' Brother Joe walk away. He came out into the yard carryin' a lantern, all dressed in his hat and coat, with his travelin' saddle bags and other gear slung over his shoulder, like we was goin' on another trip.

"Come on, Old Charlie!" he whispered to me when he got to the gate. "We're goin' to ride tonight, boy." He put the lantern down and rubbed down my head and ears, then led me into the stable. Old Jim groaned when we walked in, lookin' right confused in the lantern light, and then he started circlin' in his box. He was wondering, I'm sure, if he and I was goin' to be hitched up to the carriage like we were many days when Brother Joe took Lady Emma and the young ones out for a ride. But Brother Joe just saddled me up, led me outside, and swung into the saddle. He hesitated a spell, lookin' at the dark house with Lady Emma and Major standin' in the doorway, and then we rode out into the lane in the dark.

We passed the temple and stopped at the house of Brother Sidney. Brother Joe tied me off outside, then went up the porch to the front door and started knockin' quiet like. "Sidney," he whispered. "Sidney!" No one was out on the streets and I couldn't see nary a light, 'cept the stars overhead. There warn't no answer at Brother Sidney's door, but then I see'd how Brother Joe walked over to the porch railin' and took a hold of the post, and started climbin' up like a lizard on a wall. Well, pretty soon Brother Joe was all the way up top, where there was another little railin' on the second story. He went over to one of the windows and started tappin' real quiet like.

I heared a squeakin' sound, and one of the windows opened up, and Brother Sidney poked his head out. I could hear Brother Sidney's deep voice kind of rumblin' and Brother Joe's voice whisperin', but I couldn't understand what they was sayin'. They went back and forth at the window for a spell—whisper, rumble, whisper, rumble—and then Brother Joe shinnied back down the post and landed on the porch. Then we jest waited. A couple of little lights went on in Brother Sidney's house, while Brother Joe walked around behind Brother Sidney's house. I thought that was strange, and I stood there in the dark, jest lookin' across the street at the dark shape of the temple, kind of glistenin' in the starlight. Then the moon came up and lit everythin' up the way it does. Presently, Brother Joe came back around the house, leadin' Champ, all saddled up. Champ was bein' difficult, as usual, kind of snortin'. I blew at him, jest to say hello, but he wanted none of that and just snorted back at me, dropped his tail between his legs, and opened his mouth, ready to bite me if I come too near. I let him have his space and jest waited. We stood there for a piece, and then Brother Joe walked back 'round the house, leavin' me alone with Champ. As soon as we were alone, he took the opportunity to come at me a bit, snortin' and leanin' in for a little bite, just to show me who was boss around his place, I guess. I snorted back and nipped him on the neck, and he backed off.

Then somethin' funny happened. When I moved, my bridle come up draggin', as I wasn't tied up properly on the hitchin' rail. Anyway, I was loose, and I rambled off a bit in the moonlight, first to stand clear of Champ, but then wandered 'round the side of the house to see what had become of Brother Joe. Then I got the scent of Brother Joe floatin' in the air from behind Brother Sidney's house. There was a little stand of trees behind the yard where I knowed Brother Joe was, and I just follered it, walkin' easy like, draggin' my bridle. It was mighty dark and quiet, but then I heared Brother Joe's voice, real quiet. I came up slowly to the edge of the trees, and there was Brother Joe on his knees, with his hands together, and he looked like he was talkin' to hisself! He had his back to me, and I nuzzled his head with my nose, which gave him a start. He said another word or two, then, turned and stood up, strokin' my nose. "So here you are, Old Charlie," he said, "Lookin' out for me through thick and thin." And then he stood and led me back round to the front of the house by Champ.

Presently Brother Sidney came out of the house, all bundled up. Brother Joe helped him situate his bags on Champ, and then they mounted up, and we set out in the dark.

There warn't no talkin' between Brother Joe and Brother Sidney, which surprised me some, as Brother Sidney always seemed to have his mouth open, but I guess with the late night and the cold, he jest sort of settled in on Champ's back. We rode out south at a nice clip. The moon rose, which showed the way on the road, which was dry and not too icy, except where there had been puddles of water what froze in the night. The road was hard, though, a lot harder than I was used to, with patches of old snow here and there.

We rode straight through the night, hour by hour. I could tell that Brother Joe was in a hurry, and we didn't let up until we covered fifty, sixty mile at least.

At early light we come into a little settlement. Brother Joe and Brother Sidney stopped and knocked on the door of a house. A man come out, then three more, and they was huggin' Brother Joe and Brother Sidney. The fellers all went inside with Brother Joe, but soon one of 'em come out and got Champ and me unsaddled and led around to a pasture by a leafless willow tree. Then this feller went into the house, leavin' Champ and me alone. Champ settled down as the sun was comin' up, but I jest stood there watchin' that house where I knowed Brother Joe was restin'.

WYCLIFFE – JANUARY 13

KIRTLAND, OHIO
Saturday, January 13, 1838

Wycliffe Rigdon: "[In] the winter of 1837, [Joseph Smith and Sidney Rigdon] and their families started for Caldwell County, Missouri, a distance of about 1000 miles. I was attending school in the upper part of the temple when we left. On coming home from school one day in the afternoon of the day we left, I saw considerable commotion about my father's house. I inquired of Mother what was the reason. She said nothing that concerned me. In the evening I saw several men come to our house and whisper a time and go away. I wanted to know of Mother what was the trouble, but could get no reply; and was at last ordered to bed. And I and my brother Sidney went to bed. Along in the night, I was awakened by a man trying a pair of shoes on my feet. I asked what he was doing. He said he had gotten me a new pair of shoes. I said that was all right, but had he not better wait till morning, then I could try them on better. He said, "You go to sleep and don't ask questions." I did so. Not long after this, my brother and I were awakened and told to dress as we were going away. I asked where we were going, and he said to a land flowing with milk and honey that I had heard talked so much about. Well, I thought, if I was going to that land which was flowing with milk and honey, it was a pretty good place for me to go. And I

wanted to go. That night about twelve o'clock we started in our open wagon. . . . We rode all night. ."[33]

Wycliffe was awakened by a sound outside his door. He lay awake in his bed, listening hard. Bare tree branches scraped the side of the house in the cold wind outside, but otherwise the night was silent, except for the even breathing of his older brother, Sid, lying on the other side of the bed.

Wycliffe closed his eyes. Yesterday had been a strange day. He had attended school as usual in the upper part of the temple. On coming home there was a considerable commotion in his father's house. Many horses were tethered outside, including the Prophet's black stallion, Charlie, and the door to his father's study was closed, with the sound of many voices within.

"What is going on?" Wycliffe asked his mother.

"Nothing to concern you, dear," said his mother. "Now get ready for supper."

At supper Wycliffe's father was unusually quiet, and then while the children were getting ready for bed, more men came to the house and drew his father aside in whispers, then left. His father remained closed in his study.

Sid came in from caring for the horses. "What is it?" he asked his younger brother.

"I'm not sure, but something is happening."

---

[33] Wycliffe Rigdon History, 28-29

Wycliffe found his mother in the hallway. "Mother, I know something is going on. What is it?"

"I can give you no reply, my boy. Now you and Sid go to bed."

Wycliffe was just drifting off to sleep when he heard a soft sound of footsteps in the hallway and the hiss of whispers. The door opened and someone slipped inside in dead silence. A dark figure approached the bed, and Wycliffe felt a hand take hold of his bare left foot under the covers. He tried to pull his foot back, and then felt a shoe being pulled onto his foot.

"What are you doing?" said Wycliffe in alarm.

A man's voice answered. "I have just gotten you a new pair of warm shoes, and I'm trying them on you."

Wycliffe was astounded. "All right," he said. "But hadn't you better wait until morning, so I can try them on properly."

"You go back to sleep, boy, and don't ask questions." Then the man left the room.

Sid woke up and rubbed his eyes. "What's the matter?"

"I don't know. Someone is about the house, but I was told we should just go to sleep."

Sid didn't answer, having fallen asleep again. Wycliffe closed his eyes and had just started drifting into slumber when the door opened again. This time two men came inside carrying candles. One of them went to the boys' wooden dresser and Wycliffe heard the scrape of a drawer being pulled open. The other figure came right up to the bed and started shaking the boys.

"Wake up, boys!"

"What is it?" asked Sid.

"You're to get dressed warmly. You're going on a long journey tonight." Wycliffe recognized the voice as that of his brother-in-law, George Robinson."

"George? Is that you? Where are we going?" asked Wycliffe.

"To a land which is flowing with milk and honey," said the other man, bringing clothes from the dresser. "Your father has gone ahead and sent orders that you and your mother and sisters and little brother are to follow."

"Father? Isn't he here in the house?"

"No," said the man with the candle. "He rode out of Kirtland two hours ago with Joseph Smith."

"When do we leave?" asked Sid.

"Now. We have a wagon waiting outside."

LITTLE JOSEPH – JANUARY 13

KIRTLAND, OHIO
Saturday, January 13, 1838

"Wake up, children!" said Emma Smith. "We're going on a little trip."

Little Joseph opened his eyes. It was still dark in the little bedroom he shared with Julia. His mother was standing, all dressed, holding a candle in one hand. In her other arm she held eighteen-month-old Frederick on her hip.

"Where are we going?" asked Julia.

"To Far West," said Mother.

When she said *Far West*, Little Joseph felt a thrill of excitement in his heart. *Finally, I'm going to the far west*, he thought. "Will we take my new red wagon?" At Christmas, after his return from Missouri, Father had given Little Joseph the red wagon built by Alexander Badham and Arthur Millikin. It was red, two-wheeled, and built to be pulled by a pony. Father had put it in the barn and promised to get a pony to pull the wagon in the spring.

"I'm sorry," said Mother. "We must leave your red wagon here. We'll ride in the big wagon. Jim will pull us."

"What about Charlie?" asked Little Joseph.

"Your Father has ridden on ahead on Charlie," said Mother, "We'll meet him on the road. But we mustn't talk.

We will leave right after we pack and eat. And Joseph, you can help your grandfather hitch up Jim to the wagon."

"What shall we take?" asked Julia, who was already dressing.

"Just your clothes and one or two other little things, as you may choose. We won't have room for much. Sister Rigdon and her children will travel with us."

Grandfather Smith had a heavy cough. Little Joseph could hear it as he went outside to help with the horses. It was a frosty morning, and Little Joseph's breath went up in great drafts of steam. Grandfather brought Jim out of the corral. The ground was hard and icy cold, and Little Joseph saw that there was a ring around the moon. There was the faintest glimmer of morning on the eastern horizon.

The wagon, which was a small one about ten feet in length and covered with a canvas top, was already piled with bundles of clothing and food for the journey. By the wagon was one of Grandfather's horses, a clay-colored gelding called Jasper. "Now Little Joseph, I'm counting on you," said Grandfather, backing Jim into the right side of the long wagon shaft. He then, with a little difficulty, backed Jasper into the left side, then connected the harness traces to the single tree. "I'm counting on you to be the man on this journey. Of course you need to obey your mother, but you need to watch out over your mother, your sister, and your little brother. Do you understand?"

"Yes, sir," said Little Joseph, reaching up and patting Jim's jet-black flanks. Jim was a gentle and obedient horse.

"You are the man of the house until you meet your father again," Grandfather continued, "if there is anything needing to be done, such as feeding Jim, or gathering firewood, or keeping an eye on your little brother. Okay?"

"Yes, sir," said Little Joseph. Grandfather smiled and patted his head.

"Here," said Grandfather. "I have something for you." He reached in his pocket and brought out a smooth, round stone and handed it to Little Joseph. Little Joseph turned it over in his hand. The stone was white, with tiny veins of gold running through it. It had a little hole drilled on one side, and a little strip of deer hide tied through it. "This is a lucky stone I brought all the way from Vermont. I found it and a few others like it in a streambed running down from a mountain. It was about the time your father was born. Anyway, I kept a few of them and want you to have this."

"Why is it lucky?" asked Little Joseph, holding the stone in his fist.

"It might be that it will give you inspiration or protection when you wear it around your neck or hold it in your hands. Or at least, it might remind you where your family came from and how much they love you. Sometimes love is luck enough."

"Thanks, Grandfather," said Little Joseph. Grandfather tied the little leather around the boy's neck. Little Joseph held the stone out to look at it, then tucked it under his coat and shirt.

Mother came out the back door, carrying a box in her arms, which Grandfather took from her and placed carefully in the bed of the wagon. "These are Joseph's papers," she said. "Let us lose any belonging in the world but those."

Mother went back inside the house one last time and came out carrying a basket covered with a cloth. She placed it in the wagon, and Little Joseph could smell the aroma of her freshly baked cornbread.

Grandmother Lucy Mack Smith also came out of the house with Julia, followed by Aunt Lucy leading little Frederick by the hand. Frederick was still unsure and stumbling in his walking.

"Well, let's be off," said Mother helping little Frederick to a seat on the wagon box and then climbing up herself. Grandfather lifted Julia in the wagon with a cheerful grunting noise. It was cold outside, and Grandmother and Aunt Lucy packed blankets around the children.

"Where's Major?" asked Little Joseph with concern. "Major!" he called. The huge white mastiff dog came bounding around the corner of the house. Little Joseph climbed into the back of the wagon. Major stood on his hind legs, tail wagging, and licked Little Joseph's face. "You follow along behind, boy," said Little Joseph.

Mother clicked her tongue and they rode onto Chillicothe Road and headed south, passing the cemetery and the temple.

At the house of Sidney and Phebe Rigdon, Emma Smith drew up her small wagon, and they waited. It was not yet sunrise, but soon would be and Little Joseph's mother was anxious to be on the road.

There was a huge wagon in front of the house, with four horses hitched up, and already loaded with boxes. More than eighteen feet long and covered with a high white canvas cover, it dwarfed the Smith's tiny wagon.

Emma and her children watched as the Rigdon family finished loading the wagon. They were a big and a noisy family: The oldest daughter Athalia was married to George W. Robinson, the general recorder for the Church. George was loading boxes into the large wagon. The younger Rigdon children, eight of them, were coming in and out of the house: fifteen-year-old Nancy, fourteen-year-old Eliza, twelve-year-old Sarah, nine-year-old Algernon Sidney (who the boys all called "Sid"), seven-year-old John Wickliffe (called "Wickliffe" by the boys), six-year-old Lacy, three-year-old Carvel, and Dorcas, almost two.

The two Rigdon boys, Sid and Wickliffe, though older than Little Joseph, had been good pals. Little Joseph jumped out of the wagon. "Can Wickliffe and Sid ride in the back with me in our wagon?" asked Little Joseph to his mother.

Mother eyed the Rigdons' large wagon and the number of little Rigdons running in and out of the house in the pre-dawn light. "I think that would be all right," she said.

Julia turned to her mother. "May Lacy Rigdon ride with us?"

Mother looked at her daughter for a long moment, then said, "I suppose so," and Julia immediately jumped down from the wagon. "If she behaves herself!" Mother called.

Largely through the efforts of George Robinson, the Rigdon wagon was loaded, and Athalia and George were situating the children in their places. Sid and Wickliffe climbed in the back of the Smith wagon with Little Joseph.

"Good morning," called Mother to Sister Rigdon, who came out on the porch, bundled up and carrying little Dorcas in her arms.

"Hello, Emma," said Sister Rigdon. "We'll be ready to set off momentarily."

"Mother!" called Lacy Rigdon. She was standing on the porch with Julia Smith. "Can I ride with Julia?"

"Yes, dear," said Sister Rigdon, who then glanced at Emma Smith. "But only if it's all right with her mother."

Emma nodded and gave a little smile.

"Mother!" called Lacy Rigdon again. She had a loud voice for a little girl. "Can I bring my horse? Sid told me it was too big, but I want to bring it for our new house in Far West." Lacy had dragged a large wooden rocking horse onto the front porch.

"It won't fit!" said Wickliffe, now sitting in the back of the Smith wagon with Little Joseph.

"Father can get you a new one in Far West," said Athalia.

"Mother!" said Lacy, "I want this rocking horse! It's my favorite."

"Lacy, dear," said Sister Rigdon. "I think they're right. It's probably too big. Especially after we meet up with your father."

"But I want it!" said Lacy. "Please!"

"No, dear. I'm sorry."

Little Joseph then watched in amusement and surprise as Lacy Rigdon began crying and wailing. Julia, standing beside her, watched in fascination.

"I'm sorry, sweet," said Sister Rigdon, looking helpless. "It just won't fit."

Lacy Rigdon cried louder and louder. Finally she threw herself down upon her back on the floor of the porch and began pounding her heels on the floorboards, and then finally bumping the back of her head.

"Lacy, you'll hurt your head!" cried Sister Rigdon in alarm.

Lacy continued to scream and bumped her head even harder on the floor.

"Lacy!" cried Sister Rigdon. "Oh, Lacy, you'll get hurt."

The screams and the banging head continued for a moment, and then Sister Rigdon said, "Okay, dear! We'll take the rocking horse! Please stop! George, please get the horse!"

George Robinson rolled his eyes and went to the porch to get the rocking horse, which he stowed in the back of the wagon. Lacy stood up and took Julia by the hand and skipped happily toward the Smith's wagon.

LUCY – JANUARY 13

KIRTLAND, OHIO
Saturday, January 13, 1838

Lucy Mack Smith: "Soon after Joseph left, the constable, Luke Johnson (who had formerly been a member of the Church), came to our house and served a summons on Mr. Smith which requested him to go to the magistrate's office. Johnson said that no mischief was intended, and that it was of a peaceable nature. Mr. Smith was then sick, and I begged Johnson not to take him away among our enemies, for I knew by experience that their design was generally false imprisonment, and that their civil writs too often proved to be very uncivil. Johnson paid no attention to what I said. . . . After Mr. Smith arrived at the office, he was informed of the cause of his being arrested, and what would be necessary to escape from imprisonment. He was taken . . . For marrying a couple. As the apostates and the mob did not consider him a minister of the gospel, they contested his right to perform such a ceremony, and he was fined the sum of three thousand dollars, and in case he should default in paying this, he was sentenced to the penitentiary. Luke Johnson bustled about and seemed to be very much engaged, preparing to draw writings for the money . . . But at the first opportunity, he went to Hyrum . . . And told him to take his father into a room which he pointed out to him. Luke said, 'I will manage to get the window out, and he will be at liberty to jump out and go when and where he pleases.' Hyrum and Mr. Smith left the company, and Luke told the mob that they had gone to consult together about raising the money. By deceiving them in this way, he kept

them still until Mr. Smith crept out of the window, with the help of Hyrum and John Boynton (who said he was our friend at this time). . . . When Luke supposed that my husband was out of their reach, he started up and ran into the room where he had left him, saying that he must see after the prisoner. Upon finding that the prisoner had fled, he made a great parade, calling out that he was gone and hunting in every direction for the fugitive. He came to me and inquired if Mr. Smith was at home. This frightened me very much and I exclaimed, 'Luke, you have taken my husband away and given him into the hands of the mob and they have killed him.'"[34]

Lucy Smith waved at Emma and watched the wagon ride away in the morning light, then turned towards home with her parents.

"I hope they meet up with Joseph soon," said Lucy as the three entered their house.

"They'll find him, sure enough," said Father Smith. "I'm more worried about enduring the long journey to Missouri, nearly a thousand miles, with all of those young ones."

"But there are three men among them," said Lucy. "There is Joseph and George Robinson. And of course Sidney Rigdon."

"Sidney Rigdon!" said her mother, Lucy Mack Smith. "I don't think he is anywhere near the man your brother Joseph is. During the times of trouble in Kirtland, the brethren would take their stations to watch and stand night after night through all weather to guard to protect the lives of the Presidency, one of whom was Sidney Rigdon. He was

---

[34] *History of Joseph Smith by His Mother,* 351-352

always as faint-hearted as any woman, and far more than his own wife, who has great faith, patience, and genuine courage."

"God will direct it," said Father Smith, and then coughed loudly.

"Are you unwell, Joseph?" asked Mother Smith, laying the back of her hand on her husband's forehead.

"Just got a bit of cold in my chest," he said. "That's all."

"Well, I say you go to bed," said Mother Smith.

Just then there was a heavy knock at the door. Lucy went to the door and opened it to find the constable, Luke Johnson, standing there with papers in his hand. Luke looked inside the house and spoke to Father Smith. "I've got legal papers to serve upon you," he said.

"What kind of legal papers," Father Smith asked.

"You'll find out when I take you before the magistrate," said Luke.

"Luke," said Mother Smith. "I beg of you not to take my husband among our enemies."

"No mischief is intended against you," said Luke. "This is of a peaceable nature. It's simply a civil writ."

"Luke," said Mother Smith, "Their civil writs too often prove to be very uncivil."

"I have my duties as constable," said Luke. "He must come with me."

"I know that their design is false imprisonment," said Mother Smith. "If you take my husband, he is a dead man!"

Luke Johnson hesitated, but then entered the house and placed shackles upon the hands of Father Smith.

"At least let him take his coat!" cried Mother Smith. Lucy ran and got his father's coat. Luke removed the shackles to allow him to bundle up, then put them back on and took him out into the cold.

"Quick," said Mother Smith. "Go and tell your brothers." Lucy grabbed her coat and hat and ran out the door.

Lucy Smith arrived at the magistrate's office with her brother Hyrum. The office was set up as a courtroom, with a desk for the presiding magistrate, a clerk's table, chairs for prisoners and attorneys, and a long bench on the back wall for spectators. On this bench Lucy and Hyrum sat down and waited beside several other persons. Father Smith was seated on a chair beside Luke Johnson. His handcuffs had been removed during the court session. There were other prisoners seated near Father Smith. Lucy heard him cough several times. There was also a clerk sitting at his desk, checking his watch.

"Let's just sit and watch," whispered Hyrum to his youngest sister. "Don't say anything. Let's just see what becomes of this matter with Father."

"Okay," whispered Lucy.

Presently the side door opened, and the magistrate Warren Cowdery strode into the room.

"All arise," said Luke Johnson. There was a scraping of chairs and boots as the prisoners and spectators all stood on their feet as the magistrate, Esquire Cowdery took his seat. Then everyone sat down.

Lucy knew that he was the brother of Oliver Cowdery, and was now an enemy to the Church along with Sylvester Smith, Warren Parrish, Joseph Coe, and many others. Lucy looked at the other spectators in the room and realized that Joseph Coe was sitting on the other side of the room.

"First the matter of State versus Joseph Smith, Senior," said the magistrate. Father Smith stood on his feet and faced the magistrate's table.

"What am I charged with?" asked Father Smith with a hoarse voice.

"For illegally marrying a couple," said Esquire Cowdery.

"Your marriage to Mary Fielding," whispered Lucy to her brother. He motioned for her to be quiet.

"But I am an ordained minister of the gospel," said Father Smith. Joseph Coe let out a laugh.

"By what authority are you an ordained minister of the gospel?" asked Esquire Cowdery.

"By the authority of the Lord's Prophet, Joseph Smith, Jr."

"That's no authority," shouted Joseph Coe. "That scoundrel is no minister of the gospel." He then turned to Hyrum and Lucy and said, "He's fled the city, I hear. Your so-called prophet has fled and run."

"Mr. Smith," said Esquire Cowdery. "This court does not consider you a true minister of the gospel, and as such you are falsely ordained. Since the law requires ministers to be duly ordained as a condition to performing marriage ceremonies, the court finds you guilty of the charge. You are sentenced to pay a fine of three thousand dollars."

Joseph Coe laughed.

"I don't have three thousand dollars," said Father Smith hoarsely.

"Then you are sentenced to the penitentiary until you can pay," said Esquire Cowdery. "Next case!" he called, and then proceeded to deal with the next prisoner.

Father Smith sat down and another prisoner arose. Father Smith looked back sadly at his son and daughter. Luke Johnson walked to the side of the clerk's desk with his paperwork. He signed several documents, then received official court stamps from the clerk. While doing so, he raised his eyes and looked at Hyrum. Afterward he walked to Hyrum and Lucy and whispered, "When you are directed by the magistrate, take your father into that holding room over there." Here he pointed to a side door. "I have managed to get the window out of the cell, and he will be at liberty to jump out and go when or where he pleases."

"How can I take my father into that room?" asked Hyrum. "He is in custody of the court and ordered to the penitentiary."

"Just trust me," said Luke.

"Thank you," whispered Hyrum. "Luke, why are you doing this?"

Luke Johnson flushed red and bit his lip. Lucy saw that his eyes moistened. "Because I'm ashamed of what I have become," said Luke, then abruptly returned to the clerk's desk.

"Your honor," said Luke interrupting his conversation with the next prisoner. "May we return briefly to the matter of State versus Joseph Smith, Senior?"

"Yes," said the magistrate.

"I am told that Mr. Smith will consult with his son about raising the money to pay the fine. May they speak together in the holding room?"

Esquire Cowdery glanced over at Joseph Coe, who narrowed his eyes, and then shrugged. "Very well," said the magistrate.

"You stay here and watch," whispered Hyrum to Lucy. "Don't leave, or Joseph Coe will suspect something is up." Hyrum stood up and walked to the door to the holding room.

Lucy remained seated in the courtroom, observing what happened next. Her heart was beating wildly. Was it possible that her father may attempt to escape? This both made her happy and frightened her. What would happen to him? Where would he go? She sat in the courtroom with great dread.

Luke Johnson brought her father to the door of the holding room and escorted father and son inside. Luke Johnson then returned to the courtroom, standing with his back to the door. After about fifteen minutes Lucy noticed that Joseph Coe appeared to be nervous, and he motioned to Esquire Cowdery and pointed toward the door. Esquire Cowdery again interrupted his conversation with another prisoner and spoke to Luke Johnson. "Constable, why don't you see if Mr. Smith has been able to raise the three thousand dollars for his fine."

Luke Johnson opened the door and went into the room, then immediately returned to the courtroom. "He's gone!" Luke shouted.

Joseph Coe stood on his feet and ran into the room, returning back into the courtroom to shout, "The bars on the window are gone! He's escaped!"

Lucy saw that Luke Johnson made a great parade about searching the room and then running outside to search. In the confusion, she slipped out of the courtroom and returned home.

LITTLE JOSEPH – JANUARY 13

ON THE ROAD BETWEEN KIRTLAND AND
NEW PORTAGE, OHIO
Saturday, January 13, 1838

Little Joseph had the day of his life, riding out of Kirtland as the sun rose and then continuing on the road all day. For the first stage of the journey he sat in the back of the Smith wagon with Sid and Wickliffe. They had a grand time watching the Rigdon horses pulling the Rigdon wagon a short distance behind on the road, throwing a stick far into the grass on the side of the road for Major to retrieve and bring back to them, dragging long sticks to make marks in the dirt, playing knuckle bones, telling stories, and napping. Little Joseph wondered how Julia was doing up in front with Lacy Rigdon.

At noon on Saturday they passed a fork in the road at the bottom of a little valley, which George, who carried a map, said was the Cuyahoga Valley. One fork headed southwest toward Medina, Ohio. The other fork, which they took, headed south toward Norton. A short ways down the Norton road, the two wagons stopped for an hour at a little stream overhung with oak trees in a valley. There were farmhouses in the distance, but no one disturbed them as they laid out a lunch on the tailgates of the wagons. They ate dried venison jerky and Mother's cornbread, washed down with water from the stream. The boys ran up the stream to make little boats to float down in the water, and the girls made little baskets from leafless vines they found in a hedge.

During the afternoon, the boys decided to walk for a while, as their legs were getting cramped in the wagon. They decided to play "army scouts" and spy out the land before and after the slow-moving wagons. Wickliffe ran ahead a hundred yards and crouched behind a low stone wall to see if any danger lay ahead. Little Joseph and Sid, with Major bounding at their side, walked behind the Rigdon wagon to scout out any possible enemy forces to the rear of the convoy.

"Let's stand behind this tree for a spell to see if any one is following us," said Little Joseph.

"Let's pretend we have telescopes," said Sid, cupping his hands end to end and trying to peer down the empty space in the middle.

Little Joseph leaned against the tree trunk and peered through his "telescope." They were near the summit of a little hill, and the countryside spread out in a wide panorama before them. The road they had traveled lay in a long brown ribbon through the winter fields to the north. He could see the little valley where they had eaten lunch, and beyond that the fork in the road they had passed before lunch. As he watched, he saw specks on the road approaching the fork. Looking more carefully, he saw that they were horsemen. They came to the fork and stopped for several minutes, as if talking. Then two of the horsemen headed on the road toward Medina and the third came on the road the Smiths and Rigdons had traveled.

"Someone's coming," said Little Joseph excitedly.

"I see," said Sid.

"Come on," said Little Joseph. "Let's tell the others."

The two boys ran back to the wagons. "Mother," called Little Joseph. "We saw somebody behind us."

"That's nice, Joseph."

"There were three horsemen. When they came to the fork, they split up, and one of them is following us."

Mother gave her son a worried look, then clicked loudly and slapped the reins across the backs of Jim and Jasper.

Little Joseph did not see the horseman the rest of that day or night. They rode all Saturday and far into the evening, covering about forty miles. Lacy Rigdon had tired of the small Smith wagon hours ago and was asleep somewhere in her family's huge wagon. Little Joseph rode with Sid and Wickliffe in the big wagon for an hour or two, then went back to his own wagon. Major plodded behind, looking weary. Little Joseph reached his arm down over the back of the wagon, and Major licked his hand. Little Joseph fell asleep for an hour or so, rocked gently by the movement of the wagon.

By dark, there were sounds of complaint from the Rigdon children, especially Lacy, and in the Smith wagon Frederick was getting fussy. Little Joseph looked at the face of his mother, bundled up against the cold. She had a focused look about her eyes, watching the road ahead intently.

"Sister Emma," called George Robinson, driving the second wagon. "This looks like as good a spot as any to make a quick camp for the night."

They pulled the wagons side by side with a space of about twenty feet in between, where George lit a campfire. The horses were released from the traces and put out in a field of sparse winter grass for the night.

After a quick meal of Mother's cornbread and honey, she laid out blankets in the wagon box and put her three children to bed. Little Joseph lay awake a long time, first hearing the sound of voices from the Rigdon wagon, including more complaints from Lacy, then after things quieted down, listening to the gentle sound of the horses pulling at the grass and now and then blowing air out of their noses. Looking up through the round opening at the end of the canvas wagon top, Little Joseph saw the stars bright in the sky. He reached up and felt Grandfather's lucky stone on its leather strap around his neck and fell asleep.

LOVINA – JANUARY 13

Lovina watched Mary Fielding Smith setting the breakfast table. She felt great kindness toward this refined woman with the distinct British accent, but at the same time a trace of secret bitterness.

Her stepmother was trying so hard to become the mother to five children, but in every moment Lovina remembered her dead mother. When Mary Fielding made corndodger for breakfast, Lovina remembered her mother's superior cooking. When Mary Fielding lifted up little Jerusha from her nap, she remembered her mother's laughter and tender way with the tiny ones.

It was hardest of all to watch when Mary Fielding embraced or kissed her father. That was like a knife in the heart for Lovina.

Mary Fielding went to the back door and leaned out calling, "Hyrum! Breakfast!" The younger children sat in their places, and Lovina took her place. Her father came in, bringing a wave of cold from the outside.

"I've just been at Joseph's place," said Hyrum after a blessing was said and the meal begun. "He and Emma left so much behind. It's a shame that they couldn't take everything with them."

"When will we go to Far West, Father?" asked five-year-old John.

"Not until spring," said Hyrum. "We have much to do before we leave. Also, we need to make sure that Grandfather and Grandmother Smith are safely taken care of."

"Well," said Mary Fielding. "I'm glad that the crisis is over, and perhaps the persecution. We can now leave in an orderly time and manner."

Just then the door opened and Lovina's Aunt Lucy came in. "It's Father," she said to Hyrum. "He's been arrested!"

Lovina sat in Lucy Mack Smith's little sitting room, holding her hand. She had spent the day with her grandmother while she awaited news about the fate of her husband. In late afternoon the constable Luke Johnson had returned to the house, saying that he was looking for her grandfather. A short time later her father had come to the house to speak with Grandmama.

Lovina listened as Father explained to his mother how he had gone to the courtroom with his younger sister, Lucy, how Father Smith had been charged with illegally performing a marriage ceremony, how the apostate Joseph Coe had spoken out against the Church and apparently signaled with the magistrate, Esquire Cowdery, how Father Smith was fined three thousand dollars and then ordered to the penitentiary, how Luke Johnson had whispered to him about the window in the holding cell, how Luke had covered for him by telling Esquire Cowdery that they would be consulting about paying the three thousand dollar fine, how they had immediately removed the window and climbed out."

"Where is your father now, Hyrum?" asked Mother Smith.

"I don't know where he is," said Hyrum Smith.

"You don't know where he is?" exclaimed Mother Smith. "But you were with him when he escaped."

"We split up immediately to confuse any pursuers," said Hyrum to his mother. "I came home, while Father headed out of town by way of the fields across from Bishop Knight's place. We also had the help of John Boynton, who sent Joseph Coe down the road to the ford across the Chagrin River."

"Well," said Lucy Mack Smith. "You will never understand my fright when a short time ago, after fretting for hours about the safety of my husband and wondering what was transpiring in the courtroom, I heard a knock upon the door and opened to find Luke Johnson. He said he had come to inquire if Mr. Smith were home. This frightened me very much, and I exclaimed, *Luke you have taken my husband away and given him into the hands of the mob and they have killed him!* He denied this, but gave me no other explanation. He surely didn't tell me that he had helped my dear husband to escape."

"The law has ever been the favorite tool of the adversary," said Hyrum. "If the persecutors of the Lord's Prophet and the Lord's saints can bring civil suit for debt, or for wrongfully performing a marriage ceremony, or some other trifle or peppercorn, they will have the upper hand. They will then bring them before the magistrates, and if they are unable to pay, either their property will be seized or they will be sent off for prison."

Lucy Mack Smith seemed troubled. "What has happened to my husband? Kirtland seemed like such a peaceful and cultured place to me. Such a safe place."

"I realize now that Kirtland was never meant to remain the center of the Church," said Hyrum. "It was a stepping stone along the path for the long journey of the Church."

"But where will that path lead?" asked Grandmother Smith. "How can our hearts be strong when the people of God are scattered in this manner? We don't even know what has become of your brother, the Prophet, and whether he has found his way safely or not."

"We only need to know where the next step is," said Hyrum. "That is the way it always is. The Lord shines a light upon the next step in the road. And for us that next step is Far West. I hope that it is the final resting place of the saints, so close to the sacred center stake of Zion. But whether it turns out to be the ultimate home of the saints or not, I'm content knowing it is the will of God that we go there."

LITTLE JOSEPH – JANUARY 14

NEW PORTAGE, OHIO
Sunday, January 14, 1838

On Sunday morning Mother awakened them early, and after eating the last of the cornbread without a fire, the two families set off. Little Joseph wrapped a blanket around his shoulders and sat in the back of the wagon, watching the frozen landscape beneath a gray sky. The wagon wheels crunched and groaned on the icy road. Sid Rigdon walked up to ride with Little Joseph in the back of the wagon.

"George saw the horseman," he said.

"Where?" said Little Joseph.

"Back behind us about a mile. He said he made a camp behind us and then followed as soon as we set off."

"Let's go see!" said Little Joseph.

The two boys walked back behind the big wagon. They were just passing beyond a grove of trees and could see nothing except dark tree trunks with the morning sun shining through them. They continued walking beside the wagon, looking back occasionally over their shoulders. About fifteen minutes later Sid said, "Look!" In the midst of the tree trunks they could see a single horse with a rider. Instead of riding out into the open, he stopped, waiting.

Little Joseph and Sid looked at each other. "Let's tell my mother," Little Joseph said.

Mother looked concerned, but said, "Don't give it any mind, Joseph. It's probably a hunter." But again she whipped up the horses and the wagons moved forward as quickly as possible.

Little Joseph and Sid rode the rest of the day in the back of the large wagon.

They didn't see the horseman again until early afternoon. The wagons had traveled about twenty miles since early morning and they were just coming into the main settlement of Norton Township. The homes were built of logs and surrounded by good farmland and split rail fences. As they entered the settlement, Little Joseph looked back and saw the mysterious horseman galloping behind them, closing the gap, perhaps a quarter of a mile behind them on the open road.

Then several things happened at once. First, Major, who had been walking behind the second wagon, began barking loudly. Little Joseph thought he was barking at the pursuing horseman, but the big dog ran out of his sight toward the front of the wagon. Little Joseph then heard the voice of his father.

"Emma! Turn in here."

The wagons swung to the right and passed into a pretty little farmstead. There was a log cabin with a stone chimney, from which rose skyward a line of gray wood smoke, and a fenced in pasture, white with snow. Several horses stood along the pasture fence. Then suddenly the head of Old Charlie came into Little Joseph's view over the fence. The front door to the cabin opened and it was Father, running out in his shirtsleeves to greet them, his arms outstretched. Little Joseph stood up in the wagon and was swept into his Father's arms. Brother Sidney followed Father from the cabin, and the two families had a joyous reunion.

A few minutes later, as the men and boys unloaded the wagons, Little Joseph looked back over his shoulder. The mysterious horseman was nowhere to be seen.

GEORGE ROBINSON – JANUARY 16

NEW PORTAGE, OHIO
Tuesday, January 16, 1838

The messenger found George Robinson outside the cabin. It was one of Joseph Young's boys, and he had ridden on a bay mare, obviously all night. "Can you give a message to Brother Joseph and Brother Sidney?"

"From Hyrum?" George was expecting some news about the faithful back in Kirtland. They had left town so quickly that they feared for their friends. George looked at the envelope, then shook hands with the messenger.

George finished feeding the horses and checking on the wagons. It was bitterly cold outside, but the horses seemed fine in their thick winter coats. The Prophet's horse, Old Charlie was eating from the grain bag, which he had a right to, George thought. He had ridden sixty miles in less than four hours in the pitch black of night and was still regaining strength. There were seven other horses—the gray gelding called Champ belonging to George's father-in-law, Sidney Rigdon; the four horses for Brother Rigdon's wagon team; the Prophet Joseph's other black stallion, Jim; and the sweet clay-colored gelding belonging to the Prophet's father, Joseph Smith, Sr. The clay-colored horse would stay here in

New Portage with Brother Denmead, to be given later to Father Smith during his journey out of Ohio.

George had taken it upon himself to take primary charge of the horses on their upcoming journey to Missouri. He worried about the trip with so many young children and only three able bodied men. And two of those men, Joseph Smith and Sidney Rigdon, could not readily show their faces this close to Kirtland. But the Rigdon boys, Sid and Wickliffe and Little Joseph Smith, III, would be of some help. They were surely willing. George had observed that Little Joseph loved horses, particularly his father's, and even at age five could handle himself in a saddle, provided that someone would lift him up.

George had left the cabin early to ride out on Champ to see if he could see any sign of the horsemen who had followed them all day Saturday and Sunday. As he stepped outside, Major, the Prophet's huge white guard dog, stood up from beneath the Smith's little wagon and barked. Then he came padding over to the door and stood by George.

"Good old boy," said George scratching his ears. He looked out onto the road. He hadn't wanted to alarm the women, but he had seen at least five horsemen on the road. Three had followed them Saturday, splitting up to search all the possible side roads. He saw two more on Sunday, and he was certain that they now knew where the Prophet and Brother Rigdon had fled. Leaving New Portage in secret would now be impossible. He was certain that the men were armed and that they might possibly commit some violence upon the Prophet. As the secretary to the First Presidency, he was determined not to let that happen. He carried a pistol just in case.

George went back into the two-room cabin of Brother Denmead. Inside, the cabin was warm, in contrast to the bitterly cold air outside on this January morning. The Smith and Rigdon families occupied every square inch, it seemed, of the two snug rooms of the cabin. Sister Emma Smith and Sister Phebe Rigdon were making corndodgers from cornmeal, eggs, and salt, and frying them in a big iron pan over the open flame in the Denmead's stone fireplace.

"Everything is in order outside, Brother Joseph," said George. "And I have a message for you from Kirtland." Joseph Smith was sitting in his shirtsleeves with three children on his lap—three-year-old Carvel Rigdon and the two eighteen-month olds, his son Frederick and little Dorcas Rigdon. The Prophet was singing a song and bouncing the children on his knee.

"Thanks, Brother George," said the Prophet between verses, taking the envelope from his hands. He stopped his singing and bouncing and opened the message, reading it quietly. "They've arrested Father Smith," he said quietly. "There's word of our pursuers. They'll be out on the roads. We'll leave by mid morning. What's the weather like?"

"The weather is clear, but cold. I'm not sure that things are clear—in other ways, however."

"Oh? Have you seen anyone?"

"No, but I'm sure they are there. We'll have to keep an eye out on our journey and be prepared for whatever befalls us."

Brother Joseph lifted the three children off of his lap, and they ran to sit down for breakfast with their mothers.

"Well, George," said the Prophet, clapping him on the shoulder as he stood up. "I wouldn't be overly concerned about what may befall us. It's in the hands of the Lord. One thing is certain. I shall get through this all right, let happen what will. I have a promise of life for five years, and they cannot kill me until that time is expired."

ARTHUR – JANUARY 16

KIRTLAND, OHIO
Tuesday, January 16, 1838

"The printing establishment was seized 'to satisfy an unjust judgment of the county court,' and the Elders Journal, which had issued but two numbers of the first volume, was discontinued. Later the printing office with a large amount of paper and many books was sold by the sheriff to one of the 'reformers;' and on the night of the day of sale the office with its contents and also a small Methodist chapel standing nearby were burned to the ground."[35]

Fire!

Arthur Millikin awoke in the dark and saw the eerie light of burning buildings flickering on the walls of his bedroom. Someone shouted, "Fire!" again, and Arthur was on his feet.

His Uncle Nathaniel burst into the room. "All of Kirtland is on fire!" he shouted and ran from the room. Arthur jumped from his bed and grabbed his clothes where

---

[35] B.H. Roberts, ed., *Comprehensive History of the Church* (BYU Press: Provo, Utah, 1965) 1:407

he had left them draped over the back of a chair, quickly dressed, and followed his uncle outside. Glancing at the clock in the sitting room, he saw that it was one o'clock in the morning.

The streets of Kirtland were alight with red and orange light, but Arthur was puzzled, as he could see no burning buildings. The people, men and women, children and the elderly, were coming out onto the streets from their houses. "Fire! Fire!" a man was calling. Arthur looked around and around. Where was the source of the fire? A bell was ringing somewhere.

"Look to the temple!" someone yelled. Arthur spun around and looked up on the hill and saw the walls of the temple covered with a brilliant dancing light.

"The printing office!" shouted Uncle Nathaniel, who was already running up the hill. Arthur followed. Along the way every door was open, and the streets were filling with people.

As he ran Arthur thought about the swirl of events of the past several days. First the Prophet and Sidney Rigdon and their families had disappeared from Kirtland sometime on Friday night. Early Saturday morning the word had gone out, and Arthur's uncle, Nathaniel Millikin, who was one of the dissenters, met in the Kirtland Temple with Joseph Coe, Lyons, and others. Arthur had wandered up the hill to see what was going on and had happened to walk into the yard of the Prophet's home. There was no one about, and Arthur went into the barn. There was the red wagon that he had built for the Prophet's little boy, Joseph. It stood forlorn in the corner.

Later that Saturday morning a group of riders had departed along roads in all directions, searching for Joseph Smith. From daily conversations with his Uncle Nathaniel, Arthur knew there was much anger over financial losses many had taken in Kirtland when the Kirtland Safety Society failed. "There will be blood," Uncle Nathaniel had said on several occasions. "Blood and retribution."

That was Saturday. On Sunday morning after the departure of the Prophet, a notice was hammered to the door of the Kirtland Temple announcing that a meeting of "The Church of Christ" would take place the following Sabbath for purposes of reorganizing the Church. It was signed by Joseph Coe and Martin Harris.

On Monday morning, just yesterday, Arthur went with his Uncle Nathaniel to the magistrate's office, where the Church printing house was sold at auction to satisfy judgments that had been entered against Joseph Smith and other leaders of the Church. There was a large crowd there of both members of the Church and dissenters. To Arthur's surprise, the printing office was bought at auction by his Uncle Nathaniel.

"Why did you buy the printing office?" asked Arthur that evening at dinner.

His uncle had smiled and said merely, "Every church needs a printing operation to bolster its ministry."

"But the printing office already belongs to the Church," said Arthur.

"To a false church," said his uncle, taking a bite of his dinner. "An apostate church. A fallen church, led by a fallen prophet. That's what Joseph Smith is—a fallen prophet."

That was last night. Now Arthur was running up the hill with several dozen other men. The hill on Chillicothe Road was steep, and as Arthur turned the bend at the Joseph Smith Variety Store and came into view of the Kirtland Temple he saw the origin of the fire. It was the printing office his uncle had bought at auction the previous day.

The printing office was built against the side of the temple, and it was fully engulfed in flames. Already the flames were scorching the sides of the temple itself.

"Bring buckets of water!" shouted Uncle Nathaniel. "Bring water!"

"It's too far gone, Nathaniel!" shouted Joseph Coe.

The onlookers could only watch as the printing office and all its contents went up in flame. Arthur could feel the intense heat from the flames on his face, even at a distance.

At sunrise Uncle Nathaniel and the other men approached the smoldering logs of the printing office. The temple survived, but Arthur could see the smoke-blackened walls rising in the early morning light. It was still too hot in the glowing embers to search for anything left of value, but it was pretty much a certainty that there would be nothing left in the embers. It was a total loss.

That night Arthur sat in a meeting of citizens in the Kirtland Temple. There were hundreds of Church members and dissenters present. The purpose of the meeting was not to argue over doctrine, but to discuss the safety of Kirtland. The acrid smell of fire and ash was still strong in the air. The decision was made to organize a patrol consisting of twenty-one men, three for each night, who were chosen to guard the city and prevent further destruction by fire. Some of the men were members of the Church and some dissenters.

Arthur was assigned to watch every Saturday night.

GEORGE ROBINSON – JANUARY 18

NEAR DAYTON, OHIO
Thursday, January 18, 1838

Joseph Smith: "We passed through Dayton and Eaton, in Ohio, and Dublin, Indiana; in the latter place we tarried nine days, and refreshed ourselves. The weather was extremely cold, we were obliged to secrete ourselves in our wagons, sometimes, to elude the grasp of our pursuers, who continued their pursuit of us more than two hundred miles from Kirtland, armed with pistols and guns, seeking our lives."[36]

The women had been singing in the wagons all morning. It was one hymn after another, and the little children joined in on the ones they knew. The sound of their voices mingled with the whinny of horses and the grating sound of the wheels as they turned against the crust of ice in the wheel ruts of the road. It made a kind of strange and eerie music.

George Robinson had more on his mind than hymns. He was mindful only of the road ahead, the road behind, and the condition of the horses and wagons.

---

[36] HC 3:2-3

The days were long and cold on the road and were made colder by the fear of pursuit. George had continued to see horsemen following them. As a result, before setting out from New Portage, George had rigged up hiding places in the two wagons for Joseph Smith and Sidney Rigdon. Across the center of each covered wagon he made a little hidden compartment by fastening up blankets and tarpaulins, so that anyone looking into the wagon would see no one. In these compartments the Prophet and Brother Sidney rode, mile after mile, being jolted by every rut and rock in the road.

George continued to see horsemen following on the road, though they apparently never dared approach the travelers on the open and heavily traveled turnpike running west.

It was the nighttime that George feared the most. In the night someone might creep up unseen upon the campsite of the travelers and take the Prophet or do him harm, even shoot him. Major slept every night beneath the wagon, and several times over the next several days he would arise in the dark, growling fiercely, and advancing into the trees or bushes or over the open prairie toward some danger. And each time, after several minutes of fierce barking and growling, he returned. George suspected that some intruder had advanced stealthily toward their little camp, each time to be turned back by the Prophet's fierce guard dog.

In this manner the two wagons proceeded 190 miles on rough roads from New Portage to Dayton, Ohio, in a period of four days. Dayton was a large city of more than six thousand inhabitants, and given the distance from Kirtland, the travelers began to breathe somewhat easier.

As they entered Dayton, Brother Joseph emerged from his blanket cocoon and climbed out of the wagon, sitting beside his clerk.

"Sidney!" called Joseph back into the depths of the larger wagon. "I think it's safe to show our faces for a bit."

Sidney Rigdon emerged from the blankets and sat on the wagon box with the other two men.

"How far now to Dayton, George?" asked Sidney.

"Maybe five miles," he answered.

"Any sign of Lyons and the other pursuers?" asked Sidney Rigdon.

"Not today," said George. "I have kept my eyes open, and I had the three older boys drop back a time or two to watch. I made them promise to stay within sight of the last wagon, though. It's all a lark for them, but they don't know how serious it is."

"The young have sharp eyes," said Joseph. "And it will help prepare them for what is ahead."

"It's getting on towards evening," said George. "Shall we camp somewhere here in the countryside?"

"No," said Joseph. "I have another idea. I wonder if it would be best spent letting the women rest a couple of days in a public house with beds and good food."

"Do you have money enough for that?" asked George.

"I have money," said Sidney Rigdon. "And I think it's a good idea."

The Prophet hesitated. "I have a little money. Very little, actually. But we should also consider the matter of the condition of children. And especially of the women."

The Prophet looked at George, as if weighing what he would say next.

"Did you know that both Emma and Phebe are with child?"

"I suspected it," said George, his face turning red. "And I agree that we should let them sleep in a safe place for a night or two. But I can sleep in the wagon, to save money. Besides, we ought to have someone watch the little property we have."

The travelers stayed at the Newcom Tavern in Dayton for the night. It was in a large two-story log building and was the best-known tavern for wagon men and drovers in the Northwest Territory. It was known locally as the "Old Cabin," and was first used as a tavern in 1796. The food was good and the accommodations private.

There was place for the wagons and fodder for the horses in a yard behind the Old Cabin. The plan was to have the three boys—Sid, Wickliffe and Little Joseph—sleep in the little wagon with Major. The mastiff would be a fierce guard dog and better than any man with a gun. George tied down the canvas covers to the big wagon, and would check on them several times during the night.

That evening there were at least two dozen travelers in the tavern. Joseph and Sidney secured one small room for the two families and brought a good, hearty meal of roast mutton and bread for them to eat. George noticed that the Prophet counted out his very last coin to pay for the food.

The little children were tired, and their mothers soon put them to bed on blankets laid out on the floor. The adults found places on the bed and several chairs in the room, with the women, Sister Smith and Sister Rigdon, occupying the one bed in the room.

George took his place by the door and slept in his clothes.

The room occupied by the Smiths and Rigdons was upstairs at the head of a tall staircase. There were seven other guest rooms on the floor along a long hallway.

Whereas the outer walls of the tavern were made of thick pine logs, the interior walls were thin, constructed of plain pine boards. As the weary women and children began to fall asleep, the three men talked quietly, keeping their voices low so that no one could hear them.

"Brother Joseph," whispered George Robinson. "Do you have any money left?"

Brother Joseph smiled at him. "Not in my pocket," he said. "But the Lord will provide."

George noticed that Sidney Rigdon had his eyes closed, but wondered if he was really asleep. He had said nothing during the conversation about money.

George drifted off to sleep. He was dreaming of a farmhouse in a peaceful green country. There was a front porch overlooking rolling hills of green. He was awakened by the sound of a loud voice, as if right in his ear.

"Lyons! Did you bring the ale?"

"Shut up. You'll get yours," said an answering voice.

George realized the voices were coming through the thin walls. Their pursuers were in the next room! He looked over and saw that Joseph and Sidney were awake. The three of them sat in the dark listening to the voices through the wall. The only light came from moonlight shining through the glass of the small window. They could hear the sound of drinking, then there was a short knock on the door and the sound of more men entering the room next door.

"Welcome boys. So here we all are, then. Have some ale!"

"Is this all of us, Lyons?"

"Must be. The others turned back at the Indiana border. Said it's not worth their time following more than 200 miles."

"Well it's worth it to me. I lost more than a thousand dollars in that damned Kirtland Safety Society. It would be some compensation to see that Joe Smith dead."

"So, what do you think, boys?" said another voice through the wall. "Is Smith here? What are we all doing here?"

"He must be. We seen his horses and rig in the stable this afternoon and that hell hound of a guard dog, but he hasn't shown his face in the public rooms."

"Are you sure it's his horses and rig?"

"I should think so. We been following the damned thing for five days."

"Well, if you been following it, why didn't you do the job on the road?"

"Too many travelers. And every night we tried to sneak up on their camp, that blasted dog would sound the alarm."

"So the dog is with the wagon?"

"Yeah, and the three boys with him."

"That just leaves Joe Smith, the old man Rigdon, and the women and children to deal with."

"Right."

"So are they asleep in one of the guest rooms."

"That's my guess. I say we just open the doors one by one and have a look inside."

The voices ceased, but the Mormon travelers could hear the door open and footsteps in the hallway. Brother Joseph and Brother Sidney lay down on the floor with their faces in the pillows. George remained sitting in his chair, which was placed in such a way that the moonlight did not illuminate it.

Presently, he heard the soft sound of feet shuffling near their door, then saw in the moonlight how the doorknob turned slowly, and the door opened. He could see the darkened forms of two men standing in the threshold. The moonlight gleamed in their eyes, and he saw the light reflect off bright metal, a gun in the hand of the first man. Time stood still as George sat in his chair. The women and children were asleep, breathing deeply, and the figures of Joseph and Sidney remained motionless. After what seemed to George to be hours, the men in the doorway withdrew and quietly closed the door behind them.

A half hour later, George once again heard low voices in the room next door.

"Did you find him, Lyons?"

"No, did you?"

"No. We looked in all the faces, but didn't see any Joe Smith."

George sat in the dark breathing heavily. He saw that the Prophet was looking at him in the dark, lying on the floor, a smile on his face. George didn't dare utter a word, but smiled back and nodded at the Prophet.

He knew that he had just witnessed a miracle.

Julia – January 23

WESTERN OHIO AND EASTERN INDIANA
Tuesday, January 23, 1838

The road was no more than two ruts through the drifts of snow.

The bad part was that Julia's eyes hurt her when the sun was out, and her cheeks hurt when the wind blew. So she kept her head down much of the day below the wooden lip of the wagon. Also, the road wound back and forth over the little hills and down into frozen gullies like some great winter snake. Sometimes the road seemed to vanish altogether, only to reappear a mile to the west on the windswept summit of a hill.

The good part was that the country was open here and the travelers few. That gave Julia's father hope that they were no longer being pursued by his enemies. Now Father rode openly in the wagon instead of behind the makeshift screen of blankets they had set up in the wagon on the first stages of the journey.

The wagons moved slowly, and sometimes Julia wondered if they could walk faster. Father did indeed walk much of the time, holding onto Old Charlie's bridle and talking to Charlie and Jim in a cheerful, encouraging voice. Julia could tell that the journey was hard on the horses. The food was scarce, and grazing was hard or impossible to find under the blowing snow. In several villages Father bought bags of oats, which he fed the animals, but at night Julia felt sorry for them, tied up out in the wind and cold, sometimes with snow falling over their backs. One morning Julia saw Charlie and Jim covered in snow, the white almost obscuring their black coats.

Most days Father insisted that they cover forty or fifty miles, but on many days that was impossible. Once, outside of a small town in Indiana, where the narrow road passed along a steep hill, they came face to face with two men in a farm cart pulled by oxen. There was no way for either to get around the other. After speaking with the men for twenty or thirty minutes, Father helped the men unhitch their team of oxen and lead them down the steep slope, then helped the men spin the ox cart around and hitch the oxen back up. On that afternoon it would have been faster for Julia to walk. Needless to say, they didn't make forty miles that day.

There was little fun on the road for Julia, except watching the antics of her brother, Little Joseph. He was an irrepressible prankster, and most of his pranks were aimed at Father. Every morning Little Joseph helped to catch the horses and hitch them up to the wagon. One of Little Joseph's favorite pranks was to ride off over the prairie on Old Charlie before Father could catch them. Little Joseph would untie Charlie in the morning while Father was still at the breakfast fire, then lead him by the bridle to a rock or a stump, and throw himself up and over Charlie's back. Charlie didn't seem to mind, and would good-naturedly follow the little boy's commands and ride down a gully or behind a stand of small trees. Father would then walk out to where the horses had been left grazing and whistle for Charlie. Normally Charlie came instantly when Father whistled, but in the morning the horse seemed happy to go along with Little Joseph's prank, and would stay hidden until Little Joseph had him come cantering back into camp. Father would always pretend to be angry, but then would swing the little boy out of the saddle and hug him close before putting him back in the wagon.

The nights were the hardest part for Julia. She would lie shivering under the blankets until a pocket of her own body warmth calmed her. Then she would lay awake with her face upturned, looking sideways through the open canvas to the stars overhead. In those moments she would say a silent prayer, mentioning all who held a place in her heart. *Father, Mother, Little Joseph, Freddie, Alex, Old Charlie, Major, and Jim.*

Tonight Julia added a new name to her list—Julia Murdock. My other mother, she thought.

GEORGE ROBINSON – FEBRUARY 1

ON THE ROAD NEAR DUBLIN, INDIANA
Thursday, February 1, 1838

George Robinson scanned the road behind. There was no sight of Lyons or the other pursuers whatsoever.

"What do you suppose happened to the horsemen?" Little Joseph asked while the travelers rested by the side of the road. They had stopped in a little copse of trees to eat and let the little children run around.

"I think we've seen a miracle," said George. "Their eyes were blinded by the Lord so they couldn't see us."

"It's like the miracle in Nazareth," said Emma Smith, sitting on the end of the wagon with little Frederick on her lap. "After Jesus preached for the first time to his own synagogue, remember that the elders were filled with wrath, and thrust Him out of the city, and took Him up onto the brow of the hill, where there was a cliff intending to throw Him over. And we read that 'passing through the midst of them, He went his way.'"

On reaching Dublin, Indiana, the travelers met several other Mormons who had fled from Nauvoo, including Brigham Young of the Quorum of the Twelve, his brother Lorenzo, Isaac Decker, and several other families. They were all staying in a little cabin, and welcomed the Smiths and the Rigdons with open arms.

"Find any spot you can to lay your beds," said Brigham Young.

There were several other saints living in Dublin who were also preparing to follow on to Far West. One of them, Brother Tomlinson, was a prosperous businessman with a tavern in the village. The first evening he stopped by the little log cabin to greet the newcomers. He told them that he was prepared to move his family on to Far West as soon as he found a buyer for his tavern.

"What would you Brethren counsel me?" asked Brother Tomlinson, looking at the Prophet.

"My counsel is that you ask Brother Brigham," said the Prophet.

Brother Tomlinson turned his eyes on Brigham Young, who seemed surprised. But, after thinking a moment, Brother Brigham said, "If you will do right and obey the counsel, you will have the opportunity to sell soon. And I promise you that the first offer you get will be the best offer."

The next day the Prophet went out into the village to look for work, taking George with him. They had no luck until they came to a wood yard, where a heavy set man with a red beard looked them over then offered them twenty-five cents a day to cut cord wood and saw and stack logs.

"If you want the job, show up at dawn," said the man. They shook hands and returned to the little cabin where the Mormon refugees were all staying.

After a meager supper, George went outside with the Prophet and Brigham Young to stretch their legs.

"Brother Brigham," said the Prophet as they walked. "I am destitute of means to pursue my journey. And as you are one of the Twelve Apostles who hold the keys of the kingdom in all the world, I believe I shall throw myself upon you, and look to you for counsel in this case. Shall I take the job cutting cord wood and sawing and stacking logs?"

George thought that Brigham Young looked shocked at this question. "Are you in earnest, Brother Joseph?"

"I am," said the Prophet.

Brigham Young took off his hat and rubbed ran his fingers through his hair and didn't say a word for a minute or two as they walked.

"Well," he finally said, "If you will take my counsel, it will be that you rest yourself and be assured, Brother Joseph, that you will have plenty of money to pursue your journey."

"You counsel me not to work but to rest?" asked the Prophet.

"Yes, sir," said Brother Brigham. "That is my counsel."

The Prophet laughed and shook his head. "Well, all right. That's what I will do then."

That evening the travelers were all in their tiny cabin, when Brother Tomlinson came around with more food for the travelers.

"I have an offer for my place," said Brother Tomlinson happily.

"Oh really," said Brigham Young. "What was the offer?"

"It was really a miracle. I was offered five hundred dollars in cash, a team of horses and a wagon, and two hundred and fifty dollars in store goods. Your counsel that the first offer would be the best offer came to pass. This is far more than I ever expected to receive."

"How much did you expect to get?" asked George.

Brother Tomlinson laughed. "I thought I would do well to get two hundred dollars. Now I'll have five hundred, plus a team and ample supplies for my journey. I'll be a rich man!"

Brigham Young's eyes became moist, and he said, "This is the hand of the Lord, Brother Tomlinson, to deliver President Joseph Smith from his present necessity."

The next day Brother Tomlinson sold his property and gave the Prophet three hundred dollars, which enabled him to comfortably proceed on his journey.

LITTLE JOSEPH – FEBRUARY 2

ON THE ROAD IN INDIANA
Friday, February 2, 1838

Little Joseph had picked up a long stick, which he dragged behind in his right hand, feeling it bounce and hearing it strike the wood of the corduroy road with every step. With his other hand he held onto his mother. With her other hand, she held onto the hand of his little brother, Frederick, and he in turn held onto the hand of their sister, Julia. Major bounded along at Little Joseph's side, occasionally running off into the prairie when he spotted rabbits.

The going was very slow for the four walkers, as they followed the slow moving wagon, driven by Father. Old Charlie and Jim stepped gingerly from log to log, which were set in sand, but could shift suddenly, making it hazardous for horses. The ground was cold, but not frozen, and there were big stretches of water from the ice melting beneath the winter sun.

In the low, swampy stretches of the Indiana prairie, men had learned to build up little bridges. They were constructed by laying sand and logs cross ways to the direction of the road. These little bridges lifted the horses hooves and wagon wheels out of the mud, but made for difficult passing.

Mother had explained that the Indiana roads were called corduroy, because they had ridges, like corduroy cloth. Little Joseph didn't know anything about cloth, but he did know what a corduroy road felt like while riding in the wagon. The constant bouncing over the wooden ridges was tooth jarring, and it was less tiresome to walk than ride.

Little Joseph was five years old, and he knew what Mother was thinking. She thought that *he* needed someone to hold his hand. But he looked over at her swollen belly, and the hesitant and precarious way she placed her feet. So Little Joseph held his mother's hand tightly as they stepped from log to log.

They had been on the road for two days after leaving Dublin, and it was the greatest adventure of Little Joseph's life. He loved being out in the open with his family and their few belongings in the little wagon. They had each other, their horses, and Major. Little Joseph could not remember a time when he had had his father so much to himself. Father had let him help to scout out good campsites each evening, to gather wood and start the fires, to take care of the horses, and to prepare beds for the family to sleep in each night in the wagon box or beneath the wagon.

Father had an old Queen Anne musket dating back to the American Revolutionary War, which he used to hunt rabbits or other small game to cook and eat along the road. It was nearly four feet long and difficult to load and fire, but was effective in shooting rabbits. Mother always disapproved of this old rifle and forbade Little Joseph from handling it.

"I don't want you touching the rifle," said Mother sternly one morning, after finding Little Joseph sitting alone in the wagon after dinner, holding the long rifle in his lap.

"I didn't fire it, only touched it," said Little Joseph.

Father came up behind Mother and listened, but said nothing.

"But guns can be loaded," said Mother, "And even touching it can be dangerous."

"I'm too little, anyway, to hold it up or aim it, Mother," said Little Joseph.

"I'm glad," said Mother. "Someday you'll fire a gun, but that day can't be too far off as far as I'm concerned."

The next day Father gave Little Joseph a sharp little jackknife, the first one he had ever owned. It had a little leather scabbard, which he could tie to his belt. Father showed Little Joseph how to hold the knife in one hand and a stick or piece of wood in the other and to slice off long slivers from the wood. Thereafter Little Joseph had spent many hours trying to carve pieces of wood into various shapes.

ARTHUR – FEBRUARY 2

KIRTLAND, OHIO
Friday, February 2, 1838

Benjamin F. Johnson: "At this time, town property and real estate [in Kirtland] went up to almost fabulous prices, and a general rush was made into business of all kinds."[37]

Charlotte Haven: "We called on Joseph's mother . . . Madame Smith's residence is a log house very near her son's. She opened the door and received us cordially. She is a motherly kind of woman of about sixty years. . . . I looked . . . To the old lady, but could detect nothing but earnestness and sincerity on her countenance."[38]

Joseph Smith, Sr., the aged father of the Prophet, was arrested in Kirtland on January 13, 1838, just hours after his son, the Prophet, had escaped on horseback. Hours later the elder Smith escaped from jail and fled from the city. He was in hiding outside the city from January until May, when he traveled to Far West with the rest of his family. His wife, Lucy Mack Smith, wrote: "Mr. Smith [Joseph Smith, Sr.] crept out of the

---

[37] Benjamin F. Johnson, My Life's Review (Independence, Mo.: Zion's Printing and Publishing 1947), 27

[38] Charlotte Haven, "A Girl's Letters from Nauvoo," January 3, 1843, The Overland Monthly (December, 1890), vol. 6, no. 96, 623-24.

window, with the help of Hyrum and John Boynton (who said he was our friend at this time). . . . In a short time . . . I found out where my husband was and sent him money and clothes to travel with. . . . Runners were sent through the country to watch for him with authority to bring him back in case they found him. But despite their utmost exertions, he eluded them and succeeded in getting to New Portage, where he remained. . . . After Mr. Smith had [been in New Portage] about two weeks, we became very uneasy about him, not having received any intelligence of him since he left us. Accordingly, [my son] William resolved to go in pursuit of him to see how he was situated; whether he had met with friends and was comfortably provided for, or had fallen into the hands of his enemies and been murdered by them, for we had as much cause to fear the latter as to hope for the former."[39]

The gray cat arched her back and hissed.

Arthur pushed open the gate and walked through Lucy Mack Smith's flower garden, the summer blooms and stems all now laying flat and sodden beneath the dirty winter snow. His heart was beating like a bass drum in his chest, his breath coming in short bursts, like a swimmer coming up for air. The gray cat watched him walk up the porch, her eyes wary.

The door opened and young Lucy Smith stepped out onto the porch wearing a red dress. Arthur almost held his breath as he saw the vivid blue eyes.

"Are you Arthur?" she asked.

---

[39] Lucy Mack Smith, *History of Joseph Smith by His Mother* (Salt Lake City: 1996) 352-53

"Yes, ma'am," he said. "I mean, yes. I'm Arthur. Arthur Millikin."

Lucy smiled, her blue eyes looking at Arthur in amusement. "I'm not a ma'am, you know. But thanks for coming up to the house—will you come in? My mother is waiting."

"Yes, ma'am," Arthur stuttered. "I mean, yes, of course."

It was warm inside Lucy Mack Smith's house, with a fire crackling in the fireplace. Arthur smelled something fresh and delicious. "Come in, young man," said an older female voice. "Do come in! Lucy, fetch this young man something to eat. Please sit down."

Arthur sat down on the one small, upholstered settee in the room, where the older woman had motioned for him to sit. The gray cat jumped up on the table by the settee and seemed to regard Arthur for a moment, then set to licking its paws.

"Mr. Badham said you sent for me," said Arthur, swallowing hard and trying to keep his eyes on Lucy Mack Smith. But he was really watching the motion of the younger Lucy in his side vision.

"Yes," said the old woman. Her hair was pulled back severely in a tight bun, but strands of gray hair had come loose and fallen over her white forehead. "I am in need of some assistance, and Mr. Badham suggested you may be able to help. He said you are starting out in the business of wagon fixing and outfitting."

"That's right," said Arthur. "I am just newly qualified, having finished my apprenticeship with Mr. Badham this past December. Yes, I'm looking for work. What can I help you with?"

Lucy Smith brought over a little plate with small pieces of cornmeal bread on it, hot from the oven. She held out the plate for Arthur to take a piece, then sat down by her mother.

"We'll be needing some help with our wagon," said Lucy Mack Smith, taking a piece herself. "After we eat, I'll take you out and show you what's to be done. The axletree is broken and the spokes on one wheel are stove in and cracked. Also, the harness and traces need refitting, and the axels are about rotted out and need to be replaced. Can you do all that?"

"Yes, of course," said Arthur, eating the cornbread. It was delicious. Truth be told, it was the first home baked food he had eaten in a while, since he had moved out of his Uncle Nathaniel's place and taken a room from Mr. Badham in the shed behind the blacksmith shop. *It will just be for a few weeks*, he had promised his former employer, *until I find steady work*. Those few weeks were now stretching into two months, and still he had no steady work, only odd jobs here and there referred to him by Mr. Badham.

"How soon would you be needing the work done?" Arthur asked.

"Oh, as soon as you can do it," she said. "We'll be leaving for Far West as soon as the spring weather comes and roads dry out. Can you start working right away?"

"Of course," said Arthur, finishing his cornbread. Lucy Smith smiled at him and held out the plate and offered him a second piece.

"How much will you be charging, then?" asked Lucy Mack Smith.

"Well," said Arthur, "It'll be forty-five cents a day. If that's acceptable."

"Yes," said the older woman. "Yes, of course. But can you wait until we've sold our place for payment? We don't have much cash money right now."

"Well," said Arthur. "Maybe."

Lucy Smith smiled at him again and the old woman said, "In the meantime, we could offer you meals at our table on the days you are working."

Arthur didn't dare tell her that he needed the money now for his rent and for food, but looking into young Lucy Smith's blue eyes, he smiled awkwardly and said, "That would be just fine."

Lucy – February 3

KIRTLAND, OHIO
Saturday, February 3, 1838

Lucy Mack Smith: "When William arrived at New Portage, now called Norton, it was some time before he could learn exactly where his father [Joseph Smith, Sr.] had gone. But as soon as he obtained the necessary intelligence, he went immediately to him and had the pleasure of finding him in good health, although in great anxiety about the family, for he did not know how we were situated, nor where we were, since we had designed moving to Missouri soon after he left us. . . . William told his father that we should set out for Missouri soon, and we wished him to be ready to go with us."[40]

Through the narrow windows of Mama's sitting and sewing room, the light of the winter sunset spilled across the floor, throwing orange and red stripes upon the white walls opposite. The walls had been covered with hanging quilts and little miniature portraits, but now stood bare, the little nails seeming forlorn and desolate without their former images.

---

[40] *History of Joseph Smith by His Mother*, 353

Lucy sat upon a little stool beside a wooden chest, which bore the initials, L.M.S., marked by evenly spaced brass nails. She was sorting through a pile of old papers and documents. Across from the chest Mama was holding a swatch of quilting fabric against her knee, stroking it gently back and forth with the palm of her hand and looking vacantly out through the glowing windowpane. The evening meal was over—young Arthur Millikin had joined them once more after a day of laboring on their poor old wagon— but there was much work yet to be done.

"What are you thinking, Mama?" asked Lucy, placing the documents neatly in the bottom of the chest and reaching for a small pile of books.

"Oh, nothing, really. Just feeling wistful to leave this house."

"How soon will we leave?" asked Lucy.

"When God wills, child. When God wills. We have much to do yet. First the packing and sorting and cleaning in here. Then young Arthur has to finish with the fixing of the wagon and carriage. And we need to somehow buy or borrow a new draft horse for the journey. And then we need to wait for news of your father."

Lucy's older brother William had been gone from Kirtland for five days, looking for her father. They had no certain news as to his whereabouts, or how they might rejoin him to start a journey to Far West.

"I'm sorry we have to leave," said Lucy. "We've been here so very long."

"Six years," said Mama. "You were but a girl of ten when we came from New York. Do your remember that trip?"

"Yes," said Lucy. "I remember some of it. I remember crossing what I thought was the sea on a big boat. It was winter. And I remember the boat finding an opening in the ice to allow us to sail through."

"That was in Buffalo Harbor," said Mama, smiling at her daughter. "I remember telling the saints who were sailing with us that if they would raise their prayers to heaven, that the ice would be broken before us, and we would be at liberty to go on our way. Well, at that moment, a noise was heard like bursting thunder! And the captain cried out to his crew, 'Every man to his post!' and the ice parted, Lucy. The ice parted, leaving barely a pathway for our boat. It was so narrow an opening that I remember as the boat passed through, the buckets that were hanging over the side of the boat were torn off. When we had passed safely through the avenue, the ice closed together again."

"I remember, Mama," said Lucy, looking into her mother's gray eyes. "I remember. And now, we are moving on again. Do you think the ice will open up before us?"

"It will, child, if necessary. It will."

Outside they heard the neighing of a horse, and then footsteps on the wooden planks of the porch. Lucy put down her books and ran to the front door, her Mama moving slowly behind her. It opened wide, and her brother William burst inside, bringing a blast of cold air and a swirl of snow with him. Behind him she saw the last rays of the yellow sun on the pale bare branches of the trees.

"Did you find Papa?" said Lucy.

"Yes," said William.

"Is he in good health?" cried Mama. There were tears in her eyes.

"Yes, he's well. He's staying with Mr. Woolley in New Portage and is comfortably situated."

"Thank the Lord," said Mama. "Thank the Lord."

Later that evening, after Mama had fed William, the three sat around the roaring fire and talked about Papa and Joseph and Hyrum and the new babies coming and about the long trip to Far West, which lay ahead. They told William of the progress Arthur Millikin was making on repairing the wagon, and William told them this story:

"While I was in New Portage with Papa, it became known that William Smith, the Mormon Apostle and younger brother of Joe Smith, the Mormon Prophet was in town. A part of the inhabitants were very anxious that I should preach to them, and so I agreed to do so. But Papa told me that there were men present who had declared publicly to the Gentiles in New Portage, that if I preached the Mormon doctrine in public, they would tar and feather me. One of the men who had so sworn was Mr. Bear. He was truly a bear of man—a person of extraordinary size and strength. Well, I went to the house where I was appointed to speak, and Papa and Mr. Woolley whispered to me that besides Mr. Bear, there were three others entering the room, no less strong than Mr. Bear, who were fixing to take me and tar and feather me if I opened my mouth. Well, as they walked in I was just beginning my speech, and I told the assembled citizens of New Portage that I would be speaking on the subject of 'The Poor Deluded Mormons.' Well, this phrase seemed to excite the curiosity of all present, and a murmur of laughter went around the room, and Mr. Bear and his companions paused inside the doorway without seizing me. I suppose they were saying to themselves, 'Wait. Let's see what this fellow will do with that subject,' and they waited and listened to me speak. I guess they waited so long that they either forgot what they came for, or they changed their minds altogether, for they made no further move towards me."

"That's wonderful, William!" said Mama.

"And you know, after I finished, that Mr. Bear came up to me and frankly confessed his conviction of the truth, and asked to be baptized."

Lucy laughed and clapped her hands, and Mama just beamed. Lucy was not sure she believed every word her brother was saying—there was a tendency in the Smith family to exaggerate from time to time, especially William, and also Mama—but Lucy smiled her approval upon her brother William. He was, after all, the father of two of the precious *pearls* in Lucy's necklace—Mary Jane and little Caroline—and he was her own flesh and blood.

OLD CHARLIE – FEBRUARY 5

BETWEEN INDIANA AND ILLINOIS
Monday, February 5, 1838

Brigham Young: "On reaching Dublin, Indiana, I found my brother Lorenzo and Isaac Decker, and a number of other families who had stopped for the winter. Meanwhile the Prophet Joseph, brothers Sidney Rigdon and George W. Robinson came along. They had fled from Kirtland because of the mobocratic spirit prevailing in the bosoms of the apostates.

"Here the Prophet made inquiry concerning a job at cutting cordwood and sawing logs, after which he came to me and said, 'Brother Brigham, I am destitute of means to pursue my journey, and as you are one of the Twelve Apostles who hold the keys of the kingdom in all the world, I believe I shall throw myself upon you, and look to you for counsel in this case.' At first I could hardly believe Joseph was in earnest, but on his assuring me he was, I said, 'If you will take my counsel, it will be that you rest yourself and be assured, brother Joseph, you shall have plenty of money to pursue your journey.'"

"There was a brother named Tomlinson living in the place, who had previously asked my counsel about selling his tavern-stand. I told him if he would do right and obey counsel, he should have opportunity to sell soon, and the first offer he would get would be the best. A few days afterwards brother Tomlinson informed me he had an offer for his place. I asked him what offer he had; he replied he was offered $500 in money, a

team, and $250 in store goods. I told him that was the hand of the Lord to deliver President Joseph Smith from his present necessity."

"My promise to Joseph was soon verified. Brother Tomlinson sold his property and gave the Prophet three hundred dollars, which enabled him comfortably to proceed on his journey."

"The day Joseph and company started, Isaac Seeley and wife arrived. The house was pretty well littered up. I sat writing to my wife, but I welcomed them to the use of the house and what was left of it. Brother Samuel H. Smith came along, who tarried with me until my brother Lorenzo returned from Cincinnati, and brother Decker from Michigan, whose families had gone forward with Joseph. We prepared to follow, and started on, overtaking the Prophet four miles west of Jacksonville, Illinois, where there was a Branch of the Church[41].*"*

Brother Joe believes in livin' plain. I reckon he don't want none of the Brethren thinkin' he's better than them. But here on this journey to Zion, I figure he's gone and overdid things some. Here it seems he's mostly livin' worse than any of the Brethren.

First off, it was frightful cold outside, and I 'spect Lady Emma and the young'uns was about done in by the journey. Every horse in our little company was sufferin' from hunger, and most of 'em could hardly pull the wagons, a-slippin' and a-slidin' in the snow and frozen mud. And it appeared to be not much better for the men and women and little ones. Brother Joe had his one rig, pulled by Jim and me. We

----

[41] Eldon Jay Watson, ed., *Manuscript History of Brigham Young* (Smith Secretarial Service: Salt Lake City, 1968) 24-25

did our best to keep goin', but I could tell Jim was about ready to drop in his tracks.

After days of uninterrupted drivin', we finally rested a spell in a town they called Dublin. When we arrived we were met out on the road by that peculiar feller, Brigham. I say he's peculiar 'cause somehow he don't act like most of the other Brethren, always hot or cold in their work, or hot or cold in their friendship for Brother Joe. Brigham's a young feller, not tall, but strong. He's forever leavin' on missions and then comin' back, leavin' and then comin' back. And when he's back, he's always doin' somethin' or other, mostly buildin' houses and barns. And he's got a sharp tongue and is awful hard on horses. I see'd him whip his team somethin' terrible, and he don't properly know how to sit a horse. But I confess that I know him to be a true friend to Brother Joe and one to never let him down. That means somethin', though I don't want him ridin' me none. He's that hard on a horse.

Dublin's only a tiny place, with farms strung out on four roads and meetin' again at a dirty crossroads with a tavern or two. But even at the crossroads there's a feelin' of safety in that little place, as all the saints has started flockin' there in their wagons and stayin' at these two little log houses, laid side by side between the creek and a nice stand of trees, with pastures on all sides. There are older fellers like Brother Sidney, and younger ones like Brother Joe and Brigham, but also dozens of other fellers with their wives and kids and babies, lots of young ladies and boys, all sorts, and of course a whole herd of horses and other animals, cows and pigs and the like.

After we'd been in Dublin a few days, I see'd that the horses was all in high spirits, even in the cold. We was strung out in several pastures around these two little log houses, all the horses rompin' about and in high spirits and havin' a good time, as if they had all come together to have a grand old time, forgettin' that some of 'em nearly died of hunger and cold a few days back on the road.

Brother Joe done parked his wagon beside the bigger of the two cabins where he and Brother Sidney and several others had their families all tucked inside, with wood smoke always pourin' from the stone chimney and the candlelight burnin' far into the night. Brother Joe's big white watchdog, Major, found hisself a snug spot beneath Brother Joe's rig.

At first Brother Joe seemed worried, and he come from the cabin in his work clothes and saddled me up and rode out into the forest on a narrow track to a big clearin' in the trees, with men all a cuttin' with axes and sawin' with long saws. There we stopped for a spell, and I heared Brother Joe talkin' to a big man about cuttin' wood for him, for pay, but then we rode back, and Brother Joe seemed real sober and quiet, like he was mighty disappointed. Later that night I see'd Brother Joe walkin' around outside the cabin talkin' with Brigham, and after that Brother Joe seemed to rest and enjoy hisself a little, playin' with all the children in the yard, or takin' long walks through the trees or along the creek. Whenever he come out he'd more likely than not have one of the Mormon brethren with him, and he'd kind of introduce them to me, sayin', "This here's Old Charlie," and they'd pat me, and they would talk on and on.

But Brother Joe didn't always have people around him. Each day, more likely than not, he would get away and be alone with me, ridin' through the farm country or out in the prairie, in the cold air, with the sun a red ball in the mornin' haze. I can still remember the enjoyment of just trottin' easy along those roads, with never a signal needed from either of us, 'cause we each knew just what the other wanted, and never a thought of hard ridin' or escapin' in the nighttime, like we done back in Kirtland. We come to know those roads and paths for miles around the little log houses in Dublin, and sometimes Brother Joe would stop on a little hilltop, and I'd be grazin' patches of winter grass while he'd jest sit easy and stare across the open prairie. Brother Joe often seemed real sad in his thoughts when sittin' alone, but then he would mount back up, and we would gallop back to the log cabin in Dublin, where he would lift Julia or Little Joseph high in the air, bringin' 'em real quick to laughin', and then slap the backs of the men, and fill the air with his happy, laughin' voice. That's the side of Brother Joe I love to hear, but I can't forget the times when he seems most sad and alone in his thoughts.

A few days after we pulled up in Dublin, Brother Brother Sidney got to complainin' about how tuckered out he was getting', so he jest said to Brother Joe, "You go on ahead." I wasn't sorry to move on and leave behind that gray gelding, Champ, as he had an ornery disposition. Brother Joe spent much time fiddlin' about his little wagon, adjustin' boxes of gear hear and there, and he also made sure that Jim and me were fed well, and I knew that we would soon be movin' out.

We left one clear mornin', cold but sunny. Brother Joe hitched Jim and me up to the wagon, and then he loaded in Lady Emma and the children—Julia, Little Joseph, and Frederick—and we set out. There was still a passel of Mormons and their horses at the two cabins in Dublin, and it seemed everyone came outside to see us off and wave their hats and bonnets at us and shout *Hurrah* and *Hosanna*, but we soon left 'em behind and rode maybe twenty mile, takin' it easy, stoppin' for a bite to eat around the middle of the day, and then went on another twenty mile and finished up pretty early before dark.

Me and Brother Joe been to Missouri and back two times before, so I recognized the road and didn't look forward to the place called Indiana, where there were lots of stretches of mighty low ground, swampy and wet. In the summer or fall these roads is filled with water up to the hocks, so the men cut down thousands of trees and lay logs side by side to lift the horses and wagons up off of the mud. The passin' here was dry, but the roads were bumpy, and more likely than not the people would walk rather than ride in the wagons along these roads.

Little Joseph liked walkin' alongside the wagon, and he brung me and Jim bundles of the best grass he could find. At night he would come to where Jim and me was out grazin' and climb up on a stump or a rock and brush us down and talk to us real quiet like, jest like he seen his father do.

After a few days on the road, we heared a whoop and a holler behind us, and soon I see'd Brigham ridin' up on his horse beside us. I was mighty glad to see him, knowin' how much help Brother Joe needed on the trail. With Brother

Brigham were two other families with wagons, includin' Brother Samuel and his family.

One afternoon we made camp, and Jim and me was hobbled together in the best grass, while the family gathered 'round a cook fire. Little Joseph wandered over by me and Jim and set himself down on a rock and pulled out a pocketknife and started whittlin' on a little piece of wood. This put me in mind of that young feller, Pete, who first rode me when I was a colt and loved to whittle on pieces of wood with his pocketknife.

After that day when I got curious about Pete and walked over to sniff him all over, things changed up some. Pete would come out into the little field every day and sit on his rock, and I would leave the other foals and walk right over to him. And every day he would have somethin' new with him. One day he pulled a harmonica out of his pocket and played for me—the first time I ever heared one. Then another day he brung out a big white tarpaulin under his arm and stretched it out on the grass and sat in the middle with a piece of apple on his palm. He whispered to me, "Beau. Come on Beau. Come on son. Come get your apple," and he jest kept talkin' to me real slow. I was mighty curious about that tarp, and kind of fearful. I sniffed it good and walked all around it, and then after a bit I stepped onto the tarpaulin to get that piece of apple on Pete's palm. Another day he brung four long poles and laid them in a row on the grass, me on one side and him with the apple on the other. He called me and I walked gingerly over those poles, careful not to hurt my legs or knock them over any. Then another day he brung a big basket into the field, and after I ate my apple, he put the handle of the basket in my mouth and then called for me to follow him. We walked around the field a bit, me followin' him with the basket in my mouth. Then Pete opened the gate and led me up the hill to the big house. There was a lady workin' in the garden, and Pete called out to her, "Hey, Ma. Here's Beau. He brought you your basket!" The lady started laughin', and then four or five little kids come runnin' out on the porch to see. "You tease," the lady said to Pete. But she reached in her apron pocket and handed me a lump of sugar. And then I knowed that sugar was the sweetest thing I could ever eat!

I ain't certain of jest when I was saddle broke by Pete. Truth is, I get the feelin' he was jest preparin' me all along to bear the saddle. Jest the way he stroked my back and would lean in on me and put things over my back. One day he threw an old blanket on my back, and then I follered him around for a spell. The next day he looped a little rope around my neck jest to get me used to the feel, and then he walked along, up and down the field, with me follerin' right along, hopin' for that piece of apple. Then one day he jest popped that saddle up and over, real quick, and jest left it, not cinched up or anythin', but jest danglin'. Then another day, he jest swung into the saddle, and it startled me, but only a little. Every day it was somethin' different, somethin' new, what with blankets and bits and reins and straps and whatnot. Before I knowed it, I was wearin' the saddle and bridle and all the gear. He was that gentle with me that I don't recall ever gettin' spooked or shook up by it all.

After that, it warn't no time at all 'til Pete was ridin' me in the saddle. One day Pete jest climbed right up on my back, took the reins, and we was ridin'! After that we rode almost every day in the little field. Then one day, he opened the gate and rode me out on the little paths around the big house, then further and further away.

Pete was mighty good company in them days, and every new step was like a game, but I see now how he had a purpose in it all. He was aimin' at makin' me feel like a smart saddle horse and gettin' me to work along with him and feel like we was workin' together.

Once Pete figured he was through trainin' me, his father, Henry, the boss of the whole place, used to take me out and ride me hisself nearly every day. After ridin' with Pete, Henry felt very calm and sure. I loved ridin' with Pete, 'cause he was all fun and adventure, and he was always a-keepin' up a steady stream of talk while we rode. "All right, Beau, let's go!" "C'mon Beau! C'mon son!" Pete kind of made me feel daring, like I could run anywhere or do anythin' with him in the saddle. But Henry was different. He made me feel calm and quiet and safe. Jest the way he held the reins, I jest knowed that he was experienced. I liked Henry—the smell of him, the feel of his hands. It was the same with other horses that I seen him ride. Even jumpy horses, when they was with Henry, they got theirselves right calm and subdued. Horses most often act differently when they is ridden by different men. If a man's always nervous in his ways, it makes the horse he rides nervous. Funny thing, though, the men never seem to know that. It never seems to occur to them that the horse acts the way he does. So, I figure I growed up frisky and adventurous because that's the way Pete was hisself, like the wind in the grass. But Henry was as solid as a rock mountain.

Funny thing is, both of them fellers—Pete and Henry—was somethin' like Brother Joe in their own ways, frisky sometimes and solid other times. It took some time, but little by little I learned from them two fellers! I 'spect that Pete and Henry was gettin' me ready, in their own ways, to work someday with Brother Joe.

LITTLE JOSEPH – FEBRUARY 12

ON THE ROAD NEAR PARIS, ILLINOIS
Monday, February 12, 1838

Little Joseph watched out the front of the wagon as they rode between the first buildings. There was no one on the street, although there was smoke coming from most of the chimneys.

It was bitterly cold, and Little Joseph rubbed his gloves together to keep his fingers from freezing. Freddie lay under a blanket in the wagon, too cold to even cry. Julia sat hunched on the seat between the heavy coats of her parents. Beyond them, Little Joseph could see the black backs of Old Charlie and Jim, plodding steadily forward.

"What town is this?" asked Mother.

"It should be Paris," said Father.

Throughout early February the weather had taken a terrible turn for the worse. Day after day the wagons plodded along, and the only horse seemingly unaffected was Old Charlie.

The travelers had found it increasingly difficult to find places to stay, so in Indiana the company had split up into two groups—one part which went on ahead immediately led by Little Joseph's father, and the other part, which rested a few days, led by Sidney Rigdon.

Father and his family had continued on in their wagon alone. Even after separating, it became difficult for Father and Mother to find lodging.

"It doesn't look like the Paris I've read about," said Mother. "But I could stand some French cooking. Anything warm will do."

It was getting dark. There were three taverns in town. Father rode up to the first one and went inside while Little Joseph waited in the wagon with Mother and Julia and Freddie.

"They say they have no room for Mormons," said Father, coming back to the wagon.

"Well, I never!" said Mother. "Did you tell them your wife is with child?"

"Yes. But never mind. We'll try the other tavern."

But there it was the same story. There would be no room for Mormons.

At the third tavern, Father found the main door locked. He pounded on it, and a window opened above. The innkeeper opened up and leaned out.

"What do you want?" he called down.

"We need a place to stay for the night," said Father. "my wife and three children."

"And where you be coming from and where you be a going?"

"We come from Ohio, and we are going to Missouri."

"You aren't them Mormons, are ye?"

"Yes, sir," said Father.

"Well, we haven't got any room for Mormons."

Little Joseph could see that his father was getting angry.

"I'll tell you what, my good man!" shouted Father. "I have a wife with child and three children who are freezing to death. I have money to pay, as good as any Catholic or Methodist. We don't want to bring religion to your house that may be offensive to you; we simply want to survive this night in warmth. But I will tell you this. If you do not open this door and let my family stay in your establishment of hospitality, I will burn down this tavern, and every other tavern in this city, and we shall warm our hands by the heat of that great fire!"

The man's head disappeared from the window and presently the front door opened.

"Thank the Lord," said Mother. Little Joseph looked at her face. For the first time in his life he thought he saw fear in those gray eyes.

WYCLIFFE – FEBRUARY 18

PARIS, ILLINOIS
The week of February 18, 1838

John Wycliffe Rigdon: "We [separated from] Joseph Smith in Indiana and got along all right till we got to a town called Paris, Illinois, where we stayed overnight. In the morning there was a great snowstorm. It would be called a blizzard now."[42]

Snow was falling.

Wycliffe sat on the wagon box with his brother-in-law, George Robinson, and scanned the horizon. It was flat prairie all the way around, except for a little place a few miles off to the north, where he could see a little rocky hill punching its way up through the prairie grass and a tangle of little bare trees.

"How many miles have we gone today?" Wycliffe asked.

"Ten, maybe. Fifteen." said George, holding the long reins in his hands. "We'll need to make at least twenty-five by dark."

---

[42] *Keller, ed., John R. Rigdon History, 29*

Wycliffe's father was lying in the back of the wagon behind a blanket. They were passing strangers on the road every hour or so, and he still feared being taken by his pursuers from Kirtland.

"Looks like we have clear riding for a bit," said George, bundled up with a red scarf covering the bottom half of his face. "It's cold but the road is hardened ice, so the horses' hooves and wagon wheels won't sink."

Wycliffe looked around the side of the wagon. Brother Darrow's team was following right behind. The horses had had a warm week in the snug stables of the public house in Terre Haute and seemed ready to move.

The Wabash River was frozen solid, and George Robinson's carriage followed by the two wagons made their way precariously across, then set out on the road to Paris, the sun painfully bright in a deep blue sky with the vast white reflecting snow between. Wycliffe's eyes hurt when he looked too long at the horizon, and he squinted from between his scarf and his cap.

They made record time, covering the last ten miles to Paris in a little more than an hour, the wheels of the wagon crunching over the frozen snow.

Paris was a small town, really just two main roads crossing each other on the prairie, the buildings crowded thick at the intersection. They pulled the loaded wagon up to a large wood frame building on the corner. The sign said "McSorley's Tavern."

"Wait here," said George handing the reins to Sid and Wycliffe. The boys watched as the men disappeared into the door of the tavern.

"I'm cold," said Lacy. "Can we stop and make a fire?"

"We're going to try to get a room in the tavern, dear," said Mother, stroking the little girl's long blonde hair.

Ten minutes passed and Wycliffe began to wonder what had become of his Father. Maybe there would be no room in the inn, like the story in the Bible. Then suddenly the door to the tavern opened and Father and George came out laughing.

"We're getting the best room in the house," said George Robinson. "The proprietor told us that we are the second Mormon travelers in a week to stop here, and we are most welcome."

The next morning Wycliffe walked out of the door of the public tavern and to the wagons. Snow was blowing through the empty streets of the town they called Paris, Illinois. There was just the hint of the sun glowing dully behind the cover of morning clouds, like a single candle behind a curtain.

It had been several days since Joseph Smith and his family had separated from Wycliffe's family in Indiana. They had ridden together for hundreds of miles out of Ohio and into Indiana. Then, in Dublin, Indiana, they had met up with another wagon driven by Brother Darrow and his boys, and two fresh spans of horses. From Dublin they had all ridden together, five wagons and extra horses, but they had found it almost impossible to find places for such a large company to sleep. Most nights they stayed in public inns or taverns, or in the homes of farmers on the way.

Wycliffe blew upon his mitten-covered fists. They were already feeling cold. In fact, he had not been fully warm for weeks, and he was hungry.

"It's looking like a storm is about to hit," called George through the wind.

"I think it will be all right," called Father. "We have a long road ahead. The next town is only ten miles from here. If the snow hits we can surely make that today."

George looked skeptical and then turned to help the others into the carriage.

Mother and the girls and their three-year-old brother climbed into the carriage with George. In the middle wagon were Brother Darrow and his two boys; Sid and Wycliffe rode in the last wagon with Father. This wagon was loaded with most of the household belongings of the Rigdons and was covered with a large piece of gray canvas, spread out over four tall wooden hoops. It was as cold inside the canvas as out, so the boys rode up front on the bench beside their father.

Wycliffe stepped on the big wooden wheel hub and climbed onto the wagon. There was a skiff of snow on the bench, and he brushed it off with the sleeve of his coat. Sid climbed on beside him. Father's horse, Champ, was pulling on the reins, ready to set out, and poor Mamie in the harness with him didn't want any part of pulling the wagon today.

The convoy of three wagons pulled away from the tavern and west down the main street, soon entering the open prairie. The wind was howling, and out on the prairie it cut right through their layers of clothing.

A rider on a snow-covered horse approached from the west. He called out to George in the carriage. "You best turn back to Paris! The road is filled up with snow ahead."

George stopped the carriage, and then Darrow and father stopped the two wagons.

"We want to make Oakland today or tomorrow," said Father. "We thought we would press on before any heavy snow hits."

"You don't know this country like I do," said the man on the old horse. "You have ten miles of open prairie before you're in the trees again, and then another ten miles to Oakland. When a snow storm hits these parts, out on the open prairie, you can't see the road, and you're likely as not to wander off the road and get lost."

"But the road has horse and wagon tracks in it," said Father. "We can follow those all right."

"You won't see them ten minutes after the snow starts in earnest," said the man. "And it's about to hit us."

Wycliffe looked up into the sky. There was a slate gray covering of clouds, and the air felt much warmer than it had the previous day under clear skies. Up ahead he could see, many miles off, the trees on the other side of the prairie.

His father was also looking up into the sky. "Much obliged," he said to the man. "But I think we'll trust in God and go on towards Oakland."

The man looked at the carriage, containing Wycliffe's 80-year-old grandmother and all the women, then shrugged his shoulders, and said, "Suit yourself. I wish you success, though I advise against it."

"Thank you, but I feel differently," said Father.

They moved on, but only a short time later the storm commenced in earnest. At first there were intermittent snowflakes, but then they fell with a flurry in great numbers. Soon the backs of the horses were covered to the depth of several inches. All traces of travel on the roads were erased. There was no road to be seen. All Wycliffe could see through the falling snowflakes was the back of Brother Darrow's wagon. Then, as the snow increased, Darrow's wagon became indistinct and then vanished completely from view.

Wycliffe had never seen such a snow. It felt wonderful to him, like a dream of being in a cloud. The air was not too cold. It was if the temperature raised slightly as the cloud cover settled over the prairie, like a blanket on a bed. Not only did things look differently, but the sound was altered somehow. There was a soft, muffled quality to everything, from the jingle of the harness to the soft thuds of the horses' hooves in the deep powder.

Then, the snow deepened on the road, so that the lower legs of the horses were completely buried. The wagon wheels crunched along, buried up to the hubs, and the movement started to slow down.

Suddenly there was a cracking sound, and the wagon pitched violently to the left, throwing Wycliffe and Sid onto their father, and then out into the deep snow.

"What happened?" said Sid, sitting up in the snow.

"Wheel came off," said Father, getting up slowly from the ground. He had lost his hat and was rubbing his shoulder painfully. "Help me find it." Then he yelled into the blowing snow, "Hey! Darrow! Robinson! Hold up!"

The boys searched the snow, now more than two feet deep, and finally found the loose wagon wheel when Sid bumped into it with his feet. "Here it is, Father!" called Sid.

The three of them lifted the wagon wheel and rolled it back to the wagon, tilting sideways into the snow. "How are we going to lift the wagon?" asked Wycliffe. Father unhitched the horses and brought them around to the rear of the wagon so they could find some way to lift up the front axle to replace the wheel.

Just then another wagon passed them going east. "The road is wiped out by the snow," said the man in the wind, snow swirling around him. "You best turn around and go back to Paris with me. You'll be lost for sure and then freeze to death."

"I think you're right," said father. "What about my wagon?"

"Leave it here. You can get it when the storm blows over. Just hitch your horses to the back of my wagon and climb in."

"What about my friends ahead?" shouted Father.

"I already told them about the road and told them to follow me. I expect they are turning around now."

Wycliffe and Sid and their father tied Champ and Mamie to the wagon and climbed in.

There were other wagons following, and the caravan made its way slowly back to Paris. Wycliffe kept turning around to see if he could see the Darrows' wagon and George's carriage, but it was too hard in the blowing snow. The intensity of the storm increased, and by the time they were back in Paris, the streets were filled with three feet of snow.

By the time they returned to McSorleys, Wycliffe was so frozen that two men had to carry him inside. The tavern was filled with travelers, standing around the log fire. Wycliffe was set down on a stump by the fire and given a mug of hot tea.

"Where's George?" asked Sid, looking with worry at the door. No travelers had come in for a half an hour.

"I expect they had to wait for the convoy of wagons to pass to turn around," said Father, "then had a job getting the rigs turned in the snow. They'll come along."

But they did not come. Wycliffe had thawed out and thought about his mother and sisters, and little brother Carvel, and his 80-year-old grandmother.

"Should we go back and look for George and Brother Darrow?" asked Sid.

The innkeeper said, "No one should go out in this. The storm is at its height and the night black. You would have no chance of surviving."

All night long Father paced up and down the common room at the tavern. Wycliffe could not sleep, as there was great excitement from the huge press of people jammed into the tavern, travelers stranded or waiting for news from friends through the storm.

In the morning the storm was over, but it was still very cold. Sidney Rigdon and his sons set out to find their lost ones. They rode Champ and the other horse out to the wagon, reattached the wheel, and continued in the morning light. They could see across the prairie, but there was no road to be seen. After about two and a half hours, they got across to the timber on the other side of the prairie. There was a little house standing on the bank of a small stream, and they went to inquire if any wagons had come there the day before. They were overjoyed to learn that an open wagon and carriage had stopped to get warm, but they had no accommodations to keep them overnight. The travelers in the carriage and wagon had continued on to a house about five miles from there, and Wycliffe and his father and brother were told that they would probably find them there. They made haste to the house, and when they got there they found them well, except Darrow's sons, who were badly frozen.

JULIA – FEBRUARY 27

SALT RIVER, MISSOURI
Tuesday, February 27, 1838

Young as he was, Little Joseph never cried, but Julia could see the strain etched on his handsome little face. In fact, it touched Julia that her brother could try to be as brave as Papa.

Her brother. Even thinking the words brought her thoughts up short. Was he truly her brother? And what of the other brothers Aunt Lucy had told her about—the ones named Orrice and Johnny Murdock. And what of the three babies who shared a birthday with Julia, but had died— Thaddeus, Louisa, and another Joseph? The thought gave Julia chills and filled her mind with wonder, and she gazed vacantly out over the icy landscape passing before her eyes.

After crossing the Mississippi River, the little wagon train moved over the fertile but frozen ground of Missouri. Julia sat hour by hour on the wagon box with her father, watching the untiring labors of Old Charlie and Jim, steady in the wagon harness. Ahead were the wagons of Brother Brigham and behind them the wagons of the other families in their little company, the Mileses and the Richards. With each mile Julia felt both exhaustion from the long journey, but also excitement about approaching Far West, where

Mother and Father had promised her peace and a new home in the wilderness.

Then one evening, just before sunset, they came to the Salt River, a large stream where the ice had already broken up. Julia could see huge cakes of ice floating down the stream, white and almost blinding in the sun.

"How will we ever cross this?" asked Mother, climbing down from the wagon and shielding the glaring sun with her hand, as they watched the movement on the river. It was as if the frozen ground was alive and moving from right to left at their feet. They could hear the distant grinding and snapping as the ice cakes moved against each other, and flowed slowly downstream. There was a ferryboat on the river, but it was sunk, with one end lifted high above the ice and water and the other sunken deep beneath the stream. The travelers surveyed this sight without saying a word, and then went about the task of making camp before dark.

That night the company sat around their campfire with solemn hearts and little conversation, then one by one the families went off to bed.

"Will we be stuck here?" whispered Julia in the dark as she and Little Joseph lay in the bed of their wagon.

"I hope not," said Little Joseph. "But maybe Father will find a way for us to cross."

"But there's no ice to step on," said Julia. "And we can't swim across."

Little Joseph was quiet. Julia lay for a long time thinking, and then said a silent prayer. "Heavenly Father. Please help us to find a way once more to cross the ice. Amen."

The next morning the company stood around the campfire, warming their hands against the March cold.

Father turned suddenly to Brother Brigham and said, "Let's go and look more carefully at the ice on the river."

After breakfast they two of them left the camp and walked down toward the river. About an hour they returned, with smiles on their faces.

"We think there is a way for us to cross," said Brother Brigham.

"What?" exclaimed Mother. "But the water is flowing downstream already. How can we find a foothold between floating cakes of ice?"

"The cakes of ice are floating," said Father. "But the thickest part of the ice is still intact and has simply sunk beneath the surface of the water two or three feet. At that level it is still as solid as ever and has not broken up."

Brother Brigham added, "By taking our wagons two or three feet into the water, we can gain the solid ice beneath the surface of the river."

After breakfast, with much trepidation, the travelers packed up their wagons, hitched up the teams, and climbed in. Julia held her breath as Old Charlie and Jim plunged into the river to a depth of two feet, and then miraculously continued to move across the ice, through the slow-moving stream of water and blocks of ice to the other side. On the far bank, they landed directly in the woods on a very steep hill. Here they managed to get their wagons out of the river and up the bank.

LITTLE JOSEPH – MARCH 5

NEAR THE MISSISSIPPI RIVER AT QUINCY, ILLINOIS
Monday, March 5, 1838

Brigham Young: "After stopping a few days and resting, we proceeded to Quincy, where we found the river frozen over, though it had been broken up. . . . [W]e passed over . . . with great difficulty. . . . We proceeded on our journey to Huntsville. . . . We arrived at Far West, March 14, 1838."[43]

Little Joseph was a happy boy. There was quite a caravan of wagons and more children to play with along the road. He and Julia were constantly climbing in and out of the wagon as it rolled along, day after day, and scampering over the snow between the wagons.

At night Little Joseph loved to sit around the campfire in the cold evenings and listen to Father talk with Uncle Samuel and Brother Brigham. Little Joseph whittled as he listened, letting the wood shavings fall into the coals and burst into flame.

---

[43] *Manuscript History of Brigham Young, 25-27*

Brother Brigham looked like a watchdog, he could build like a beaver, and he had the courage of a lion. He was the sort of man Little Joseph's father loved to sit and talk with or work beside.

In the next stage of the journey, the weather turned bitterly cold, and the travelers bundled up with every coat and scarf and blanket they possessed. The hours passed monotonously in the wagon for Little Joseph, especially when Julia objected loudly about Little Joseph carving wood in the wagon and leaving wood shavings on her blanket.

Seven hundred miles out of Kirtland, the little wagon train arrived at the Mississippi River in Quincy, Illinois. Father stopped the wagon and got out to walk down to the riverside, followed by Little Joseph. Little Joseph saw that the river was one solid mass of ice.

Brother Brigham walked up behind them. "Frozen solid?" he said.

"Looks that way," said Father. "But it has been broken up already this season. See how the blocks of ice have piled up one on another."

"Let's go down and take a closer look," said Brother Brigham.

Little Joseph followed his father, who turned around and said, "You wait here, Joseph. It's too dangerous on the ice."

Little Joseph stood on the riverbank and watched Father and Brother Brigham make their way carefully over the frozen ice. There was a flat river barge that had obviously been beached with one end on the bank in warm weather, but was now firmly frozen in ice, its far end protruding out into the frozen river. Father and Brother Brigham each held long poles, and here and there they probed the ice to see how thick it was. In several places their poles thrust easily through the thin ice on the surface. They walked over the thin ice near the shore, then climbed up onto the flat boat and walked further out onto the river ice, where huge blocks of ice had been created by movement in the freezing and thawing Mississippi. Little Joseph stood watching for more than an hour and watched as they ventured far out onto the ice of the river, until they were no more than two dark specks in a field of blinding white.

When Father and Brother Brigham returned, they all walked up to the wagons, where the horses had been unhitched, a camp had been made, and a warming fire built.

"Can we cross?" asked Uncle Samuel.

"It's possible," said Father, warming his hands over the fire. "The ice has been broken up, but is now frozen again. We went past the center of the river, where the main channel flows in summer, and it is frozen solid in the middle sufficient to carry our wagons."

"It's the sides of the river which pose the problem," added Brother Brigham. "There the ice is very thin, having thawed in weeks past where the ice meets the warm earth."

"There is a flat boat beached against the bank," said Father. "Perhaps we can run the wagons over it, and thus reach the heavy ice further out in the river."

"We can do it," said Brother Brigham. "But we will have to take great care. The ice will support us, but we need to spread out so as to not concentrate all our weight together. I suggest we take the wagons first onto the ice, and situate them some distance from each other, then take the families, and spread them out as well, and finally the horses."

"That will be the most difficult," said Samuel. "The horses weigh the most and have a very narrow hoof width for their weight."

"We can lead the horses onto the ice one by one," said Brother Decker. "We'll start with the smaller horses, and end with the largest. That way, if a horse falls through the ice, at least we will have gotten as many safely on the ice as possible and be able to pursue our journey to Far West."

Little Joseph heard this and looked over to where the horses were grazing on the prairie grass. Old Charlie was obviously the largest horse of all. He tried not to picture Charlie falling through the ice into the cold waters of the Mississippi River.

OLD CHARLIE – MARCH 6

ON THE BANKS OF THE MISSISSIPPI RIVER
Tuesday, March 6, 1838

Brigham Young: "Joseph and I went down to the river and examined the ice. We soon learned that by going through the flat boat which lay the end to the shore and placing a few planks from the outer end on the ice, we could reach the heavy ice which had floated down the river a few days previous sufficient to bear up our teams. We hauled our wagons through the boat and on to the ice by hand, then led our horses on to the solid ice, and drove across the river by attaching a rope to the wagon and to the team, so that they would be some distance apart. The last horse which was led on to the ice was Joseph's favorite, Charlie. He broke the ice at every step for several rods."[44]

Early in the mornin', while most of the people was still asleep in the wagons, I looked out through the cold mist and see'd Brother Joe and Brigham jest sittin' by the fire on two barrels. Brother Joe's big white dog, Major, had set hisself down by Brother Joe's legs, and Brother Joe was

---

[44] Eldon Jay Watson, ed., *Manuscript History of Brigham Young* (Smith Secretarial Service: Salt Lake City, 1968) 25-26

scratchin' behind Major's ears. Well, them two men was both jest settin' on them barrels, talkin' quietly back and forth, kind of disputin' amongst theirselves. It was jest gettin' light and I see'd the Big River stretched out behind our camp. I recognized everythin' jest as I see'd it in the fall, when Brother Joe and me rode this way with Brother Sidney and Champ and the others. There it all was, jest as I remembered it—the road, the ferry, and the Big River all spread out as far as you could see. 'Cept now the river was all covered over with ice, which was startin' to shimmer and shine in the early mornin' light.

I heared Brigham sayin' that they should wait until the ice broke up, but Brother Joe was urgin' him to try to cross today. Well, I perked right up as I heared that, as I warn't specially anxious to go walkin' across no ice pullin' a wagon! 'Twas enough to unsettle any horse, and I was afeared of fallin' through that ice.

As I listened to Brother Joe and Brigham talkin', Little Joseph poked his head out from behind the wagon cover and looked around. Pretty soon he climbed down on the wagon wheel with a blanket wrapped around hisself and came over to the fire and set hisself on his Pa's lap.

"The ice won't hold the horses and wagons, I say," said Brigham.

"You may be right," said Brother Joe. "But what if we empty the wagons and let the horses walk over one by one."

Brigham thought this over some. Jest then I heared a great crackin' noise, and the men looked over towards the river. It was them great chunks of ice groanin' and cracklin' as they moved one agin' the other.

Brother Joe see'd me standin' there watchin', and he set Little Joseph down on the barrel and up and walked over to me. He took my head in his hands and started in on rubbin' my cheekbones, then scratchin' behind my ears.

"We're going to cross the ice, Charlie," he said, real soothin' like. "You can cross the ice! Trust me!"

As Brother Joe talked to me, standin' there lookin' out over that Big River, all covered over in ice, I started to remember the first time I crossed a river and how I first learned to trust a man. One day when I was still a young colt and after I had been broke to the saddle, Pete and his Pa, Henry, took me and two, three other young horses to the big city called Cincinnati, across a river from the place I was born and raised, which they called Kentucky. All the day I felt like a wire strung up between two trees.

Back then Pete called me "Beau," and right before we crossed, he talked to me, jest like Brother Joe did this mornin', tellin' me everythin' would be okay and to trust him. Then I went down with Pete to cross that river.

'Course, since then I seen bigger rivers and crossed bigger rivers than the Ohio River, but at that time it was the biggest piece of water I ever seen or dreamed of. It was the scariest thing I'd ever knowed up to that point in my young life. Nothin' like a big river to make a horse afeared! Pete and Henry helped some other fellers load me and the other horses in a flat boat, which they pulled across the water on ropes, with some help by two fellers with poles as long as trees. I was skittish from the get go, but Pete stood by my head and kept me calmed down, and pretty soon we reached the other shore.

After we crossed, we rode into a bigger town than I ever seen, with buildings, horses squealin' up and down the streets, the rattle of wheels on roads pieced together with little rocks. Then we come to this big place where there were scads of other horses. If it hadn't been for Pete, I reckon I would have snapped my reins and bolted. It was strange all around—strange smells and sounds, so many men, and so many horses. Later on I would live in a big city and get used to such things, but it was a mighty disturbin' experience for me that first time.

Then we come to a little openin' amongst all the buildin's. Pete led me out into that open space, which he called the racetrack. A band was playin' music, with banjos and horns and what all else. That's the first time I ever heared a banjo. And the smells there was so strange. Fact is, everythin' was strange to me—strange horses, strange men, smoke, tromped up grass. Lucky I was close by Pete and Henry. They brought me up to a fence strung out in a circle with a bit of grass in the middle. Outside the first fence, there was another fence. I see'd how there was a big crowd of fellers, black and white, leanin' up agin' that fence and all watchin' a lot of horses with their riders circlin' around that inside fence when a gun was fired—BANG!, like that— follered by a perfect tornado of noise, halooin', jumpin', and clappin'. Well, I was led into this paddock with Pete with all sorts of men shoutin' and jostlin' together, and then Pete mounted up on me, and we lined up with eight or ten other horses. I remember one of them 'specially, a low, long-backed shaggy horse, with a small saddle, and dirty legs and withers, his legs like pillars and his monstrous, shaggy head set low on a short, straight neck. And then the gun went off and the other horses set to gallopin'. I reared up, and nearly pitched Pete into the dirt, but he urged me on, sayin', "Come on, Beau! Come on, Beau! Go, son, Go!" and I got the idea, and took off after the other horses.

We come up to a big curve, and the other horses leaned in with their left shoulders agin' the fence, and by that time I caught up, and we had a long stretch ahead, 'bout a quarter mile, and I passed one and then another of the other horses. And you should have see'd the crowd, black men, white men, hats flyin', some of 'em whistlin', and hallooin' like I never heared in my whole life. Well, I passed the last horse when the loudest roar of all surged from the men onto the field, and Pete and I passed a feller holdin' a black and white checked cloth hung on a stick.

After that the men all raced out onto the track, and surrounded Pete and me. Henry was there, too, and I see'd him takin' little green pieces of paper from a lot of other fellers, and he had the biggest grin on his face that I ever seen on him.

After that, we passed through some gates, and I remember a big man standin' in one of the gates with another horse, and I froze up, in the gate. The man started yelling, and cussing, and I reared up and nearly pulled my bridle off. Henry got me all calmed down.

Finally, I got led out in front of everybody, and a big fellow with a white hat put some sort of ribbons on me.

Pete was always for the fun of it. After the ribbons was all over and done, he got up on my back, and rode me over to this big sheet of canvas, the same color as the one Pete used to play with me on the grass back home, except this canvas was high, set up on tree trunks with pegs and ropes. Pete called it a tent. Well, what do you know, if Pete didn't ride me straight into that tent. I was awful jumpy inside, but Pete jest clicked his tongue at me and dug his heels in, and on inside I went. "Go on, Beau! Go on, son!"

A crowd of men inside all set to laughin', when they see'd us. They was all sittin' or standin' around, glasses in their hands, or singin' and yellin'. Then all inside just went quiet, and they stared at me. Then Josh walked me up to a long table with a man behind it and spoke to him, and the man handed him a glass. I just stood still, my reins slack on my neck lookin' at the tromped up grass under my hooves. I dropped my head down for a sniff, but it warn't any good, tromped up and foul. But Pete, he jest sat on my back, drinkin' his glass, and then we walked out of the tent.

Henry was outside, and he was mighty angry at Pete.

"Are you crazy, boy?" he yelled, "Taking Beau in the tent like that?" Pete was jest real quiet, and I stood there, pawin' my fore hooves a bit in the grass.

Finally Pete said, "Sorry, Pa. I just wanted to see if Beau would go inside, if he trusted me enough to do anythin' that I asked him to do."

Henry jest frowned, with his big arms crossed over his chest.

"Well, Pa," said Pete. "Beau trusted me. He trusted me completely."

I reckon that was the first time I ever truly trusted a man, when I walked into that tent with Pete. I don't trust many men, but I sure did trust Pete.

And I trust Brother Joe.

LITTLE JOSEPH – MARCH 7

On the Missouri bank of the river, the travelers had taken shelter behind a grove of little, stunted evergreen trees just off the road. The wind was whipping wildly through the canvas coverings of the five wagons.

"We need to start a fire," shouted Brigham Young through the wind. "My wife and several of the Miles children are chilled through to the bone!"

Within an hour, the five families were standing around a blazing fire, warming their hands. The men were bringing in more wood to last the night, and the women were working on cutting potatoes and carrots and onions into silver dollar shaped slices and dropping them into a cauldron of boiling water. Some beef jerky and salt pork was added to the water, and Little Joseph's mouth started watering as he smelled the savory stew.

Later that night, Little Joseph closed his eyes and lay cocooned in his nest of blankets, his belly filled with food and his mind racing with memories of the adventures of the past few hours.

The morning after their arrival at the banks of the Mississippi, the five men—Father, Brother Brigham, Uncle Samuel, Brother Miles, and Brother Decker—had spent several hours building an earthen ramp from the bank, running onto the long flat boat, and then they laid several planks from the outer end of the boat out onto the ice. Then, one by one, they pulled the wagons by hand through the boat and onto the ice.

Little Joseph and Julia stood on the riverbank watching the men pulling the wagons with great difficulty out onto the ice. Julia reached over and took Little Joseph's hand.

"Do you think the ice will hold us all?" she asked.

"If Father says it will," said Little Joseph. "I'm sure we won't fall through the ice."

"I really meant the horses," said Julia. "Jim and Old Charlie are so big and their hooves so small. Do you think they will be able to walk on the ice without falling through?"

Little Joseph thought this over, then looked nervously back at Old Charlie, standing with the other horses. As he looked, he reached into his shirt and held Grandfather's lucky stone in his hands.

"Time for the mothers and children to cross," called out Brother Decker from down on the bank. Little Joseph walked down the bank with Mother, Julia, and Frederick. The other families followed. Brother Decker and Uncle Samuel helped to tie ropes around each of their waists, and then they walked out onto the flat boat. The wood was old and rotted in places, but it provided a safe place to walk. Little Joseph could hear the echoing sound as their feet struck the wood. There was obviously water directly beneath the boat.

At the end of the flat boat, there were half a dozen long planks from the end of the boat onto the ice below. This was the trickiest part, as the planks were only ten or twelve inches wide. One by one, Mother with Frederick, Julia, and then Little Joseph descended the planks, holding their arms out for balance. Father and Brother Brigham stood by the side and helped them the final few precarious steps. Once safely on the thicker ice, they stood a few rods away from the wagons and turned back to watch the other families cross the flat boat and the planks, walking one by one.

Now the four men returned to the bank to bring the horses. Little Joseph stood with his mother, sister, and brother and watched. His heart was beating wildly.

First the men brought the smaller horses, one by one. They walked without problem down the bank, and over the flatboat. But then they had to balance on the planks. By giving the horses encouragement, one by one they walked down the planks and onto the ice.

The smallest horses walked onto the ice without problem and were led ahead of the wagons at a distance from each other. But once the larger horses started to descend the plank and walk on the ice, a distinct cracking sound could be heard. *The ice is not thick enough*, Little Joseph thought.

There were two horses left. Jim and Old Charlie. Father led Jim to the planks at the end of the flat boat, and he walked right down onto the ice, which popped and groaned and cracked, but held him as Father rapidly brought him further out on the river, where the ice was the thickest and safest.

Finally, Father returned to the bank to Old Charlie. Little Joseph watched as his father stroked his neck and spoke into his ear, then led him out onto the boat and down the plank. Father walked ahead of old Charlie onto the ice, then turned around and called to him.

"Okay, Charlie! Come on, boy! You can do this. Come on, Old Charlie!"

Old Charlie looked at Father, then with perfect balance and sureness, ran down the plank and out onto the frozen river. As Old Charlie stepped onto the ice, it broke. Little Joseph caught his breath. He could see the splash of water from the between the broken cakes of ice. But Old Charlie kept moving, breaking the ice every step for ten, twenty, thirty, forty, then fifty feet. In several places Charlie could be seen to begin sinking, but scrambling on all four legs and hooves, and by continuing to move forward, he saved himself time and again, until finally he stepped onto the solid ice over the main part of the river.

Little Joseph realized that he was shaking. He took Julia's hand, and she was shaking as well.

With all horses, wagons, and passengers safely on the ice, the men then attached long ropes to each wagon, and allowed each team to pull its wagon across the mile-wide, ice-bound Mississippi. The families followed on foot, many dozens of feet behind their respective wagons. Thus, in a long string, the company struck out over the ice. The passage took several hours, and each wagon and family crossed separately. First Brother Brigham's family, team, and wagon, then Father's, then Uncle Samuel's, then Brother Decker's, and finally Brother Miles'. Each family crossed in the tracks of the other, but it was with great difficulty and risk that they all got across, many times having to separate from each other a great distance and get onto the solid cake of frozen ice. Many times the ice was very near to breaking up as the travelers passed over. In this way, they passed safely over the river into Missouri.

By the time they set up camp on the Missouri side of the river, it was already getting dark, and Little Joseph was surprised to realize that the process of crossing the river had taken an entire day. They traveled about six miles from the river and camped that night, both horses and men weary and still shaking from the exertion and excitement of the day.

Before going to bed, Little Joseph went over to the horses, and stroked Charlie's flanks. "Good boy," he said. "Smart boy."

The snap of a breaking branch woke Little Joseph. He poked his head out of his nest of warm blankets and saw the fur-covered bear, Brother Brigham, standing by the fire in the dark, putting new wood on the fire. The branches and logs crackled and sparked as they caught fire. He could smell the rich, piney smell of the burning logs. Little Joseph lay back and watched the pink and orange light dance on the canvas cover of the wagon.

LOVINA – MARCH 7

The next few weeks were busy ones for Lovina Smith and her family. It was extremely cold in Kirtland, and there was great concern in the entire Smith family and in the Church for Uncle Joseph and his family. The Prophet had been forced to flee on horseback one night at midnight, his family leaving in the darkness a few hours later. There had been scant news from them since, and Lovina wondered what had happened to them. Sometimes at night she would lie awake in their snug home in Kirtland, with the wind howling around the eaves of the house, and think about her little cousins, Julia and Joseph and tiny Freddie. Where were they sleeping? On the cold ground? Did they have enough warm blankets? Lovina shuddered, and snuggled deeper beneath her down comforter. Lovina knew that it was only a matter of time until her family, too, would follow Uncle Joseph on the thousand-mile journey to Missouri.

Lovina's family remained in Kirtland until the end of March, as there was important church business for her father to attend to. With her Uncle Joseph and his first counselor Sidney Rigdon gone, there were few leaders left to lead the saints.

Over a period of several weeks Lovina's father made quiet preparations to leave and travel with his family to Far West. He also exercised great care over his mother and his brothers William and Don Carlos to make sure they would be able to move their families safely.

Lovina was busy helping Mary Fielding and Aunty Grinnel with the packing. They were able to send the furniture and farm equipment ahead by riverboat through the Ohio and Erie Canal to the Ohio River, where it was taken in freight barges to the Mississippi River and up to Quincy, Illinois. They would require several teams and wagons to transport the family and all of their furniture and tools, as well as seeds of every kind for planting in Missouri. Lovina's father also arranged to take with them much of her Uncle Joseph's and Aunt Emma's furniture and personal belongings, which they had been obligated to leave behind in their hasty departure from Kirtland.

In addition to Lovina's immediate family, including her new stepmother, Mary Fielding Smith, they would be taking with them the faithful Aunty Grinnel and Old George, who would be much help both on the road and in settling a new home in Missouri. Also, Mary Fielding Smith's sister, Mercy Thompson, and her husband, Robert, who had recently come from Canada would travel with them. This would make eleven people traveling together in several wagons. Since there were only three men in the group, Hyrum Smith, Robert Thompson, and Old George, Lovina's stepmother and Lovina herself would be required to do much of the work handling the teams.

Julia – March 10

HUNTSVILLE, MISSOURI
Saturday, March 10, 1838

Joseph and Emma Smith and their children arrived in Far West, Missouri, on March 14, 1838. After their arrival, they stayed for several weeks in the home of George and Lucinda Morgan Harris, while preparing their own house on the town square of Far West.

When Julia Murdock Smith heard Major barking, she somehow knew the end of their journey was near. As they sat at breakfast, Julia suddenly heard the dog let out a long, baying howl, then begin barking furiously. They were still a hundred and twenty miles from Far West near Huntsville, Missouri.

We're getting close, Julia thought. A wave of relief flowed into her heart. *It will be good to be warm again.*

"Someone's coming," said Brother Brigham, standing upon the tongue of one of the wagons to get a better view. "It's a carriage."

Soon Brother John Barnard drove into the camp on a fine carriage. It was filled with fresh food and supplies.

Brother Barnard insisted that Julia's family ride the rest of the way in the carriage. At first Father said, no, but after repeated entreaties he agreed. Brother Barnard moved his horses to the wagon, and Father hitched up Old Charlie and Jim to the new carriage. It had wide seats of fine leather and springs over the axles to ease the violence and jarring as they passed over bad roads and trails.

Julia rode on the back seat at the side and felt like a princess as they rolled smoothly over the prairie. Major ran along by the side, often barking at rabbits and other animals, and darting out into the prairie happily in pursuit. It was cold, but the sky was clear, and the sun felt good on the dark leather seats of the carriage.

One day, not long after they began riding in the carriage, they crossed a large prairie, with no trees in sight and many miles from any house or settlement. It was cold, and the ground was frozen. As they crossed a small stream, Julia heard a loud bang and then a scraping noise and felt a shudder go through the body of Brother Barnard's carriage. Father stopped the carriage, and all the men left their wagons and horses to gather around to look at the underside of the carriage.

"You've sprung one of the axletrees," said Brother Barnard, lying upon his back and looking up at the underside of the carriage.

"I'm sorry," said Father. "It was riding fine and then without warning it sprung."

"'Tain't your fault," said Brother Barnard. "But I'm sorry you can't travel in the carriage any longer. I'll help you move back to the wagon, and I'll wait here and get back as best as I can."

"Brother Barnard," said Father. "I'm certain that I can spring that iron axletree back so that we can go on our journey."

"I hate to disagree with you," said Brother Barnard. "But I'm a blacksmith and am used to working in all sorts of iron, and that axletree is bent so far around that to undertake to straighten it would only break it. It will be necessary for me to remove the wooden cap from the axletree and then heat the axletree in a smithy so that the bent portion can be brought gradually back around and then tempered in the blacksmith's fire."

"And I hate to disagree with you," said Father, "but I'm certain that I can bend it safely back around."

Brother Bernard looked doubtful, but Brother Brigham put his hand on the man's shoulder and whispered something in his ear.

"Okay, President Smith," said Brother Bernard. "I'll have faith in you. Go ahead a try. But don't tell me afterward that I didn't warn you."

Father went to their wagon, and rummaged around in the bottom of the wagonload, bringing out a long, iron pry bar. He then took off his coat, rolled up his sleeves, and lay down beneath the wagon, placing the pry bar solidly against the axletree, then pulled back with all his strength. Suddenly, Julia heard a loud clicking sound and felt the carriage right itself beneath her.

"There," said Father.

"Well, I've never seen anything like that," said Brother Barnard, climbing under the wagon to look. "I'll never again say that a thing can not be done when a Prophet says that it can."

"Let's see how that rides," said Father.

They got back into the wagon and proceeded on their way and rode the final hundred miles to Far West without it giving them any more trouble.

They arrived in Far West a few days later. Hundreds of the saints had ridden out over the prairie for miles to greet them, including the brass band. It was a grand parade, with Father and Mother leading the way in Brother Barnard's carriage, pulled by Jim and Old Charlie.

PART III

"HE SMELLETH THE BATTLE AFAR OFF"

"Hast thou given the horse strength?
Hast thou clothed his neck with thunder?
Canst thou make him afraid as a grasshopper?
The glory of his nostrils is terrible.
He paweth in the valley, and rejoiceth in his strength.
He goeth on to meet the armed men.
He mocketh at fear and is not affrighted,
Neither turneth he back from the sword.
The quiver rattleth against him,
The glittering spear and the shield.
He swalloweth the ground with fierceness and rage,
Neither believeth he that it is the sound of the trumpet.
He saith among the trumpets, 'Ha! Ha!'
And he smelleth the battle afar off,
The thunder of the captains, and the shouting."[45]

---

[45] Job 39:19-25 (Within the immediate family of Joseph Smith, Jr., this scripture was deemed a fit description of Old Charlie)

JULIA – MARCH 29

FAR WEST, MISSOURI
Thursday, March 29, 1838

Letter of Joseph Smith to the Saints in Kirtland
March 29, 1838
Dear and Well Beloved Brethren,

Through the grace and mercy of our God, after a long and tedious journey of two months and one day, my family and I arrived safe in the city of Far West, having been met at Huntsville, one hundred and twenty miles from this place, by my brethren with teams and money, to forward us on our journey. When within eight miles of the city of Far West, we were met by an escort of brethren from the city, viz,: Thomas B. Marsh, John Corrill, Elias Higbee, and several others of the faithful of the West, who received us with open arms and warm hearts, and welcomed us to the bosom of their society. On our arrival in the city we were greeted on every hand by the Saints, who bid us welcome to the land of their inheritance.

Dear brethren, you may be assured that so friendly a meeting and reception paid us well for our long seven years of servitude, persecution, and affliction in the midst of our enemies, in the land of Kirtland; yea verily our hearts were full; and we feel grateful to Almighty God for His kindness unto us. The particulars of our journey, brethren, cannot well be written, but we trust that the same God who has protected us will protect you also, and will, sooner or later, grant us the privilege of seeing each other face to face, and of rehearsing all our sufferings.

We have heard of the destruction of the printing office which we presume to believe must have been occasioned by the Parrish party, or more properly the aristocrats and anarchists.

The Saints here have provided a room for us, and daily necessaries, which are brought in from all parts of the country to make us comfortable; so that I have nothing to do but to attend to my spiritual concerns, or the spiritual affairs of the Church. . . .

Brother Samuel H. Smith and family arrived here soon after we did, in good health. Brothers Brigham Young, Daniel S. Miles, and Levi Richards arrived here when we did. They were with us on the last part of our journey, which ended much to our satisfaction. They also are well. They have provided places for their families, and are now about to break the ground for seed.[46]

Julia dreamed that she was back in Kirtland. It was summer, and she walked in Mother's garden holding little Freddie's hand, and she looked up into her favorite apple tree and saw two strange boys there, whom she somehow knew were her older brothers. As she tried to see their faces, the sun moved behind them, blinding her eyes.

She awoke with a dagger of sunlight pouring through the window onto her bed. *We're in Far West,* she thought with sudden remembrance. Julia pulled the blanket up over her face and luxuriated in the warmth of her narrow bed. Father had piled straw in a corner of their little room and shaped it like a bird's nest. Father and Mother and their three children had a single room in the upstairs of the house belonging to Brother and Sister Harris. The house was two

---

[46] HC 3:10-12

storied, built of logs, and snug in the cold March nights. Over Julia's little nest Father had laid two blankets, and now she did not want to leave the warmth.

"Get up now, Julia," whispered her mother. She opened one eye the smallest little crack to see her mother's figure, now very pregnant, leaning over to straighten the bedding of the larger nest Little Joseph and Frederick had been sleeping in.

Julia pretended to be asleep. Mother glanced at her and smiled, deciding to let the little girl sleep, then went about her work, dressing the boys and tidying up their room.

"Is she still asleep?" asked Father.

"Maybe," said Mother. "Let's let her lie there a while more. It won't hurt." Mother and Father quietly got the boys up and left their six-year-old daughter alone in the room.

Julia smiled, knowing that there would be no wagon journey today. No campfires. No finding a private place to take care of the duties of nature, no riding in a bouncing or teeth-jarring wagon, no walking on the cold prairie, no picking burrs and thorns from her dress, no sore feet, no fear of pursuing horsemen. She was in a safe and warm place. That was all that mattered.

Julia already liked Far West, though it was on the edge of civilization, facing the vast unexplored emptiness of the new American territories. In Ohio they had everything one could want from a civilized society—all the freshest foods and even delicacies brought on the canals and lakes and turnpikes from New York, New England, and even from Europe. There were music concerts and dances and books. Julia had been one of the youngest pupils in Eliza R. Snow's

Select School for Young Ladies, with her Smith cousins Lovina and Mariah. There she had begun to learn to read, using *Murray's English Reader* and *Pieces in Prose and Poetry Selected from the Best Writers*. But in Far West, Mother said, they wouldn't have very many of the nice and genteel blessings of culture. "But that will be all right," said Mother. "You can learn to read and write and sing and dance as well in a wilderness as in the salons of Europe." Julia didn't know what a salon was, but she liked the idea of starting over in Far West.

ARTHUR – MAY 1

KIRTLAND, OHIO
Tuesday, May 1, 1838

Lucy Mack Smith: "When we were ready to set out for Missouri, I went to New Portage with a conveyance to bring my husband to the rest of his family, and we were shortly on our way together, right glad to meet again, alive and in good health, after so many perilous adventures."[47]

One long, muddy road ran over the hills and down through the vivid green valleys where they drove. Down the center of the wide valleys ran noisy streams, clear as strings of diamonds in the sun. In the distance lay the green carpet of endless woods to the south and east.

"Are you still listening, my boy?" asked Mother Smith as Arthur drove the team in the newly repaired carriage.

"Yes, ma'am," he said, holding the reins and surveying the road ahead over the rumps of the two matching white mules.

---

[47] *History of Joseph Smith by His Mother*, 357

"Good," she said. "The scripture which says, 'Your old men shall dream dreams,' was literally fulfilled in the case of my husband, for he had many visions, which I'll relate to you." And then the old woman embarked on another long tale of her life with her husband, Joseph Smith, Sr., and their nine children, whose names Arthur now knew by heart— Alvin, Hyrum, Sophronia, Joseph, Samuel, William, Katharine, Don, and Lucy. And that was not counting the two sons who died as infants. Arthur knew everything, it seemed, about this family, although he admitted to himself that at times his mind wandered as the two odd companions continued their bumpy journey over the roads of Ohio.

His mind wandered, that is, until Lucy Mack Smith told any story that involved her youngest child, Lucy Smith. Whenever Lucy was mentioned, Arthur perked up his ears and soaked in every detail, imagining Lucy's bright blue eyes as she spoke.

The two traveling companions were driving fifty miles southwest of Kirtland to find Joseph Smith, Sr., the patriarch of the family, who had been in hiding since the day his son, Joseph Smith, the Prophet, rode out of Kirtland on his black horse in the middle of the night to escape his persecutors. Arthur had also heard this tale told a hundred times since he began working on the repair and outfitting of Mother Smith's carriage and old wagon. Mother Smith had fed him as he worked and promised him forty-five cents a day before they left for Missouri. She now owed him four dollars and fifty cents, but Arthur didn't particularly care when he was paid. Just seeing Lucy Smith was payment enough for him, and if the truth be told, he had taken twice as long on the job as he ought to have, just to see her shining blue eyes.

The wagon was all fixed and being loaded up now in Kirtland, while he had agreed to drive Mother Smith to fetch her husband and meet the other travelers on the road.

Working for Mother Smith had not been Arthur's only occupation in the spring. There had been an unexpected flood of cash and business in little Kirtland, and he had picked five or six small jobs to fix wagons and make wheels. Alexander Badham had not only taken Arthur in as a regular boarder, but had allowed him to use his tools for twenty-five cents a week. Arthur had been able to save a few dollars, and things were looking up for him.

That night they stopped at dusk ten miles outside of New Portage. "We'll have to camp here tonight, young man," said Mother Smith. "I'll sleep in the carriage and you can sleep by the mules. If you make a fire and go shoot us a rabbit or squirrel, I'll make a little supper."

The stars came out as they were finishing a savory stew. Lucy Mack Smith sat down on a round stone close to the fire across from Arthur. The two were silent for a while as it grew dark and the net of stars moved slowly overhead.

Arthur threw a large log on the coals and it crackled and popped as it caught on fire.

"Do you know my son, Joseph?" she asked.

"A little," Arthur said. "Leastways, I know his black horse, Charlie. I've shoed him a time or two."

"Do you believe that my son Joseph is a Prophet?" she asked.

Arthur was silent for a moment. "I don't know," he finally said.

"If you had seen what I have seen, you would know," she said.

"When did you first know that he was a Prophet?" Arthur asked.

"The night after he saw the angel," she said. "My family was all young, then. Joseph was only seventeen years old and my little Lucy was still a little toddler. When Joseph came in that evening, he told the whole family all that had passed between him and the angel while he was at the place where the plates were deposited. We all sat up very late and listened attentively to all that he had to say to us, but his mind had been so exercised that he became very much fatigued. When my oldest son, Alvin saw this, he said, 'Now, little brother, let's go to bed. We'll get up early in the morning and go to work so as to finish our day's labor by an hour before sunset. Then if Mother will get our supper early, we'll then have a fine, long evening and all sit down and hear you talk.'"

"Well, the next day we worked with great ambition and were ready by sunset to give our whole attention to my son and his story of obtaining the plates. I think we presented the most peculiar aspect of any family that ever lived upon the earth, all seated in a circle, father, mother, sons, and daughters, listening in breathless anxiety to the religious teachings of a boy seventeen years of age who had never read the Bible through completely in his life."

"But how did you know he was telling the truth?" Arthur asked.

"We were convinced that God was about to bring to light something that we might stay our minds upon, something that would give us more perfect knowledge of the plan of salvation and the redemption of the human family, and we rejoiced in it with exceeding great joy. Arthur, the sweetest union and happiness pervaded our house. No jar nor discord disturbed our peace, and tranquility reigned in our midst."

The old woman ceased speaking and both of the travelers were silent. Arthur gazed into the flames of the campfire, swirling up, the sparks flying heavenward toward the network of bright stars. He found himself envying the family that could sit in a circle with such unity and peace and tranquility, and he wondered if he would ever find something to stay his mind upon.

Lucy – May 2

KIRTLAND, OHIO
Wednesday, May 2, 1838

Lucy Smith traveled from Kirtland to Far West between May and July of 1838 in a wagon company consisting of nineteen travelers, all members of the family of Joseph Smith Sr., who was sixty-six years old, and Lucy Mack Smith, sixty-two. Besides Father and Mother Smith and Lucy, there were eight other adults in the company: Sophronia and her second husband, William McCleary, whom she had married a few weeks earlier after being a widow for two years; William and his wife, Caroline; Katharine and her husband, Wilkins J. Salisbury; and Don Carlos and his wife, Agnes; as well as eight children six years of age and under: Mariah Stoddard, six; Mary Jane Smith, four; Lucy Salisbury, three; Solomon Salisbury, two; Agnes Smith, twenty-one months; Caroline Smith, twenty-one months; Sophronia Smith, a few days old; and Alvin Salisbury, who would be born on the banks of the Mississippi River on June 7, 1838.

Mother and Father Smith would welcome five new grandchildren in the turmoil-filled year of 1838. Agnes, Don Carlos's wife, gave birth in New Portage at the start of the trip to little Sophronia; Katharine Smith Salisbury was eight months pregnant at the start of the journey and would give birth at the Mississippi to a son, Alvin, on June 7. Joseph and Hyrum and Samuel's families had already moved to Missouri some weeks before. Emma Smith would deliver a son, Alexander, on June 2 in Far West; and Mary, Samuel's wife, would deliver a son, Samuel, on

August 1 in Marrowbone, Davies County, Missouri; and Mary Fielding Smith, Hyrum's wife, would deliver a son, Joseph F. Smith, in Far West on November 13. That made for one new niece and four new nephews for sixteen-year-old Lucy in 1838.

Lucy Smith sat in the box of the wagon, reading from her school reader to her nieces and nephew. There were four little girls between the ages of one and six, and little two-year-old Solomon, who sat happily on her lap. The wagon was freshly painted with new wheels and axles. Arthur Millikin, the strangely quiet young man from Kirtland village, had spent many days working on the wagon and on Mama's carriage. Now all was repaired and ready for the journey to Far West. Lucy felt a sudden, inexplicable flood of happiness as she sat in the wide and spacious wagon with her little *pearls* surrounding her. *The Lord will open the way for us*, she thought. *He'll even part the ice on the waters, if need be.*

Lucy opened her English Reader. "Be quiet now," she said. "I'm going to read you about the cataract of Niagara, in Canada, North America."

"What's a cataract?" asked little Mariah, age six.

"It's a waterfall, now shush," said Lucy gently. "You'll hear all about it if you'll listen." "This amazing fall of water is made by the river St. Lawrence, in its passage from lake Erie into the lake Ontario," she read. "The St. Lawrence is one of the largest rivers in the world: and yet the whole of its water is discharged in this place, by a fall of a hundred and fifty feet perpendicular."

"What's perpendicular?" asked Mariah.

"It means up and down," said Lucy, keeping her eye on the door, where her brother William and brother-in-law Wilkins were carrying out the last box and placing it in Father Smith's wagon. "The water falls down one hundred and fifty feet."

"Will we fall down perpendicular?" asked Mary Jane, age four.

"No, Mary Jane. Now shush and listen!" Lucy continued reading. "It is not easy to bring the imagination to correspond to the greatness of the scene. A river extremely deep and rapid, and that serves to drain the waters of almost all North America into the Atlantic Ocean, is here poured precipitately down a ledge of rocks, that rises, like a wall, across the whole bed of its stream. The river, a little above, is near three quarters of a mile broad."

"Is the river really a mile broad?" asked Mariah. "The Chagrin River in Kirtland is so small that the boys can throw rocks across it."

"Well, the Niagara is a mile wide," said Lucy. "And so is the Mississippi, which you'll see for yourself in a few weeks."

"How will we cross the Mississippi?" asked Mary Jane.

"In ferry boats," said Lucy. "Now, let me continue reading: "The cataract is not straight but hollowing in wards like a horse-shoe, so that the cataract, which bends to the shape of the obstacle, rounding in wards, presents a kind of theater, the most tremendous in nature."

As she continued to read, Lucy's mother, Lucy Mack Smith, and her sisters Sophronia and Katharine came out of the house. Katharine moved slowly, being eight months pregnant, and was helped up into the wagon containing all of the little ones by her husband, Wilkins, and brother William.

"Let's gather for a prayer," said her brother, William. "A prayer before we set out." They all bowed their heads and folded their arms and the men removed their hats. Lucy helped the little ones keep quiet during the prayer until the "Amen."

After the prayer, there was a final bustle before the wagons began to move. The men inspected the wagons to make sure that everything was tied down securely. The women ran back and forth from the house, bringing last-minute items to take along for the journey. And two or three of the children called out that they had to use the outhouse one more time. Finally, Lucy's brother William called out in his booming voice, "Let's start moving."

As the wagons began rolling out of the beautiful farmyard, the reality finally hit Lucy, lodging like a knot in her throat. She was leaving her home! She swallowed hard and turned to watch as the dear old homestead disappeared from view. She loved everything about it—the house, the porch, the barn with its sagging room, the old apple tree with its branches almost touching the ground beside the wooden fence. Tears ran down Lucy's cheeks and fell onto the fabric of her coat.

"Why are you crying, Aunt Lucy?" said a little voice. Lucy looked down to see tiny Mary Jane gazing up at her, concern in her eyes.

"No matter," said Lucy smiling and brushing away the tears with her sleeve. "Let's play a game on the road!"

There were three wagons in the little Smith family caravan, and slowly they rumbled along the main road, to the top of the hill, past the grand Kirtland Temple, past the farm houses of all their dear neighbors, and out onto the open country south of the city.

Along the road, Lucy glanced back one final time to catch a glimpse of the spire of the Kirtland Temple, then returned to entertaining her little brood of nieces and nephews. It was a joyous time, despite their departure from dear old Kirtland. Almost every person in the world she held dear was loaded in these wagons. Hopefully they would be joined in New Portage by Papa, who had been in hiding from the mob since January, and Mama, who had ridden to New Portage the day before with Arthur Millikin as her driver. Lucy's brother Don Carlos and his wife, Agnes, and their one-year-old daughter, Agnes, and new little daughter, Sophronia, would also join them in New Portage. And then, in Far West, a thousand miles away, Lucy hoped to be reunited with her dear brother Joseph and his family.

Katharine's husband, Wilkins, drove one wagon, and her brother William drove the second, and the third was driven by her sister Sophronia's new husband, William McCleary. The road southwest of Kirtland was wet, but the fields were green under the morning sun. It seemed that all of the colors that Lucy had been missing during the winter found their way onto the wide fields of Ohio, in shades of green, yellow, rose, and violet. Overhead the sky was a deep blue, and as the sun began to set on that first day, Lucy pointed out to her little nieces and nephew how a line of clouds, tinged with yellow and crowned with gold, stood brightly against the deepening blue and purple sky.

They were on their way to Far West.

Old Charlie – May 14

FAR WEST, MISSOURI
Monday, May 14, 1838

Joseph Smith, May 12, 1838: "President Rigdon and myself attended the High Council for the purpose of presenting for their consideration some business relating to our pecuniary concerns. We stated to the Council our situation, as to maintaining our families, and the relation we now stand in to the Church, spending as we have for eight years, our time, talents, and property, in the service of the Church: and being reduced as it were to beggary, and being still detained in the business and service of the Church, it appears necessary that something should be done for the support of our families by the Church, or else we must do it by our own labors. . ."[48]

Joseph Smith, May 14, 1838: "I spent the day in plowing my garden."[49]

Spring's a good time. I was out just croppin' some fresh grass, nice and easy, in the pasture behind the log house they say belongs to the man called Harris. He's got one of

---

[48] HC 3:31

[49] HC 3:33

the biggest houses in Far West, but more and more are bein' built every day. Seems like I can hear the bangin' of hammers from dawn to dusk. This is nice country, this Zion, in the spring. The roads are pretty flat, more certain for my hooves than them bumpy corduroy roads in Indiana. Here it's all open prairie, with lots of trees down in the creek bottoms, but open spaces on the tops of the rollin' hills, and fields and fields of standin' grass and crops. There aren't no mountains, and no big rivers. Far West sets atop a big hill, between two streams, one they call Goose Creek and one they call Shoal Creek. I already know most of Far West, as Brother Joe likes to ride out every day to "take the prospect," as he says.

After such a frosty winter, the spring rains and green felt mighty good to a horse, especially seein' what a warm land Missouri is. It's hard to explain, but somehow the air seems wetter. But the wet air makes the grass greener, and I was havin' a fine feed among the tender grass behind Harris's house. Harris has a nice string of horses and a wagon and carriage for them to pull around. One of them is an old stallion Harris calls Commander. He is big and strong and keeps to hisself, but like any stallion wants to assert himself now and then, so Jim and I keep our distance. But the funny thing is there are these mares who also belong to Harris, and Commander gives in to the mares every time. He just obliges them when they want a spot of grass. Old Commander also likes to play with the colts and even the young foals. There are a few of those in Harris's field.

While I was grazing, Brother Joe come out of Harris's house, where he and Lady Emma and the young'uns are stayin', and hitched me and Jim up to his old wagon, the one he brung all the way from Kirtland. At first I wondered if we was headin' off to another camp, or maybe even back the whole way to Kirtland, but then Lady Emma and the young ones—Julia, Little Joseph and Freddie—all come outside without their bags and what not, and I knowed we was jest goin' out for a ride. Lady Emma walked mighty slow and looked very big around the middle. Brother Joe piled the young'uns in the back with two or three shovels and hoes and other man tools he brung down from Harris's barn and some canvas bags stuffed with somethin', and we headed off. Old Major follered right along behind the wagon.

Harris lives a mile west from the main part of Far West. The streets is nothin' much, just sticks in the ground and some prairie dirt kicked up and smoothed over, but here and there are men bangin' and workin' on stacks of wood they are makin' into houses. Brigham seems to be workin' on every house bein' built in the city, includin' the one that belongs to Brother Joe.

I really enjoy jest grazin' alongside Brother Joe when he's workin'. He's ridden me over to his new house most days, and he has done a mighty lot of work, helpin' Brigham, knockin' in nails, plowin' the ground, and draggin' boards here and there. He's laid out a vegetable garden and planted a tree or two. He's jest settin' to rights everythin' about this new place. Brother Joe seems to enjoy workin' with his hands, and on the days he is here at his new place, he has an easiness about him.

It's only now and then that Brother Joe has the time to be hammerin' nails. He's too busy ridin' out with me to see the men and women pullin' up in wagons and buildin' houses of their own, or speakin' at meetin's here and there in the countryside.

Brother Joe parked the rig by the new house and unhitched Jim and me. Brigham and a couple of other fellers were there, bangin' away with their hammers, liftin' up boards, and knockin' in nails. The new house is made out of wood and is already high off the ground, with a big porch and lots of windows. Jim stayed by the wagon in the shade of the building, grazin', but I followed Brother Joe and Lady Emma and the little ones around to the back, where there is a big piece of prairie that has had a plow run through it.

I was just grazin' easily near Brother Joe as he worked with the hoe and shovel in his hands. The young ones were scamperin' off down the furrows, and Lady Emma had a long hoe in her hands and was workin' the ground right gingerly, stoppin' now and then to put her hand on her stomach. The wind was blowin' warm, and her hair came loose a bit on top, and she lifted her hand to brush it from her face.

Brother Joe stopped his diggin' a bit and turned to Lady Emma and said, "All we had to do back in Kirtland was to light a cook fire and put out the dog." Then he laughed. "But this settling a new country is a different matter." Then he laughed again.

Lady Emma smiled and said, "I prefer settling."

JULIA – MAY 16

FAR WEST, MISSOURI
Wednesday, May 16, 1838

Lacy Rigdon sat on her rocking horse eating an early strawberry. It was afternoon, and Julia had been sent to play at the Rigdons by Mother, who wanted to rest. Mother was getting very close to delivering the new baby and seemed very tired, especially since Father had left to ride to the north country. Julia sat on the floor, playing with one of Lacy's many dolls.

The Rigdons lived in a new house directly across the street from the temple square on West Main Street.

"I found out more about you," said Lacy, rocking back and forth and looking at Julia. "About your parents."

"Well, I don't want to know," said Julia, putting the doll down. "It's none of your business who my parents are. Joseph and Emma Smith are my parents."

"My mother said that they're not your parents," said Lacy. "They adopted you."

"Well I don't want to talk about it," said Julia, angrily, standing up. "They're my parents, and I have two little brothers, and my mother will soon have another baby, and she'll be my sister, or if it's a boy, he'll be my brother."

Sister Rigdon walked into the house and removed her sunbonnet. Her stomach protruded very visibly from beneath her long, calico dress. "Well hello, Julia," she said.

"Hello, Sister Rigdon," said Julia, still standing on her feet, her cheeks flushed with anger and hurt and fear. "I'm just leaving."

"Oh, I'm sorry. You must tell your mother hello for me. I hope all is well with her baby. We will have new babies close to the same time!"

"Mama," said Lacy, still riding her rocking horse. She had finished her strawberry, and her lips were red and a trickle of juice ran down from the corner of her mouth. "Julia doesn't believe the secret about her."

Sister Rigdon looked sharply at her daughter and tilted her head slightly. "I don't know what secret you mean, Lacy."

"You know, Mama."

Sister Rigdon was staring into her daughter's eyes and shook her head very subtly.

"Lacy, you shouldn't . . ."

"You know, about her not being born to Sister Smith."

Sister Rigdon sat down on the chair and closed her eyes, then opened them and looked at Julia, who had tears running down her cheeks.

"I don't want to know," said Julia.

"You should know, dear," said Sister Rigdon. "And I'll tell you."

Julia stood facing Sister Rigdon. She could feel her hands shaking.

"When you were born, you had a twin brother. And then your real mother died, and your real father gave you to Joseph and Emma Smith to raise, because they had just had twin babies who had died."

"Where are my other brothers?" Julia felt the tears pouring down her cheeks.

Sister Rigdon hesitated. "I don't feel right telling you. I'm sorry Lacy said anything. Maybe you should ask your mother."

"I can't ask my mother," said Julia. "I just can't."

"She's not your mother," said Lacy Rigdon.

Julia Smith ran from the room and out into the sunlight.

OLD CHARLIE – MAY 18

FAR WEST, MISSOURI
Friday, May 18, 1838

Joseph Smith: "Friday, May 18. I left Far West, in company with Sidney Rigdon, Thomas B. Marsh, David W. Patten, Bishop Partridge, Elias Higbee, Simeon Carter, Alanson Ripley, and many others, for the purpose of visiting the north country, and laying off a stake of Zion; making locations, and laying claim to lands to facilitate the gathering of the Saints, and for the benefit of the poor, in upholding the Church of God. We traveled to the mouth of Honey Creek, which is a tributary of Grand River, where we camped for the night. We passed through a beautiful country the greater part of which is prairie, and thickly covered with grass and weeds, among which is plenty of game, such as deer, turkey, and prairie hen. We discovered a large, black wolf, and my dog gave him chase, but he outran us. We have nothing to fear in camping out, except the rattlesnake, which is native to this country, though not very numerous. We turned our horses loose, and let them feed on the prairie."[50]

"Thursday, 24. This morning the company returned to Grove Creek to finish the survey, accompanied by President Rigdon and Colonel Wight, and I returned to Far West."[51]

---

[50] HC 3:34
[51] HC 3:37

"Monday, 28. The company started for home, and I left Far West the same day in company with Brother Hyrum Smith and fifteen or twenty others, to seek locations in the north, and about noon we met President Rigdon and his company going into the city, where they arrived the same evening. President Hyrum Smith returned to Far West on the 30th, and I returned on the 1st of June, on account of my family, for I had a son born unto me on June 2nd."[52]

In 1838 Apostle David W. Patten was chosen as captain of the cavalry in the predominantly Mormon Caldwell County Militia. The Saints were soon calling Patten "Captain Fearnot" because of his boldness and bravery.[53]

Joseph Smith, III: "While I can remember some things which happened at Far West the fall I was six years old, the incidents of the . . . settlement there seem very obscure. I seem to see a two-story frame building standing broadside to an open space like a square, and some excitement going on outside. I remember Father starting away from the house and our white dog, Major, jumping from an upper window to a platform below to follow him off."[54]

This mornin' I was grazin' in Brother Joe's prairie meadow, right 'longside that feller Harris's house,

---

[52] HC 3:37

[53] Linda Shelley Whiting, David W. Patten: Apostle and Martyr (Cedar Fort: Springville, Utah 2003) 129, 144, 146.

[54] *The Saints' Herald,* November 6, 1934, 1414

where Brother Joe and all is stayin'. It was fine weather in Far West, and I could see the blue sky with nary a cloud any which way I turned. Harris's place is all wood and fresh-smellin' white, with lots of windows and a big front porch where Lady Emma likes to sit in a rockin' chair. She is gettin' right stout in the middle and moves slowly here and there, and she loves jest settin' out on that porch of an afternoon, watchin' Brother Joe work in the garden or while the young uns' play in the prairie grass. Above Lady Emma's porch there's this little roof and two windows above that. Through the block and across Main Street from the house is a big square, where the fellers is diggin' this big hole in the ground. What the hole is for, I couldn't tell you, but every day two or three of 'em is over there diggin' away. Next to the hole is a new schoolhouse, where the saints also gather of a Sunday for preachin'. Jest through the square is Brother Sidney's big new house, with eight, ten windows lookin' out over the square. I could hear the sounds of hammers bangin' away on other new houses here and there. I knowed Brother Joe was inside the house, and I couldn't help wonderin' what he could be a-doin' all mornin'. He usually come outside early for a long ride 'round about Far West, but I ain't seen a sign of him since yesterday.

The back door to the house opened, and Little Joseph come runnin' out, with the white dog, Major, follerin' right along behind him, barkin'. It was sorta comical to see them two—Little Joseph barely as high as my hind leg and that durned dog, bigger'n most men I ever seen. But Little Joseph knew how to handle the critter. I watched from the meadow fence as Little Joseph picked up a big stick and threw it as far as he could, then Major would run out barkin', tryin' to catch the dad-burned thing. After he brung it back to Little Joseph, they started the same thing over—throw, fetch, throw, fetch.

Suddenly I see'd the dust of horsemen comin' up Main Street. Turned out there was ten, twelve of 'em, ridin' right up to Brother Joe's house. Well, when they got close in, Major jest set to barkin' and growlin', like he always does when strangers come to set foot on Brother Joe's place. First thing I noticed, the horses was loaded up for a trip. That was plain, 'cause there was bedrolls and saddlebags and whatnot slung over behind all of the saddles. Among the riders, I see'd Brother Hyrum, ridin' on Sam, and a bunch of others I knowed from Kirtland. All the men dismounted and tied up in front of Brother Joe's place, but Major warn't happy about it and was growlin' somethin' fierce. Pretty soon Brother Joe come out of the house and shouted at the big dog, "Major! Shush! Shush!" And Major quieted right down. Then Brother Joe turned to Little Joseph and said, "Take Major inside and shut him in the upstairs room."

Little Joe took Major inside, and then Brother Joe walked over and said hello to all them fellers, slapping a few of 'em on the back and whatnot. I noticed one of the men who was the last to dismount kinda' holdin' back, I guess. He was wearin' a dusty soldier's uniform, all blue with yellow buttons and a blue hat, and he gave his horse to one of the other fellers and walked over to Brother Joe, who threw his arms around him.

"David!" said Brother Joe as he clapped him on his back! "But I hear they're all callin' you Captain Fearnot now!"

The man in the blue uniform looked kinda embarrassed, and he took off his hat and smiled, scratchin' his head. I see'd that he was covered in dust from head to foot, and when I looked at his horse, I could see they'd come far.

Well, Brother Joe took Captain Fearnot and Brother Hyrum and all them other fellers into his house for a spell. I could hear 'em all through the open windows downstairs, talkin' and laughin' and I could hear the clink of glasses and plates, so I knowed Lady Emma must be feedin' 'em all somethin'. From upstairs, I also heared Major a-barkin' away, and I see'd him a time or two jumpin' up to the open window, so I knowed Little Joseph must've locked him in the room so as not to bark at them fellers visitin' downstairs.

After a while Brother Joe came out of the house with Captain Fearnot and all them other fellers. I could tell that we was ridin' out, 'cause Brother Joe had his gear all slung over his shoulder. He saddled me up and said goodbye to Lady Emma and the young'uns and we started out. There was Brother Hyrum ridin' Sam, Brother Sidney on Champ, and about ten, twelve others.

Well, we hadn't ridden spit down Main Street, when I heared a holy racket behind us. It was Major barkin' like thunder up in the window of Brother Joe's place. He turned me around to look, and I see'd Major jump right out of the window onto the porch roof, and then down off the roof onto a pile of wood leanin' by the side of the house and come runnin' to join up with us. All the men laughed. Little Joseph came a runnin' to fetch Major back to the house, but Brother Joe said, "It's all right, Joseph. Let Major come with us. Ride with me a spell and then go back home. You can watch out over things while we're gone."

Outside Far West Brother Joe set to ridin' between Captain Fearnot, ridin' a big chesnut gelding called Hannibal, and a short, little man called Wight, who was ridin' a big smoky black stallion, real young and barely saddle broke, called Fireball. That black stallion started off real jumpy and excited, but settled down on the road.

I said road, but there really warn't no proper road, only the rollin' hills of prairie with the weather clear, all calm and nary a cloud in the sky. And all the horses was just spread out, gallopin' easy. Then, Sam let out a snort, and reared sideways, then kind of roared. The others rode near, and I seen on the ground a long snake, with his tail just a quiverin', and lettin' out a rattle. So we watched the ground real careful after that, and now and then see'd snakes, but they didn't bother us none, so we let 'em be.

We came to a little creek, then rode on through, the water not even touchin' our bellies, and come up on the other side. There we smelled somethin' comin' down the wind, somethin' strange and wild, and at the same moment Major started up a barkin' like I never heared from him, and took off on a full run up and over a little hill. Brother Joe, who is never one to shy away, kicked me up, and we follered on a gallop, and over the rise I see'd a big, black wolf on a full run, with Major in his tracks. We chased him for a quarter mile, but the wolf outran us, so Brother Joe and me turned around and trotted back to the others, with big Major runnin' beside.

There we stopped for the night, and the Brethren rolled out their bedrolls and tents and started up their cookin' fires. They set us loose on the prairie, and Sam and me and the others just grazed.

About sunset, I just stood on the hill, with no saddle, feelin' free. Before he turned in, just as the stars was comin' out, Brother Joe walked out over the prairie to where I stood. I nuzzled him, and he stroked my neck and reached out a nice piece of molasses candy from his pocket.

LITTLE JOSEPH – MAY 23

FAR WEST, MISSOURI
Wednesday, May 23, 1838

Joseph Smith, III: "There comes to mind a circumstance which occurred about this time which was attended by some degree of mystery. It was my habit to take a nap in the afternoons upon a bed or couch in the bedroom. The house had two rooms, one the living or 'keeping' room and the other a bedroom. Into this latter the door leading from the keeping room opened inwardly, opposite a window in the end of the building. My mother was washing in the larger room and I, lying upon the bed in the chamber, was awakened by someone coming through the door and across the room past me. It was a man apparently from thirty-five to forty-five years of age, sparely built, wearing dark clothing somewhat shabby, and having on his head a rather tall-crowned hat, napless as was the custom of the time. He passed to the window and turned to come back toward the door, saying as he did so, 'We will all have to go to the land of Voree.' Reaching the door he turned again and came back toward the window. As he turned at the window the second time to again pass by the bed he repeated what he had said before, 'We will all have to go to the land of Voree.'. . . When the man returned to the door the second time he passed out, as I supposed, into the room where my mother was. I called to her and asked her who the man was. She wanted to know to what man I referred. I told her about the man I had seen in the room and repeated what he had said. She had not seen him, nor did either of us see him after, though we went at once to the door to look for him. He was fairly tall,

being a little over medium height, and had a clean-shaven face. I relate the circumstance because it impressed me at the time and because it is a mystery that has never since been solved."[55]

"Will you bring me a bucket of clean water from the well?" called Mother from the doorway of their house. "I'm going to wash a few clothes."

"Yes, Mother," said Little Joseph, who had been playing in the yard with his cousin, John Smith. "John will help me." John was just Joseph's age and the son of his Uncle Hyrum.

The two little boys carried the largest bucket from the side of the house to the well and lowered it down the shaft with a long rope into the darkness, then brought it back up. They each took a side of the handle and carried it into the house.

"Don't let the water slop on the floor," said Mother. "Thank you, boys."

Later that afternoon, Little Joseph was sleepy, and he decided to take a little nap on his parents' bed, which was his habit most afternoons. Father and Mother's new house in Far West stood about two hundred yards from the temple foundation and had two rooms. One was the living or "keeping" room, where the family gathered for meals or for visiting or work of various kinds. For example, Mother sat for hours sewing in the keeping room with Julia and with many women who came to visit. Or she would prepare food.

---

[55] The Saints' Herald, November 6, 1934, 1415

Or, like today, she would do the wash. Father would shell peas, or slice fruit, or do other chores for Mother. And some days he would work on his Church papers. Since they arrived in Far West, he had begun to write a personal and Church history, and Little Joseph loved to watch him sitting at the table writing or dictating his history to Brother George Robinson, his scribe. Little Joseph loved to whittle, using a little jackknife that his father had given him. Mother made him lay out a handkerchief on the floor to catch the shavings, which he would later throw in the fire or carry outside.

The second room in the house was a bedroom, where straw mattresses were set in wooden bed frames. Little Joseph shared a bed with his little brother, Freddie. Julia had a little bed. And Mother and Father had a large bed, covered with a blue and white patterned quilt, which Mother had made. Little Joseph loved to lie on this quilt to take naps every afternoon. It was cool and quiet, and he loved lying on the quilt listening to the gentle sounds of quiet conversation coming from the keeping room or watching the pattern of sunlight reflecting through the panes of the window.

There was a door leading from the keeping room to the bedroom, which Little Joseph closed, and then he climbed up onto his mother's bed. There was a window opposite the door, through which soft light came from the outside. The window was open, letting in a gentle breeze. Little Joseph drifted off to sleep.

Suddenly, he was awakened by someone who came through the door from the keeping room and walked past the bed. Little Joseph opened his eyes and saw a strange man. He was about thirty-five to forty-five years old, wearing very shabby dark clothing. On his head he had a very tall hat.

Little Joseph sat up in surprise as the man walked to the window opposite the door. Then he turned around and walked back toward the door. As he walked past Little Joseph the second time, he said, "We will all have to go to the land of Voree."

"What?" said Little Joseph.

The man walked to the doorway, then turned and looked at Little Joseph. He was fairly tall and thin, with a clean-shaven face and had very bright, dark eyes. He then walked to the window, then turned again and walked back to the door. "We will all have to go to the land of Voree," he repeated. He then walked through the door into the keeping room.

Little Joseph sat on his bed in astonishment. He had never seen this man in his life. After a moment, he climbed off the bed and ran to the door.

In the keeping room, Mother was working, wringing out clothes from the wash bucket.

"Who was that man, Mother?" asked Little Joseph.

"What man?"

"The man who just walked into the bedroom, then back into the keeping room.

"I haven't seen any man, dear."

Little Joseph told her about the man. They both stepped outside into the yard and looked up and down the streets, but could see no one.

"Maybe you were dreaming," said Mother as they returned to the keeping room.

"No, I was awake. I'm sure of it."

Little Joseph pondered this mystery, but had no answer for it.

Julia – June 1

FAR WEST, MISSOURI
Friday, June 1, 1838

Joseph Smith: "President Hyrum Smith returned to Far West on the 30th, and I returned on the 1st of June, on account of my family, for I had a son born unto me on June 2nd."[56]

Julia stood out on the prairie on a little hill along the road. From here she could see all the roofs and chimneys of Far West and the big, open square in the center of town. There was a great hole in the ground, where the men had been digging a cellar for the new temple. She could also see Lacy Rigdon's big house facing the square.

Lacy Rigdon. Julia thought about Lacy and her mother. Sister Rigdon knew who Julia's older brothers were. Everyone must know. Everyone but Julia herself. She felt the anger rise in her throat, like some nasty tasting medicine, and she felt the tears come again to her eyes.

"Julia," called a familiar voice behind her. "Julia."

---

[56] HC 3:37

She turned and saw Father on Old Charlie, riding down the road. Major barked and came running into the yard. The big dog bounded up to her and licked her face.

"Climb up, and I'll give you a ride home," said Father. He reached down from the saddle and with a strong arm lifted Julia up into the saddle in front of him.

"Are you crying?" he asked. "What happened?"

"Nevermind," said Julia, turning to hug her father.

At home, Julia's father hugged her mother and her brothers, then they all sat in the keeping room. Mother was tired and rocked quietly in the chair.

"How are you feeling?" Father asked.

"Big," smiled Mother. "Tired. Glad to see you. That's all."

Father said, "Let me tell you children about a place called Adam-ondi-Ahman."

"What does that mean?" asked Little Joseph.

"I'll tell you," said Father. "It's a place where we have laid off a new stake of Zion for the gathering of the saints. When we left here last Friday, we first traveled to the mouth of Honey Creek, which flows into the Grand River."

"Does it taste like honey?" asked Freddie.

"Shh," said Mother to the little boy. "Let Father tell us."

"No, Freddie," said Father. "But it tastes clean. We passed through a beautiful country as we rode north. Most of it was prairie, but there are groves of fine trees. The prairie is thickly covered with grass and wild flowers. There is plenty of game, such as deer and turkey and prairie hen.

On the first day we discovered a big black wolf, and Major chased him."

"Did you catch the wolf?" asked Little Joseph.

"No. He outran us. We camped on the prairie. You should have seen the sunsets. We had nothing to fear, except a few rattlesnakes here and there. We just turned Old Charlie and the other horses loose and let them feed on the prairie the first night."

"Did the wolf and rattlesnakes come back?" asked Freddie.

"Nope," said Father. "We slept like babies. The next day we struck camp and rode in a single line across the Grand River. It's a wide, beautiful, and deep stream. Old Charlie had to swim across in the deepest part. Then we went in a line up the other bank through timber about eighteen miles until we arrived at the cabin of Colonel Lyman Wight. We arrived there Saturday night and camped for the Sabbath."

"Is there a church there?" asked Little Joseph.

"No. But there is a beautiful hill shaped with high rocks, which I called Tower Hill, and there were the remains of an old altar. I suppose it was a Nephite altar. It was a very special place. Before sundown on Saturday I went further up the river about a half a mile to a place Brother Wight called Spring Hill. But as I was there, I had a revelation." Here the Prophet swallowed.

The family was silent, and looked intently at Joseph Smith.

"I had a revelation on that hill, that by the mouth of the Lord the place is named Adam-ondi-Ahman, because it is the place where Adam will come to visit his people."

"Why will he come to visit his people?" asked Julia.

"Because we are his children," said Father. "Adam and Eve are the father and mother of all mankind."

"Joseph!" called Mother, her face twisted in pain.

"What is it, Emma?"

"I think it's time!"

"What time, Mother?" asked Julia.

"The baby will come soon," said Mother, as Father helped her stand up and walk toward the bedroom. "You're going to be a big sister again."

LUCY – JUNE 4

INDIANA
Monday, June 4, 1838

Lucy Mack Smith: "We traveled on through many trials and difficulties. Sometimes we lay in our tents through a driving storm. At other times we traveled on foot through marshes and quagmires, exposing ourselves to wet and cold. Once we lay all night in the rain, which descended in torrents, and I, being more exposed than the other females, suffered much with the cold, and upon getting up in the morning, I found that a quilted skirt which I had worn the day before was wringing wet, but I could not mend the matter by changing that for another, for the rain was still falling."[57]

The crack of lightning awoke the family in the night, and then a torrent of rain descended. Lucy woke up with a start. Two-year-old Solomon woke up, too, and started to cry. Lucy crawled over to him and picked him up to comfort him. The other children all awoke and peeked out from under their blankets with wide eyes. Lucy thought they looked like little baby robins in their nest, looking out and waiting for mother to come feed them or comfort them.

---

[57] *History of Joseph Smith by His Mother, 358*

Through the canvas top of the wagon, Lucy heard the men, her brothers William and Samuel and Don Carlos and her brother-in-law Wilkins calming the animals and tying down wagon tops more securely as the rain began to fall in torrents.

They were nearly a month on the road, moving slowly with so many little children, and were somewhere in Indiana. Lucy was bone weary, and she was sure all the others were as well. During the journey, she had adopted the role of supervising the older children together, and space had been made in Papa's wagon for them to sleep with Lucy. This freed the mothers and fathers to tend to their own wagons and get good rest, as the days were long and the journey exhausting.

Suddenly a gust of wind tore the cover off of Papa's wagon, and the children started to get drenched in the rain.

"The wagon cover!" shouted William, climbing up on the side of Papa's wagon. "Don Carlos! Help me!" Lucy gathered up the children in the center of the wagon, where they sat huddled together as their uncles tied the wagon top down again with strong ropes.

"Is this a cataract?" asked little six-year-old Mariah.

"Yes," laughed Lucy. "This is a cataract."

"And the rain is falling perpendicular," laughed Mary Jane, hugging Lucy.

"You're right," said Lucy. "It looks perpendicular to me, too!"

"I can feel it blowing sideways," said three-year-old Lucy, "right into my face."

Several of the children laughed nervously, but most of them were frightened and clung to Lucy.

The rain fell in great drops, which soon churned up a deep mud all about. Lucy's sister Katharine, due to give birth any day, was lying in the second wagon, and her sister-in-law Agnes was lying in the third wagon with her new baby and one-year-old daughter. There was no more room in the wagons. The men and Mama were making do outside in the rain.

"Mama! Climb into the wagon with me and the little ones!" called Lucy to her mother.

"No," said Mama. "There's no room!"

"We can squash up!" shouted Lucy, but even as she said it she knew it wouldn't work. She was sitting by the open end of the canvas and was already getting soaked as it was.

"No," said Mama. "I'll be fine out here. The little ones need to keep dry. You stay there with them. I'll climb under one of the wagons and make do with this tarpaulin." Lucy bit her lip and watched with alarm, as her parents crawled slowly beneath William's wagon, and covered themselves with a small piece of canvas. The rain was blowing sideways and the tarpaulin was doing little good, and the water was running in rivulets on the ground. Mama and Papa were literally sitting in mud on the ground.

In the morning, Lucy emerged from underneath the wagon cover. It was growing light, and everything was quiet and bitterly cold. It had stopped raining, but everything— the ground, the trees, and the canvas wagon covers—was wet. The horses and mules were huddling together in bunches behind Don Carlos's wagon. The sky was still threatening, and Lucy watched as patches of dark clouds raced across the dim glow of approaching sunrise. It looked to be another very wet day on the road in Indiana.

Then Lucy saw her mother, who was trying to crawl out from under William's wagon. She struggled through the mud and stood up. Papa followed her and soon had started a fire. Lucy watched as her Mama stood by the growing flames, shivering quietly. She was wearing her long, quilted skirt, out of which she was wringing water as she stood.

"Mama," called Lucy quietly, so as not to wake the little ones. "You're soaked through to the skin!"

"No matter," said Mama, twisting the hem of her skirt again, which produced great drops of water on the ground. "I'm all right. Just a little water. Water never hurt anybody."

Lucy – June 7

ON THE BANK OF THE MISSISSIPPI RIVER
Thursday, June 7, 1838

Lucy Mack Smith: "I took a severe cold and was very sick, so that when we arrived at the Mississippi I was unable to sit up at any length and could not walk without assistance. After we crossed this river, we stopped at a Negro hut, a most unlovely place, but we could go no farther. Here my daughter Katharine gave birth to a fine son."[58]

For the next three days the travelers pressed on through storm after storm. They were unable to stop for more that a few hours or to change clothes, as all of their belongings were soaking wet.

Lucy noticed that her mother was coughing now. "Mother," said Lucy. "You've taken cold."

"I'm fine, daughter," said Mother Smith.

But Mother Smith was unable to sit up for any length of time, and could not walk without the assistance of her husband or one of the other men. She lay in one wagon bed, and Lucy's sister Katharine, who was already experiencing the birth pains for her child, was lying in another wagon.

---

[58] *History of Joseph Smith by His Mother,* 358

They had traveled all the way to the Mississippi River, and waited several hours until a ferry could carry the three wagons and teams safely across the wide river.

"Is this river a mile wide?" asked Mary Jane, wide eyed, as the men drove the wagon onto the wooden ferry.

"It's more than a mile," said Lucy.

"Is there a cataract here, too?" asked Mariah. "Will we fall over the edge perpendicular?"

"No, dear," smiled Lucy.

On the other side, as the wagons were being driven up the bank, Katharine called out sharply. Lucy could tell that she was in serious pain.

A short distance from the bank Wilkins called out in alarm, "We need to find a place now. The baby is coming!"

The other travelers stopped and looked around in alarm. "There is no place!" said Samuel. "We are far from any settlement."

"There is a hut over there on the prairie," said William McCleary.

"It's the only place," said Sophronia. "It will have to do."

It was just a little hut, patched together of drift logs and blocks of prairie sod. As the Smith wagons rode up in front, Lucy was surprised to see an African man and woman step outside from the low doorway, looking frightened. They were wearing the simplest of clothes, obviously hand woven.

"No trouble! No trouble!" cried the man, smiling at the travelers. "We want no trouble, now." As he spoke, a little girl, wearing a brown homespun shift, walked out between her parents and stared at the Smith family.

"They may be slaves," whispered Wilkins Salisbury. "Or more likely, free blacks trying to make a start."

"My daughter is about to deliver a baby," called Mama to the man. "May she find shelter in your house?"

He stood there looking uncertain.

"We don't mean you any harm," said Don Carlos, climbing down from the wagon and shaking the man's hand. "See? My sister is having a baby. She's having a baby, and needs a place."

Katharine gave out another cry of pain as a new contraction started.

"Oh, a baby!" said the black woman, realizing what was wanted. "A baby coming?" Lucy nodded at her. The woman smiled and took control of the situation, helping Katharine down from the wagon and leading her through the low doorway, into the hut.

Lucy waited outside with the little children, while the men made a camp not far from the hut. Lucy tried to keep the children occupied with games. They stood in a circle and played several games of "Drop the Handkerchief" and then "Blind Man's Bluff." The little black girl came and joined in. All the while, Lucy could hear the voice of her sister, crying in pain but with a resolute quality in it. Sophronia, Agnes, and Mother Smith were with her.

After only an hour or so, Lucy heard the cry of a baby, and everyone outside clapped and cheered.

That evening Lucy went in to see her new nephew, Alvin Salisbury. Inside the hut, Lucy found a place to sit. It was small, with no glass windows, only a hole to allow in air and light. There was a chimney made of rough stone and mud, and the floor was dirt. But it was out of the cold. There were two candles lit in the room, and through the soft candlelight she saw the smile of her sister.

ARTHUR – JUNE 8

KIRTLAND, OHIO
Friday, June 8, 1838

Benjamin F. Johnson: "The Bank having issued its currency in confidence now began to comprehend that its specie vaults were empty, with no possibility to realize upon collateral to replenish them. The spirit of charity was not invoked, and brethren who had borne the highest priesthood and who had for years labored, traveled, ministered and suffered together, and even placed their lives upon the same altar, now ere governed by a feeling of hate and a spirit to accuse each other, and all for the love of Accursed Mammon. All their former companionship in the holy anointing in the Temple of the Lord, where filled with the Holy Ghost, the heavens were opened, and in view of the glories before them they had together shouted, 'Hosanna to God and the Lamp', all was now forgotten by many, who were like Judas, ready to sell or destroy the Prophet Joseph and his followers. And it almost seemed to me that the brightest stars in our firmament had fallen."[59]

Uncle Nathaniel was angry. Arthur saw that at once. As he entered his uncle's house, Nathaniel Millikin

---

[59] Johnson, *My LIfe's Review*, 28-29

shoved away his breakfast of fried eggs, bacon, and bread with drippings of grease and looked at Arthur coldly. Beside him Warren Parrish sat with his feet up on the table beside an empty plate. He looked as if he found the scene amusing.

"So, what are you doing, nephew, helping the Josephites to slip out of Kirtland without paying their debts."

"What do you mean, Uncle," said Arthur.

"Just as I said," the old man said. "You've been fixing the wagons of those that owe me and others money, and then they ride out of town in the night."

"I only do an honest day's work for an honest wage, Uncle."

Nathaniel Millikin considered this for a moment, and then picked his fork back up and went back to eating his eggs.

"Your Uncle just wants to know where you stand, Arthur," said Warren Parrish. "Since you left home, he's not sure whose side you are on."

"I'm on no one's side, Uncle. I do my work. That's all."

"Hmmph," said Uncle Nathaniel. "Well, I'll be wanting you to do me a favor. Can you do that?"

"Sure," said Arthur. "I'm indebted to you for your kindness to me in years past. What can I do for you?"

"You can tell me who is fixing to pull up stakes and flee Kirtland. That way I can—what shall we say?—'help' them dispose of their property before they leave."

Arthur stood and stared at his Uncle as at a foreigner whose language he didn't understand.

"What he's trying to tell you, Arthur," said Warren Parrish, chewing on a toothpick, "Is that you and him and all of us can advance ourselves a little through all of this. We can pick up some bargains here and there instead of leaving things to the Bank."

"I don't really understand what you're wanting me to do," said Arthur. "But I don't want any part of it. I'm a craftsman, plain and simple. I want a simple wage for a simple day of labor."

"You've been seduced by the false doctrine of the Josephites!" shouted Nathaniel Millikin. "My brother would be ashamed of you, as I am."

"I haven't been seduced by anything or anybody," said Arthur, his voice rising. "And I'm not going to be ordered about by you or anybody, meaning no disrespect. I'm a grown man now and will make my own decisions."

Arthur left his uncle's house and put on his hat. Out in the street a group of boys ran past him toward the river with fishing poles in their hands, but otherwise the street was empty. He walked past the Whitney store, which had hardly a barrel on the porch. Money was tight in the village and trade had plummeted to almost nothing. No one was paying, and no one was earning, and everyone was feeling it. He walked up the hill to Badham's blacksmith shop and saw his old boss sitting on a barrel on the street.

"Any business for you today, Arthur?" he called out, squinting one eye in red face in the bright sunlight.

"Not much, sir," said Arthur. "I'm helping Joseph Young with his wagon wheels, but nothing much is coming in."

"That reminds me," said Mr. Badham. "Your rent is coming due again, and you still owe me for last month."

"I know," said Arthur. "I promise I'll pay. I have promissory notes for thirty-five dollars in my pocket."

"You told me already," said Badham, squinting at him. "Promissory notes from folks that can't pay—or have already up and left and followed Joseph Smith to his land of Zion."

"I promise to pay," said Arthur again, and then walked back to his little shed behind the shop. Inside, the light from a single pane of glass cast a patch of sunlight on his low bed. He sat down and surveyed all of his earthly belongings—two pairs of boots, two pairs of trousers, three shirts, a sharp jackknife, a wooden box holding his carpentry tools, and a small bookcase holding a few books. What he hadn't told Mr. Badham was that he had no work this week, and maybe none next, that he had no money, and no food. Arthur ran his fingers over the spines of the books—Murray's English Reader, an Almanac from 1835, and a copy of the Book of Mormon with a deeply scratched cover. He pulled this from the shelf and opened it up and read aloud: "Wherefore, whose believeth in God might with surety hope for a better world, yea, even a place at the right hand of God, which hope cometh of faith, maketh an anchor to the souls of men."

He closed the book and sat in silence on his bed as the patch of sunlight moved from the bed to the opposite wall and then disappeared altogether. *An anchor*, thought Arthur. *What is my anchor?* As it grew dark, Arthur laid his head down on his ragged pillow and closed his eyes and thought of a girl far away, riding over a distant road, a girl with radiant blue eyes.

LUCY – JUNE 10

MISSOURI
Sunday, June 10, 1838

Lucy Mack Smith: "I washed a very large quantity of clothes with as much ease as though I had not been out of health at all. When the company was all gathered together, we started on our journey again and arrived at Far West without any further difficulty. Here we met Joseph and Hyrum in good health. They had heard by William and Carlos, who went into Far West before us, of my sickness and were surprised to see me in such good health as well. We moved into a small log house, having but one room, and a very inconvenient place for so large a family. When Joseph saw how we were situated, he proposed that we should take a large tavern house, which he had recently purchased from Brother Gilbert, and we did so. Samuel previous to this, had moved to a place called Marrowbone, Daviess County. William had moved thirty miles in another direction. We were all now quite comfortable."[60]

On Sunday, the sun finally came out.

Lucy Smith and Mama sat on a tarpaulin that Lucy had

---

[60] *History of Joseph Smith by His Mother, 359*

spread out on the prairie grass, surrounded by Mama's grandchildren. It was the Sabbath, and Lucy relished the feeling of being at rest.

"How are you feeling, Mama?" Lucy asked.

"Better, child. Much better."

It had been an event-filled week. First, Mama had taken ill after being exposed to the rain for several days. Then her sister Katharine had given birth to little Alvin on Thursday, June 7, in the humble home of former slaves, who gave all that they had to the travelers in need. The next day Lucy had walked with the older children, while her father drove Katharine and the baby and Lucy's mother, Lucy Mack Smith, in an open wagon to a better house, about four miles ahead. There Katharine and her husband were left with Sophronia and her husband to care for her, and Lucy had continued on with the children and her father and brothers to Huntsville to find a place for Mother Smith to rest.

Lucy's mother was no longer able to ride in a sitting position, but lay on a bedstead in the wagon, covered up. She was continually coughing.

Papa had put his arm around Lucy. "I don't think your mother will make it to Far West," he said. "She's dying."

At Huntsville, they found a house to stay in, and Mama was able to sleep in a bed.

Then the miracle occurred. After arriving in Huntsville, the family took the children out for a little walking excursion, leaving Mama to rest. When they returned back a few hours later, they found her in the house, gathering up clothes from the wagons and preparing to do a washing.

"What has happened, my wife?" asked Papa. "You are well again, and on your feet."

"The Lord has healed me," said Mother Smith. "I had an impression that if I could find a secluded place to pray uninterrupted, I might be healed. So when you all left, I seized upon that time and walked to that dense hazel grove across the field."

"But how did you get there, Mama?" asked Lucy. "You couldn't walk or even sit up for days."

"I picked up two long staffs, and walking with them, I reached the fence, and then followed the fence into the hazel thicket. There I threw myself on the ground. And there I lay, exhausted. I thought it didn't matter how far I was from the house, for if the Lord would not hear me and heal me, I must die, and I might as well do it in a grove of trees as anywhere. I lay on the ground and rested a little, then I knelt on my knees and commenced calling upon the Lord to beseech his mercy, praying for my health and for the life of my daughter Katharine and grandson Alvin. I urged every claim which the scriptures give us, with as much humility as I knew how to show, and I continued praying for nearly three hours."

Lucy looked at her father, who had tears in his eyes.

"At last," said Mama, "I felt a sudden relief from pain. My cough left me, and I was well."

"God be thanked," said Papa.

"And I received an assurance that we would hear from our sick daughter today. And so I arose and came back to the house to prepare to receive Katharine and the baby."

Just then, Lucy heard the sound of a carriage. They looked outside, and it was Wilkins Salisbury, bringing

Katharine and the baby, as well as Sophronia and her husband.

"God be thanked," said Papa again.

LUCY – JUNE 27

FAR WEST, MISSOURI
Wednesday, June 27, 1838

Lucy Smith walked to the house of her sister-in-law, Emma Smith, carrying a basket of early sweet peas and cucumbers. The streets were filled with people walking here and there, and everywhere Lucy was met with greetings.

Lucy loved Far West. They had arrived from Kirtland to find Lucy's brothers Joseph and Hyrum and their families in good health.

It had been a year of babies for Lucy, and she smiled as she walked, counting her nieces and nephews like pearls on a string. When she left Kirtland, she had five nephews and eleven nieces. But since January her sister-in-law Agnes had delivered little Sophronia, Katharine had delivered little Alvin, and Emma had delivered another son, Alexander Hale Smith. Lucy also thought of Samuel's wife, Mary, who was expecting by the end of the summer, and Hyrum's wife, Mary Fielding Smith, who was expecting a baby in the fall.

At Emma's house, Lucy found Emma was lying down with the baby, so she sat in the keeping room and began to shell the peas. Julia sat across the table and helped her.

"What a joyous year we are having," said Lucy brightly. "We do not have wealth or property, but we have a wealth of new babies."

"Little Alex is a dear baby," said Julia happily. "I have never been so happy. Seeing his tiny face and hands and even hearing his little cry in the night is so sweet."

"He has his father's blue eyes and light hair," said Lucy. "It is certain that he is the son of Joseph Smith."

Julia was silent. She bent over the bowl and continued to break open the pea pods, dropping the lovely green peas into the bowl. Finally she whispered, "Lucy, may I ask you something."

"Do you think Father and Mother love me as much as Little Joseph and Freddie and baby Alex?"

"Of course they do!"

"Even if I'm not their natural born daughter."

Lucy walked around to the other side of the table, sat down beside Julia and picked her up, just like she had done when she was a wee child, and placed her on her lap. Julia laughed at that, and then went back to her tears, but no words were said. Lucy simply held Julia tight in her arms, and kissed her head. Finally she said, "Your mother and father love you as much as anything in this world, just like I love you. They don't care if you were born to poor Sister Murdock; they are as much your parents and you are as much their child as if you had been born to Emma."

Julia laid her head back on Lucy's shoulder and let the tears flow.

Lovina – July 3

FAR WEST, MISSOURI
Tuesday, July 3, 1838

Lovina Smith sat on a hickory stump behind her father's new house in Far West, holding a long stem of prairie grass in her hand. She absently examined the little blue flowers on its stems, with six petals and a center of bright yellow. Old George, the family handyman, had told her it was called Blue-eyed Prairie Grass. He had picked her a bouquet of blue flowers as their wagon had rolled over the endless prairie and handed them to her over the side of the wagon box.

"Here," Old George had said, simply. "These are called Blue-eyed Prairie Grass."

In Illinois and Missouri, Lovina had seen more flowers than she knew how to name. At one point in her life, she would have been beyond excitement to see and gather all the flowers, but she now only felt a dullness. She had held the blue bouquet for twenty-five miles, then thrown it into the brown waters of a little shallow creek they had crossed, watching it swirl down stream.

Flowers had always been Lovina's joy. Her mother had loved flowers and tended a neat little bed beside the white picket fence in the kitchen garden. In Ohio they raised roses and iris and geraniums, not the twisted and brilliant and strange and marvelous wildflowers of the prairie. Each fall, Mother had carefully collected the seeds of the annual flowers in little paper packets, to be planted the next spring. She kept them in a special bundle hidden in the dark coolness of the cellar. As a girl, Lovina had loved helping her mother plant flowers, tend flowers, and then gather the seeds for planting the next spring. It had been a private ritual between mother and daughter. A few days before Mother had delivered little Sarah and then fallen sick and died, Lovina had helped her mother gather up and package next year's seeds and put them in their special cool and dry hiding place in the cellar.

Lovina sat on the stump and looked around her new home in Far West. The smell of freshly cut wood was in the air, both from the wood pile and from the piles of logs, boards, and planks laying everywhere on the prairie grass. The house was only partially finished, and there were materials piled everywhere.

The house would be a good one for her little brothers and sisters, thought Lovina. The air was clear, the sun warm, and the prairie covered with wildflowers. But for her, she felt only numbness.

The other children were inside the partially finished house with her father's new wife, Mary Fielding Smith. Lovina felt guilty to admit it, but she had lately not even wanted to be around Mary Fielding. Every time she tucked in a child to bed, every time she set food on the table, and every time her father kissed his new wife, Lovina felt a stab of bitterness. That ought to have been her mother, she thought.

Lovina threw the prairie flowers to the dirt and walked to the wagon sitting still in the yard behind the house. Climbing up into the wagon, she thought of the long days from March until May when this wagon, now motionless, was endlessly moving, day after day. Besides Lovina's family, including Old George and Aunty Grinnels, they were joined on the journey by her stepmother's sister and brother-in-law, Robert and Mercy Thompson from Canada. Lovina lay down in the wagon bed and watched a huge white cloud moving slowly across the deep blue sky.

They had set out in two large wagons, piled high with furniture and farming implements. Lovina remembered the day the wagons moved away from her house in Kirtland, the only home she could remember clearly. As the family climbed into the wagon, Lovina had suddenly remembered her mother's seed packet in the cellar and had run back into the house and brought it to the wagon. She had placed it in her little bag.

Their journey had taken them first to the Ohio and Erie Canal, where Father had sent all of their household furniture by boat to Quincy, Illinois. Then, with the wagons lightened, Lovina had sat day by day with her brothers John and Hyrum and her sisters Jerusha and baby Sarah as they traveled through Ohio, Indiana, and Illinois to the Mississippi River. Day after day, the wagon bounced along the dirt roads. Night after night, Lovina sat staring into the campfire, or later, at the net of stars high overhead.

During the long journey from Kirtland, Lovina had spent many hours pondering on the radiance of her mother, Jerusha Barden Smith. Mother had been gentle, faithful, unwavering. She was the center of the family life. It was a shock, a blow, a deep wound to have her taken so suddenly from them. Lovina spent several days rethinking her mother's swift illness—the birth of little Sarah, then her mother's fever and listlessness, the calling in of the women, then of the doctors—then her death, the funeral, and soon thereafter the marriage of her father to Mary Fielding. Why had this happened? One night on the journey, while the others slept, Lovina had laid awake far into the night, with tears in her eyes, praying to God, asking Him why, pleading with him, even bargaining with Him to bring back her mother.

As the wagon jarred violently over rocks, Lovina had often questioned herself. Interrogated herself. What could she have done? What should she have done to save her mother? She had focused upon the final day when her mother was very low, barely awake, and feverish. Aunty Grinnels had sent Lovina outside to fetch medicine from the store. On the way inside, Lovina had stumbled and dropped the vial of medicine on the back step, and it had broken. She ran back down the hill and got more medicine, hurrying back up the hill to her house. When she returned to her mother's bedside, Aunty Grinnels was angry. She had said, "What took you, girl?" then filled a spoon with the elixir for her mother.

That night her mother had died. *What if I hadn't stumbled?* Lovina often asked herself. *If I hadn't stumbled, she might still be alive. I'm to blame for her death.* Thoughts such as these echoed in her ten-year old head over and over during the long journey in the wagon.

"Lovina! Lovina!" It was Mary Fielding Smith calling from the back door. Lovina remained motionless in the back of the wagon. Lately she had not wanted to see her stepmother, especially since hearing the news that she was expecting a baby in the autumn. "Lovina! Come inside! I need you!" Mary Fielding Smith called again. Lovina lay still, watching the white cloud as in slow motion it seemed to boil and swirl against the blue.

Lovina asked herself why even hearing Mary Fielding's voice seemed to irritate and annoy her, even make her angry. It made her angry that Mary Fielding would be bearing her father's child, when her own mother lay in that cold grave in Ohio.

"What you be doing out here in the wagon, little lady?" She turned and saw Old George standing beside her. "Your stepmother be calling you, child."

"I know," said Lovina.

Old George held out his hand to steady the girl as she stepped onto the hub of the axle then to the ground. For a moment the old man and the little girl stood regarding each other. Old George was smiling sadly at her. He had his hand behind his back. She stood looking up into the grizzled face of Old George, who it had been said had served in the United States Army during the war with Great Britain.

Without a word, Old George produced from behind his back a bouquet of beautiful wildflowers.

LITTLE JOSEPH – JULY 3

FAR WEST, MISSOURI
Tuesday, July 3, 1838

Luman Shurtliff: "I, with several others of my company, went into the timber of Goose Creek, got the largest tree we could and made a liberty pole, and on the 4th of July, 1838, the brethren and their families assembled in Far West to celebrate the day. . . ."[61]

They ran down the dirt street, the sun beating warm on their bare backs, and then they passed the temple square. There were four of them, including Little Joseph— four boys followed by a large white dog, his tongue lolling from his mouth in the warm July sun. As they passed the tavern house where Father and Mother Smith lived, the boys had peeled off their shirts in the afternoon heat and continued running. That may not be right, thought Little Joseph, to run through the city with no shirts on. Little Joseph's father, who had just arrived on Old Charlie to visit

---

[61] *Luman Shurtliff Autobiography, 33*

his parents, thought so too, but contented himself with cautioning them to be careful as they ran by.

Passing the last house at the south end of Main Street, they entered the open prairie and ran down the hill toward Goose Creek. Down the hillside, the prairie gave way to clumps of hazel brush and then to stands of tall trees whose roots found moisture in the creek bottom.

"Let's go watch them cut down the Liberty Pole!" said John Smith, Little Joseph's cousin. The two were only two months apart and would both turn six years old in the fall. The other two boys were Sid and Wycliffe Rigdon, the sons of Father's counselor.

"Where will they cut it?" asked Wycliffe.

"Among the tall, white oaks," said Sid, the oldest and tallest of the four. "Along the creek on Brother Musick's place."

The boys slowed to a walk as they entered the quiet of the oak grove, the white trunks of the trees soaring overhead like pillars in a cathedral.

The boys heard the sound of an axe echoing among the tree trunks. Major barked and ran ahead. The boys entered a little clearing on the north side of Goose Creek. There were fifteen or twenty men with several teams, heavy chains, and axes. Two men had scaled an especially tall, white oak tree, and were stripping the branches off with axes and small saws.

"You boys should sit out of the way, so the tree doesn't fall on you when we bring her down." Little Joseph recognized the man as Luman Shurtliff, who had often been in their home, walked over to speak with the boys.

The four boys sat down on the side of the hill on the soft, loamy soil and watched the men work. After stripping off all the branches, the men used a long saw to make a clean cut two or three feet off the ground, and the tall oak began majestically, and then with awesome power to fall, crashing through the branches of other trees to land neatly along the creek bank. The men then cut several remaining limbs away from the smooth, straight trunk, and then hitched up long chains to the tree and strong horse teams and began dragging the tree toward Far West.

The boys followed and watched through the afternoon as the men dragged the tree across the prairie and up Main Street to the town square, where they dug a deep hole and then raised the tree in the center of Far West. The pole had a block and tackle with a rope attached to the top, by which a flag could be raised. The boys watched as the men unfurled an eight-foot American flag and raised it sixty feet in the air, and then lowered it as a test.

"Boys," said Brother Shurtliff, coming over to speak with the boys. "This here is the Liberty Pole. It is a sign of our liberty from all enemies of the Church."

OLD CHARLIE – JULY 3

FAR WEST, MISSOURI
Tuesday, July 3, 1838

Joseph Holbrook: "[On July 4 the] cornerstones of the temple were laid, they having been hauled to the spot beforehand. My team helped to haul them. They were quarried from the ledge down west and were about seven feet long, four feet wide and two feet thick by the First Presidency, Joseph Smith, Jr., and counselors and others."[62]

To the west of Far West town is what Brother Joe calls the Buryin' Ground, and from there the prairie goes on forever.

That's where we rode out to this afternoon, right to the edge of the prairie, where it sort of dips down into a creek bottom they call Willow Branch. The sun was beatin' down nice and hot, and the prairie grasses was blowin' in a nice breeze. Brother Joe come out of the house with little Julia follerin' him and hitched Jim and me up to his wagon harness, and then clicked at us and we headed out down the

---

[62] Joseph Holbrook, "The Life of Joseph Holbrook," typescript (copy in the possession of the author), 39

road. Brother Joe follered right along behind us, jest walkin' along and holdin' the reins, with little Julia walkin' along next to him. I kept turnin' around to see if Brother Joe warn't out of his mind, since he'd plum forgot to hook us up to the wagon, but he looked like he knowed what he was about. Brother Joe and Julia headed us past all them new houses they is a buildin' and past the big square in the middle of town where a bunch of fellers has dug out a big hole in the ground. When we walked past, I was s'prised to see that some other fellers had brung up a big old tree trunk to the square, as long as a barn, and they was pullin' it straight up with long ropes right there in the middle of the square. It looked mighty strange—a tree without branches stuck right in the ground in the middle of town.

Brother Joe stopped Jim and me next to that tree and went over to talk some with the fellers 'round about. A big clump of 'em gathered 'round Brother Joe, and I could hear him sayin' somethin' about fetchin' some stones up out of the ground for the temple. Just then Little Joseph come runnin' up with two or three of his pals. He come over to Jim and me and started to rub my nose and pat my flanks. Then Brother Joe come walkin' back over to Jim and me with a feller I'd seen a time or two before. His name is Holbrook, and he and Brother Joe fiddled some with our harness in the back. Then Brother Joe and this Holbrook feller led us over by the big hole in the ground, where he hitched Jim and me up to a big wooden sledge.

Well, Brother Joe jest jumped right up on the sledge and grabbed the reins. "Come on, you youngsters," he called out. "Let's go." Julia and Little Joseph jumped right up on the sledge by their Pa, makin' a lot of noise. One of Little Joseph's pals, the young feller they call Wycliffe, jumped up too, and we headed out draggin' the sledge onto Main Street. It made a fearsome scrapin' sound, but moved along smooth enough. All the while the young'uns in the back was laughin' and squealin' and makin' a racket.

I heared another racket behind us and turned to see Holbrook ridin' up beside us with a big sledge and rig of his own, pulled by a flea bitten grey and a white gelding. Brother Joe shouted at Holbrook and whipped Jim and me up some, and we took off, draggin' that sledge behind us. It looked to be a race, until Holbrook backed his team off, and waved at Brother Joe, smilin' and laughin'. The young'uns in back was makin' a grand time of it, a regular lark.

Well, we went on through town, and we was trottin' along nice and steady until we come to Willow Branch. There the road ends right sudden, as the ground drops right off down in the gully by the creek. Up top it was all prairie, but down by the water the trees was right thick. There was another bunch of fellers on the edge, where the ground gets right stony, and they had been diggin' all around the stones with shovels and crowbars and had lifted three or four big flat stones right out of the ground. Holbrook jumped from his sledge and come over to start yellin' orders at the men, and pretty soon those fellers had dragged one big stone over to Brother Joe's sledge and winched it up on top. Brother Joe jumped down to help 'em lift all together. Pretty soon I could feel the weight of that big flat stone on our sledge. Little Joe and Wycliffe and Julia and a bunch of other young'uns stood about and watched the fellers work. After

Jim and me got loaded up, those fellers hoisted another big old stone on Holbrook's sledge.

After that we headed back into Far West, draggin' them sledges. But instead of a race, we was barely walkin' along, the stone was that heavy. Brother Joe stood right up top on our stone with Julia and Little Joseph with him.

As we got close to the center of town, Jim slipped some on a patch of mud in the road, and we stopped dead. Gettin' that sledge movin' again was a chore, and almost more than Jim could stand. He's a strong horse, his coat black as night, and a fine lookin' workhorse, but the problem is Jim don't *know* how strong he is, and that sometimes lands old Jim in trouble. A horse has got to *know* how strong he is in order to pull a load.

Arthur – July 4

KIRTLAND, OHIO
Wednesday, July 4, 1838

In the spring and summer of 1838, the Seven Presidents of the Seventy in Kirtland organized Kirtland Camp to assist many of the poorer Church members living in Ohio to move their families to northern Missouri, a trek of more than eight hundred miles. More than five hundred Latter-day Saints made the trek together. Kirtland Camp was the first Mormon company organized to assist in the migration of the Latter-day Saints in the history of the Church.

Members of the Kirtland Camp covenanted to live by a constitution that provided guidelines concerning the organization of the camp and a code of conduct for members.

Kirtland Camp's trek began on July 6, 1838, in Kirtland, Ohio. The main company arrived at Adam-ondi-Ahman in Daviess County, Missouri, on October 4, 1838.

The stay of members of the Kirtland Camp in Adam-ondi-Ahman was short-lived. They were there only about six weeks. Following the Mormon surrender to Missouri military officials in November of 1838, they were forced to leave Adam-ondi-Ahman and temporarily relocate near Far West. They stayed there until February of 1839, when they were forcibly moved from Missouri by order of Missouri Governor Lilburn W. Boggs.

On July 4 Arthur Millikin stood ankle deep in wood shavings in Alexander Badham's wagon shop. He had been working from early morning until late at night, six days a week, for more than a month. Scores of men had come to Badham's in recent weeks to have new wagons built or old wagons prepared, as hundreds of the Latter-day Saints were leaving Kirtland for good. And Arthur had been busy beyond anything he had previously imagined.

Arthur pondered on the great changes that had occurred in Kirtland in the past year. The streets of Kirtland were largely empty now, with few travelers, and with a look of fear and suspicion in the eyes of citizens who went quickly about their business. Arthur remembered that only a year ago these same quiet streets had been continually thronged with teams loaded with wood, materials for building houses and barns and corrals, and provisions for the market, with people coming in to buy or to trade, or with curious sightseers coming into the city to see the stately and magnificent temple. Last year the temple had been filled to overflowing every day of the week. During the week, a school called the Kirtland High School was taught in the attic story of the temple, and every Sunday worship services were held throughout the day. And the temple was filled most evenings. Every Sunday evening the singers met to practice chorale music. On Mondays the quorum of high priests met. On Tuesdays the Seventies met. On Wednesday evenings the quorum of Elders met. On Thursdays a prayer meeting was held, conducted by Joseph Smith, Sr., the patriarch of the Church.

It was at the weekly prayer meetings, that Arthur took the occasion to exchange a word here and there with the patriarch's youngest daughter, Lucy Smith, whose charm and quiet beauty and shining eyes had rather captured Arthur Millikin. He thought about those eyes as he fashioned the spokes on a wagon wheel intended for Brother Andrew Lamereaux. He loved watching those eyes, although when they turned their light upon him, he quickly turned his head, and felt the blood in his cheeks. In late May he had prepared the wagons for Patriarch Smith and his family, who left in a large group. Arthur had watched them as they rode away, two dozen members of the Smith family, with Lucy Smith laughing and talking to her numerous nieces and one small nephew.

As he watched them riding away, his mind suddenly had a crazy thought. He should follow Joseph Smith to Missouri. This was a crazy thought because his Uncle Nathaniel was instrumental in the reorganization of the Church in Kirtland, and now was one of the leaders of the group known as The Church of Christ. "Joseph Smith is a fallen prophet," said Uncle Nathaniel often to Arthur. The Church of Christ had been organized, with his Uncle Nathaniel joining with their neighbor, Warren Parrish, Joseph Coe, and Martin Harris, one of the Three Witnesses to the Book of Mormon, to form a new church. "We must go back to the Old Order," Uncle Nathaniel had repeatedly said. "Joseph Smith has deviated from the Old Order, and is in apostasy."

Arthur had attended the new Church of Christ, which held meetings each Sunday in the Kirtland Temple, but they were missing some of fire and power he had felt in years past. The number of people attending dropped off considerably, and now there were just a handful.

There had also been a controversy in March in the new Church. In a meeting Arthur attended in late March, Brother Stephen Burnett renounced the Book of Mormon. He was followed by Warren Parrish, who had been Joseph Smith's private secretary, and by the Apostles Luke Johnson and John Boynton. These four all spoke out in the temple against the Book of Mormon, calling it a false book and contrary to the Bible, and a fabrication from start to finish.

After they had spoken against the Book of Mormon, there was a silence over the small congregation. Then Arthur watched as old Martin Harris stood on his feet. He walked to the lower central pulpit and spoke with quiet energy. He said he was sorry for any man who rejected the Book of Mormon, for he knew it was true. He said he had hefted the plates repeatedly in a box with only a tablecloth or a handkerchief over them, but he never saw them, only as he saw a city through a mountain. He also said he was sorry if anyone interpreted anything he had said as casting doubt upon the testimony of the Three Witnesses or the Eight Witnesses.

While these troubles went on among the dissenters from Joseph Smith, his followers had been quietly organizing themselves beginning in March to remove all who wished to go to Missouri to be with the Latter-day Saints.

This work went on under the direction of the seven presidents of the Seventy. Arthur had been present at another meeting, this one under the direction of Elder Joseph

Young, the senior president of the Seventies, also held in the Kirtland Temple, for the saints and the dissenters both shared the building for their respective meetings, in which the decision was made to take the poor in a body to the west. They had written a constitution, with rules for everyone to abide by, and taken a list of over five hundred who wished to travel together. They then took measures to procure horses and wagons and tents and other necessary supplies for the long journey.

Arthur remembered that Elder Oliver Granger had stood upon his feet in that meeting and made an impassioned plea on behalf of the poor. He said, "I consider it would be the greatest thing ever accomplished since the organization of the Church or even since the exodus of Israel from Egypt if the saints in Kirtland, considering their poverty, should succeed in going from that place in a body."

It was decided that two good teams, one wagon, and one tent would suffice for every eighteen persons. From that time, Arthur was busy working on wagons and wagon wheels, though there was precious little money available to pay for his or Alexander Badham's services. Brother Badham himself was soon going to Missouri with his family on his own.

Arthur Millikin brushed the wood shavings off of his clothes and stepped back to look at his work. *Should I follow Brother Joseph to Missouri or stay here in Kirtland?* Arthur stood for a long while, then picked up his tools and went back to work.

Julia – July 4

FAR WEST, MISSOURI
Wednesday, July 4, 1838

Joseph Smith: "The day was spent in celebrating the Declaration of Independence of the United States of America, and also by the Saints making a 'Declaration of Independence' from all mobs and persecutions which have been inflicted upon them, time after time, until they could bear it no longer; having been driven by ruthless mobs and enemies of truth from their homes, and having had their property confiscated, their lives exposed, and their all jeopardized by such barbarous conduct. The corner stones of the Houses of the Lord, agreeable to the commandments of the Lord unto us, given April 26, 1838, were laid."[63]

Parley P. Pratt: "On the Fourth of July, 1838, many thousands of our people assembled at the city of Far West, the county seat of Caldwell, erected a liberty pole, and hoisted the bald eagle, with its stars and stripes, upon the top of the same. Under the colors of our country we laid the corner stone of a house of worship, and had an address delivered by Elder Rigdon, in which was painted, in lively colors, the oppression which we had long suffered from the hand of our enemies; and in this discourse we claimed and declared our constitutional rights, as American citizens, and manifested a determination to do our utmost endeavors, from that time forth, to resist all oppression, and to maintain our rights

---

[63] HC 3:41

and freedom according to the holy principles of liberty, as guaranteed to every person by the constitution and laws of our government. This declaration was received with shouts of Hosanna to God and the Lamb, and with many and long cheers by the assembled thousands, who were determined to yield their rights no more, except compelled by a superior power."[64]

Little Joseph bolted down his breakfast, then started out the back door with Major at his heels.

"Wait for me!" said Julia. "I'm coming, too!"

"Hurry up," said Little Joseph. "I promised to meet Sid and Wycliffe before they raise the flag."

"Wait for your sister," said Mother. Little Joseph waited impatiently by the door while Julia finished eating, then combed her hair.

"Finally," said Little Joseph, as he and Julia left the house and walked toward the center of town. It was early, but already the streets were filled with crowds of people, who were still walking into town on the roads from the north, south, east, and west.

"There must be a hundred thousand people here already," said Little Joseph as they passed the central temple square, with the Liberty Pole rising majestically in the morning light.

"There's not a hundred thousand, silly," said Julia. "But there might be two thousand. Or three thousand."

---

[64] *HC 3:34-37; Mormon Redress Petitions, Parley Pratt History of Persecution, 74*

At the Rigdons' home, they were greeted by Lacy Rigdon and her older brothers, Sid and Wycliffe.

"We've been waiting for you," said Sid. "We need to hurry or we'll miss the flag raising."

The boys ran off, and Julia started to follow.

"Don't go with them," said Lacy. "I have a better idea."

"What?" asked Julia. Lacy went inside the house and held the door for Julia.

"Let's watch from the upstairs windows."

Upstairs in the Rigdon house were two large rooms. Lacy's brothers, Sid and Wycliffe slept in one, and Lacy and her sisters slept in the other. The room had two large windows overlooking the central square of Far West. Julia brought a chair over to one window and climbed up to stand on the seat. Lacy dragged her rocking horse to the other window and climbed on the seat.

The two girls looked out east across the public square. In the center of the square was the tall Liberty Pole, and beyond it the basement for the Far West Temple, excavated the previous year. To the right on the square was the new school house, and across the street the Whitmer Hotel, and beyond it the Wamsley Hotel, where Julia's grandparents, Joseph Smith, Sr., and Lucy Mack Smith lived with Julia's aunts and their families.

As the girls watched, the flag was raised on the Liberty Pole, and a great cheer went up. Then a procession assembled on horses and paraded around the square. First, the infantry of the militia company, with their rifles cocked over their shoulders; followed by the Patriarch of the Church, Julia's grandfather; Julia's father riding Old Charlie;

her Uncle Hyrum riding his white stallion, Sam; then others of the Brethren of the Church; followed by the cavalry under the direction of Captain David Patten, who was called "Fearnot" by the saints. The cornerstones of the temple were then dragged into place and dedicated one corner at a time by a group of men. First, the southeast cornerstone was laid, assisted by the twelve members of the High Council at Far West.

"I found out more about your history," said Lacy. "Do you want to hear?"

"No," said Julia. "It doesn't matter to me. I have my family now, and I'm not sure I want to know about anybody else."

"But I found out who your real father is," said Lacy, smiling brightly at Julia.

Julia felt the blood leave her face. She was surprised to find herself angry. Angry that no one had told her that she had a different mother and father from the ones she had known and loved her whole life. Angry at her real mother and father for not being there to raise her. Angry at herself for being unworthy to have a normal family life. And most of all, angry at Lacy for knowing what she didn't know. She was angry, but at the same time she knew that she must know everything.

"Are you sure you don't want to know?" asked Lacy.

Julia thought for a moment, looking out the window. John Smith, the stake president, was speaking in a loud voice, saying a dedicatory prayer over the huge rust and gold colored sandstone block which had been dragged into place at the southeast corner of the basement excavation for the temple. Behind him, with their hats in their hands were his two counselors and twelve men, who were the high councilors in the stake.

"I can tell you, if you want," said Lacy teasingly.

"Okay. Tell me," said Julia, looking out the window to where her father sat on the wooden stand that had been built beside the temple excavation. She noticed how handsome he was, and how much taller he was than most men. "Tell me who my real father is."

"There he is," said Lacy, pointing toward the southeast cornerstone of the temple. "He is one of those twelve men."

"Which one?" asked Julia.

"The one with the bald head, wearing a red shirt with suspenders. He's the school teacher."

Julia squinted and watched the man, moving among all the others. She could hardly believe that he was her father. "What's his name?" she asked.

"John," said Lacy. "John Murdock."

"What about my brothers?" asked Julia. "Do they live with John Murdock?"

"No," said Lacy. "They don't. But one of them lives here in Far West. He lives with a family called Phelps."

"What's his name?" asked Julia.

"John Murdock," said Lacy. "The same as your father. But they call him Johnny."

As Julia watched from the window, she saw the men of the high council walking in a line before the stand. The man called John Murdock, the one with the bald head, passed directly in front of Father on the stand—Father, with his full head of light-colored hair and his handsome face. It filled Julia with sadness and dread.

What is to become of me? she thought.

WYCLIFFE – JULY 4

FAR WEST, MISSOURI
Wednesday, July 4, 1838

Joseph Smith: "The oration was delivered by President Rigdon, at the close of which was a shout of Hosanna, and a song, composed for the occasion by Levi W. Hancock, was sung by Solomon Hancock. The most perfect order prevailed throughout the day."[65]

Luman Shurtliff: "We then assembled under the flag of our nation and had an oration delivered by Sidney Rigdon. This orator became quite excited and proclaimed loudly our freedom and liberty in Missouri. Although Sidney was a great orator and one of the leading brethren, his oration brought sorrow and gloom over my mind, and spoiled any further enjoyment of the day."[66]

John Wycliffe Rigdon: "Colonel Hinkle had one company of uniformed militia. The Saints had a martial band with a brass drum and two small drums, and so a procession was formed to march, the uniform company of militia coming first and then the procession followed. We made quite a showing for a small town. After marching around the square, the militia came to the cellar and halted. There was erected a

---

[65] HC 3:41-42
[66] *Luman Shurtliff Autobiography, 33*

stand to speak from. Joseph Smith, Hyrum Smith, Sidney Rigdon and several others took their places."[67]

Look," said Sid Rigdon. "Father's about to speak."
Wycliffe, Sid, and Little Joseph had joined their sisters in the upper story of the Rigdon house. Wycliffe looked from the window of his house to the public square in the center of Far West to where his father, Sidney Rigdon, was standing at the podium.

It was the center of a hum of activity, like the center of a beehive. Beyond the houses of the city, a thousand tents had been pitched, and ten thousand saints swarmed into the city to watch the festivities. In the central square the men had raised a great flag pole, at least fifty feet high, from which fluttered the United States flag, with its red and white stripes and field of blue with white stars. The temple excavation stood ready to receive the cornerstones, which had been brought here by teams of horses. A wooden platform had been built by the carpenters, from which hung red, white, and blue buntings. The splendor of it all took Wycliffe's breath away—the throngs of people in their best clothes, the ranks of soldiers in their uniforms with muskets and rifles on their shoulders, the horses saddled up to carry the dignitaries and cavalrymen on a grand circuit of the

---

[67] Karl Keller, ed., John Wycliffe Rigdon, "I Never Knew a Time When I Did Not Know Joseph Smith: A Son's Record of the Life and Testimony of Sidney Rigdon," in Dialogue: A Journal of Mormon Thought (Salt Lake City, 1966), Volume 1:30-31

square, and the dignitaries themselves, most of all. Wycliffe saw his father, Sidney Rigdon, standing in the place of honor behind the podium. In a way, Sidney Rigdon was the center of this city and of the religion that was building it up so rapidly.

"Your father has a loud voice," said Julia Smith in the room behind Wycliffe.

"Of course he does," said Wycliffe. He's the greatest preacher of this dispensation."

"I can hear every word he says," said Sid Rigdon, Wycliffe's older brother. "We better listen, since he'll probably ask us about what he said."

"My father is also a great speaker," said Little Joseph, the son of the Prophet.

"But he's not as great as Sidney Rigdon," said Sid. "It even says so in the Book of Commandments—your father needs a spokesman."

Little Joseph didn't answer, he just stood at the window looking out over the vast crowd.

"Our cheeks have been given to the smiters," the children heard Sidney Rigdon shouting across the square, "and our heads to those who have plucked off the hair."

"What does smite mean?" asked Lacy Rigdon.

"Shh," said Sid. "It means to hit. And if you don't be quiet, I'm going to hit you."

"You will not," said Lacy. "If you do, Father will whip you."

"Shh," said Wycliffe. "I'm trying to listen."

Sidney Rigdon's voice had been raised to almost a fever pitch, and Wycliffe felt a kind of trembling in his chest.

. . . we are wearied of being smitten, and tired of being trampled upon. We have proved the world with kindness; we have suffered their abuse without cause, with patience, and have endured without resentment, until this day, and still their persecutions and violence does not cease. But from this day and this hour, we will suffer it no more!

The crowd outside let out a long shout and then clapped their hands loudly, until Sidney Rigdon held up his hands to quiet the crowd.

We take God and all the holy angels to witness this day, that we warn all men in the name of Jesus Christ, to come on us no more forever, for from this hour, we will bear it no more, our rights shall no more be trampled on with impunity. The man or the set of men, who attempts it, does it at the expense of their lives. And that mob that comes on us to disturb us; it shall be between us and them a war of extermination, for we will follow them, till the last drop of their blood is spilled, or else they will have to exterminate us: for we will carry the seat of war to their own houses, and their own families, and one party or the other shall be utterly destroyed. Remember it then *ALL MEN.*

There was an even greater cheer from the crowd. Wycliffe saw that the men on the stand, including Joseph Smith, had risen to their feet to clap.

We will never be the aggressors, we will infringe on the rights of no people; but shall stand for our own until death. We claim our own rights, and are willing that all others shall enjoy theirs. No man shall be at liberty to come into our streets, to threaten us with mobs, for if he does, he shall atone for it before he leaves the place, neither shall he be at liberty, to vilify and slander any of us, for suffer it we will not in this place. We therefore, take all men to record this day that we proclaim our liberty on this day, as did our fathers. And we pledge this day to one another, our fortunes, our lives, and our sacred honors, to be delivered from the persecutions that we have had to endure, for the last nine years, or nearly that. Neither will we indulge any man, or set of men, in instituting vexatious law suits against us, to cheat us out of our just rights, if they attempt it we say we be unto them."

Sidney Rigdon's voice was now as loud as if he were standing in the upper room with the children. It got louder and deeper and more emotional, until he practically shouted,

"We this day then proclaim ourselves free, with a purpose and a determination, that never can be broken, "no never! no never!! NO NEVER!!!"

ARTHUR – JULY 5

KIRTLAND, OHIO
Thursday, July 5, 1938

On July 5 Arthur rode his horse Dominic up past the temple to watch the Kirtland Camp assemble. It was a beautiful morning. Riding to the top of the temple hill, Arthur looked all around him. The horizon at every point was clear and unobstructed, and overhead billowy clouds were tinged with morning light. Suddenly Arthur had an indescribable feeling in his heart. He knew somehow that God was watching with a smile over the camp of Kirtland saints who were beginning to assemble for their journey.

There were already about twenty tents pitched on the grass behind the empty house formerly owned by Brother Mayhew, a few hundred feet south of the temple. Many other spectators were already gathering from Kirtland and from neighboring towns to watch the spectacle. Here and there a wagon filled with household goods and men, women, and children would pull up on the grass, and a new tent be pitched. People of all ages carried parcels to the gathering spot and found their assigned company and wagon.

Arthur stayed throughout the day, helping here and there with a wagon, and watched the gathering. By evening nearly five hundred people were gathered. At dusk the spectators left the campers in peace. Arthur stayed on. The night was clear, and the encampment and all around was utterly peaceful and calm. Arthur found himself not wanting to return home. He sat on a fence for an hour as the stars came out, watching the campfires of the saints.

He looked up at the stars and again thought unexpectedly of the light he had noticed in the eyes of Lucy Smith.

The next morning Arthur sat for a long time on his bed. His heart was beating wildly, for he knew what he must do. He quickly arose, put a few clothes in a satchel, lifted up the floorboard under his bed and withdrew the six dollars in gold coins which he had hidden there, then put on his hat, picked up his hunting rifle, and walked down the hill to Uncle Nathaniel's house. He stood in the open doorway to the kitchen. Aunt May was cooking breakfast, but looked up when she saw him. Uncle Nathaniel came through from the other room and stood staring at Arthur. Arthur stood in silence, with his satchel over his shoulder.

Uncle Nathaniel took a long look at him, then said quietly, "You're going, aren't you?"

"Yes," said Arthur.

There was silence in the room. Then Uncle Nathaniel simply said, "Well, eat some breakfast first."

At a very early hour in the morning, the people began to assemble to witness the departure of the camp. When Arthur rode up on Dominic, there were already several hundred people gathered to watch. Arthur rode right up to Elder Joseph Young, the president of the Seventy. "Do you have room for one more?" Arthur asked.

"I knew you would come," said Joseph Young. "We can use a wheelwright and wagon man."

Throughout the morning the camp packed up their tents and implements and hitched up their teams. At noon the camp began to move and passed out of Kirtland.

Arthur Millikin, riding Dominic, looked over his shoulder as they moved down the Chillichothe Road and took one final look at the spires of the temple.

OLD CHARLIE – JULY 8

FAR WEST, MISSOURI
Sunday, July 8, 1938

Luman Shurtliff: "On Sunday [July 8, 1838] a cloud came over Far West, charged with electricity, and lightning fell upon our liberty pole and shivered it to the ground. When the news reached me, I involuntarily proclaimed, 'Farewell to our liberty in Missouri.'"[68]

Sunday meetin's is held in the schoolhouse down in the center of Far West, nearby the big hole in the ground that them fellers dug up and the big tree without branches that they stuck in the ground. I never did learn what that hole was for, or that big old tree with no branches, but sometimes what men will do is mighty puzzlin' to a horse. I suppose they had some good reason for it.

I know that Brother Joe must have some purpose in mind, hisself, for he drug them big stones up to the corners of that hole, and then all the folks from miles around walked 'round and 'round with their drums bangin' and their horns

---

[68] *Luman Shurtliff Autobiography, 33*

blowin'. The men tied a big piece of cloth to the top of that there tree, all red and white with some blue in it, and it stood flappin' way up high while all the commotion went on down below. Brother Joe and the other soldiers and Brethren went to each of them four stones and spoke some words. Then Brother Sidney stood up and shouted for 'bout an hour or so, and finally all the folks started shoutin' together, and some of the fellers threw their hats up into the air, almost as high as that cloth flappin' at the top of the tree.

Well that was days ago, and since all that hullabaloo, things have calmed right down in Far West, and I'm hopin' it will be a right peaceful summer and fall, with plenty of ridin' with Brother Joe. I thought about that as I stood amongst all the other horses and carriages waitin' for the folks to finish with their meetin' in the schoolhouse. I could see it settin' all white and new in the prairie grass yonder with the windows all open, and the sound of men and ladies singin' and singin'.

I reached down for some grass to graze on, and felt the wind blow through my mane. Sam, Brother Hyrum's big white stallion, whickered, and I looked up to see a big black cloud sorta' movin' over the town. Then the sun went out, and it got dark all of a sudden like. Sam whickered again, and the other horses started layin' their ears back. I felt somethin' too and knowed we was in for a big blow, and probably some rain, but it didn't concern me none, as it was right hot, and a fine rain would feel good in the heat.

Then, all of a sudden, the black sky lit up, and a great BANG sounded. All of the horses ducked their heads and spread their feet, and then started rearin' up. I looked up, and the tree with no branches was suddenly gone, and pieces of it was fallin' to the ground all on fire. Last of all I see'd that cloth, all red and white and blue, layin' on the ground, all on fire.

Hearin' the bang of that thunder put me in mind of another bang that I heared long ago. It happened when I was still a colt, learnin' how to be a proper horse with Pete and his pa, Henry.

One day—this was after we had crossed over the river for that there race and come back home to Kentucky—Pete and his pa, Henry, brung me up permanent-like to the stable by the big house. From that day on, I never much saw the colts and other horses or my dam in the Big Field, but I spent my nights sleepin' by Henry's fine horses—trotters and racers—who kept pretty much to theirselves and didn't take too kindly when I tried to talk with 'em.

Then one day Henry and Pete took me and a few other horses on a trip twenty, thirty mile to another city, where I hadn't been before. Pete led me into this big barn that was filled with men sittin' on logs around the edges, and there was an open space in the middle where the dirt was all tromped down. The men sittin' on the logs was all talkin' and shoutin' at once, and I see'd a fat feller with a big white hat jest sittin' on this high-up platform at a little table, and he was jest a-jabberin' away while all the others shouted. There was a nice sorrel racer standin' proud next to a feller in the middle of the barn, and that feller led the sorrel 'round and 'round whilst all the other fellers shouted and talked. Suddenly the feller up on the platform stopped jabberin' and he brung this big hammer—BANG!—down on the table. The sound of the bang startled me some, but I could see that no harm would come from it. It was jest some feller bangin' his hammer down on the table for all he was worth.

I was plenty nervous, but Pete stood by me and spoke real soft in my ear and reached in his pocket for a lump of sugar. I dropped my head to sniff the tromped up ground. There was the smell of plenty of them green leaves the fellers love to chew on. Then the fat man with the white hat started yellin' again, and I heard him call out Henry's name, and then my name!—BEAU—and Pete led me out in the middle of the barn. The fat man started jabberin' out numbers—twenty, thirty, thirty-five, forty—and all the other fellers started in again on talkin' and shoutin'. Here and there a feller would raise his hand up or shout out a number. Some of the fellers seemed to be gettin' right angry and agitated with one another. Well, this went on and on, jest a yellin' and jabberin' back and forth 'til I couldn't understand what the fellers were shoutin'. Then finally, the fat man picked up his hammer and slammed it down hard on the desk—BANG!—and yelled, "Sold!" which made me jump and rear up on my hind legs.

And suddenly there was a big, tall man wearin' a funny little round cap. He had a cigar between his teeth, only it wasn't lit, jest jammed there between his teeth. He was standin' beside Henry and puttin' a stack of them little green papers in Henry's palm. Pete was real quiet, and I see'd that he had streams of water runnin' down his face. Then he handed my bridle to the tall man with the cigar between his teeth. The man took his cigar out and spat on the ground and grabbed my bridle. I jumped a bit, but calmed right down when Pete hugged me tight around the neck and whispered in my ear, "Good boy, Beau! It's all right, Beau!"

Well, that was the last time I ever see'd Pete or Henry or the Big Field where I was born and broke. The feller with the cigar 'tween his teeth—his name was Bradshaw—he done took me back over the Ohio River to that big city—they call it Cincinnati.

I've always been a lucky horse. And I suppose meetin' Bradshaw was a piece of luck, too, for it brought me along to the time when I met Brother Joe.

But that's another story.

EPILOGUE

ISRAEL SMITH

INDEPENDENCE, MISSOURI
Wednesday, September 10, 1913

The day has grown bright, with sunlight streaming through the windows, and then dark, as twilight approaches, but still Israel Smith's father continues to talk.

"After Father's death I used often to ride Charlie into the city, day after day, to watch the work being done upon the Temple. Often upon these excursions I was accompanied by my cousin John Smith, who rode his father's white horse, called Sam. We doubtless made quite an interesting quartet—the two boys and the two splendid horses, one coal black and the other snow white."

The old man falls silent as the last rays of the sun cast a yellow glow on the walls of the room. Finally, Israel walks over and switches on the lights. He starts back toward his writing desk, but then stops short. Israel has been with his father for almost four decades. He has seen him in joy and sorrow, in triumph and in defeat, but he has never seen him in tears. Israel does not return to his writing desk that day, but merely walks over, kisses the old man on his forehead, then steps out of the room and closes the door behind him.

About the Author

Daniel Bay Gibbons has aspired to be a novelist his entire life. Born in Salt Lake City, he began his first historical novel at the age of fourteen and has been writing ever since. A well-known Salt Lake City trial attorney, he was educated at the University of Utah and Willamette University. During his professional life, he was also a refugee sponsor with the Tolstoy Foundation, a long-time radio talk-show host, an elementary school chess coach, a founding member of the Holladay City Council, and a frequent guest lecturer in Ukrainian law schools. In 2001 he became a trial judge in suburban Salt Lake County, serving on the bench for ten years.

Dan walked away from his judgeship and his legal career in 2011 when he accepted a calling to serve with his wife, Julie, as an LDS mission president in Russia and Kazakhstan. He had previously served a two-year Church mission as a young man in Germany, as an ordinance worker in the Salt Lake Temple, and twice as bishop. From 2011 to 2014 Dan and Julie lived in Novosibirsk, Russia, and traveled more than 750,000 miles throughout Russian Siberia and Central Asia, as well as in Eastern Europe, the Baltic nations, Ukraine, and Turkey.

Dan returned to the United States in 2014 with a determination to make his way as a full-time writer of historical fiction, novels of suspense, and Mormon history and biography. He is the author of several books, including the *Old Charlie and the Prophet* series of historical novels, the biographical series *Remembering Seven Prophets*, and the historical mystery series

Sherlock Holmes in the Country of the Saints. He is the coauthor, with his father, Francis M. Gibbons, of two previous titles: *A Gathering of Eagles* and *Nethermost: Missionary Miracles in Lowly Places.*

Aside from his passion for writing, Dan loves reading books (he has a home library of more than 5,000 titles), learning languages (he is fluent in German and Russian, reads ancient Greek and has studied Biblical Hebrew), and running (he currently runs four to six miles a day and has completed seven marathons). He is married to Julie Glenn Gibbons, and they live in Holladay, Utah. They have five children—Annie, Jenny, Liz, Abby and Josh—and five grandchildren.

www.ingramcontent.com/pod-product-compliance
Lightning Source LLC
Chambersburg PA
CBHW070757120726
47910CB00001B/206